Tania Kindersley was [...]
up in the Lambourn Val[...]
National Hunt racing. A[...]
fourteen she grew out o[...]
London, discovered boy[...]
writing. Her life's ambi[...]
an actress and it was only when she failed
her drama school auditions that she started
writing seriously. She has lived in France,
the West Indies and at nine different London
addresses.

Her second novel, *Here for the Season*, is
published in hardcover by Bantam Press.

OUT TO LUNCH

'A snappy and witty début'
Publishing News

'Oxford graduate Tania assuredly has a
future as a comic novelist'
Daily Express

'Determinedly frivolous . . . Kindersley
writes sharp dialogue with verve'
Daily Telegraph

OUT TO LUNCH

Tania Kindersley

CORGI BOOKS

OUT TO LUNCH
A CORGI BOOK 0 552 13708 1

Originally published in Great Britain by Bantam Press,
a division of Transworld Publishers Ltd

PRINTING HISTORY
Bantam Press edition published 1991
Corgi edition published 1992

This book was set in Bembo

Corgi Books are published by Transworld Publishers
Ltd, 61–63 Uxbridge Road, Ealing, London W5 5SA, in
Australia by Transworld Publishers (Australia) Pty Ltd,
15–23 Helles Avenue, Moorebank, NSW 2170, and in New
Zealand by Transworld Publishers (NZ) Ltd, 3 William
Pickering Drive, Albany, Auckland.

Printed and bound in Great Britain by
Cox & Wyman Ltd, Reading, Berks.

To my grandmother, Oonagh, with love

CHAPTER
1

It was after Venice had been fired from her third job in a month that she decided she was simply not cut out to work. A girl with a name like Venice couldn't have been put into the world to graft, could she? Graft. Now there was a word, Venice thought to herself, wondering quite where it could have come from. Graft was not really her at all. She would simply have to find a lovely accommodating sugar daddy with more money than libido. Just the very thing.

She swung down Bond Street, light with early summer sunshine, choosing to ignore the appreciative glances and bolder whistles sent her way, pausing only to admire her reflection in the shop windows. Shop windows, Venice always thought, were so much more satisfying than mirrors. There was something so infinitely seductive about seeing one's face reflected against a St Laurent model at £1,000 a shot. At Chanel, she stopped, entranced. Chanel never lost its power to thrill her. She stalked in, tossing her best smile carelessly at the doorman, ignoring the scandalized stare of the assistant. Venice's jeans might be ripped, but she had the face of an angel, and she knew it.

An hour later, she stalked out again, having tried on everything in the shop, and found it not quite what she wanted. In fact, she had longed to say 'Charge it', like they did in the films, but who could she charge it to? It was a sad state of affairs when a girl didn't have at least one Chanel suit. She really would have to sharpen her wits and find her old man soon.

Way across London, a million miles away from the rarified atmosphere of Bond Street, Max Charlton pushed his hair off his face and tried to concentrate. His jeans were ripped too, but he thought Chanel was something they were trying to build a tunnel under. The stage was hot and dark and musty, and all he wanted was a beer and a smoke, and it didn't seem likely that he would get either for another hour.

'Don't believe you,' snapped the director. He had run out of Valium that morning, and was even more tetchy than usual. 'Do it again.'

The cast dutifully resumed its positions, muttering under its breath. Max scowled to himself. Was it really worth it? All this, and what for? A two-bit production in a one-horse suburb, that would probably only run for a month. So much for the bright lights. Still, who could tell in this business. Croydon today, Shaftesbury Avenue tomorrow, rave reviews, and a spot on *Wogan*. Reality be damned. He would just have to find himself a nice accommodating casting agent who knew talent when she saw it, and let her put him on the casting couch. Max grinned. Olivier, eat your heart out.

Still musing on the dream-like qualities of little black dresses, Venice let herself into the house. The dim

8

light couldn't quite conceal the mess. Venice never seemed to have time to clear away glasses or empty ashtrays. On every surface, the dust quarrelled with the clutter of glossy magazines, cigarette packets, half-used bottles of scent and discarded pieces of jewellery. Records littered the floor, fallen out of their sleeves, interspersed with most of Venice's forty pairs of stilettos, and a bunch of roses from some forgotten admirer shed its petals sadly onto a rug that might once have been Aubusson. Venice's sister Alabama lay asleep on one sofa.

'Al!' Venice cried in unaffected delight.

Alabama opened one quizzical eye.

'Well, hello Ven. How's tricks?'

'I thought you were still in New York.'

'So did I. I'm suffering from cultural displacement. Have you got any brandy?'

'In my knicker drawer. Medicinal purposes only.'

'So call the doctor.'

Just as Venice was the product of a well-timed trip to Italy, Alabama was the fruit of her parents' only visit to America. They hadn't liked it much. Too many Americans, they had said. They hadn't liked Alabama much either, when she chose to appear, in the middle of one of her mother's grander dinner parties. Born wayward, she had annoyed them from the moment she could talk. As soon as was decently possible, they had shown her the door, which she always said was the only thing she had to thank them for. Venice, the divine, the perfect, the blessed Venice, the apple of her parents' doting eye, had followed her sister in a cloud of righteous fury, and they had been together ever since. As different as they could wish to be, they got along fine.

'So,' said Venice now, pouring brandy into nearly clean glasses. 'How was it?'

'Exhausting. They kept calling for rewrites. The leading man has spent the last ten years pickling his brain, what there is of it, in Smirnoff, so he has great difficulty in saying anything over one syllable. I don't know how he ever graduated from *Planet of the Apes*.'

Alabama wrote sharp satirical plays that brought jaded critics to their knees, begging for more. Her first play had bought her the basement of a tiny house in the wrong part of Chelsea, the sale of the film rights had bought the rest, and her second play had paid for a few pretty things to put in it. With the proceeds of the third she had bought a motorbike, and then run out of ideas. Despite her success, she still turned up to first nights in jeans, and drank bourbon instead of Dom Perignon. Her one concession to fame was that she no longer rolled her own cigarettes.

'I've been trying to prove something all my life,' she had once said to Venice, 'but I'm damned if I know what it is.'

'Drink your brandy,' said Venice, ever soothing.

'I will. So, enough about me. Tell me about you.'

'I got fired again,' said Venice, a note of pride in her voice. 'Do you call that rather chic? Three times in a month.'

'I could think of better words for it, but we won't go into that now. I suppose you want some money.' Alabama was resigned. She had long ago accepted Venice's inability to do any kind of job that would have her.

'Well,' said Venice, assuming the voice of reason, 'you know you won't spend it.'

10

'Yes, yes,' said Alabama, lighting a cigarette and blowing smoke rings at the ceiling. 'And I know that you feel morally obliged not to let it moulder in a vault. Isn't it time you started sleeping with your bank manager.'

'Well I would, only he prefers boys.'

'Don't they all? Why do you think I cut all my hair off?'

Venice tossed her own golden mane over her shoulder in one of those careless gestures she had been perfecting since she was eight.

'I,' she said grandly, 'am going to find a sugar daddy.'

'Of course you are. A credit card with a pacemaker. I hope you like Arab food.'

'I thought I'd ring up Oliver,' said Venice, rising above this dig. Anyone with half an eye could see that Alabama had terrible jet lag. 'He knows everyone.'

'Brilliant,' said Alabama. 'I wonder you didn't think of it before. Can I come to your first night?'

Venice beamed.

'I rather hoped you might write the script.'

Full of resolve, Venice rang up her cousin. He was jet set and discreetly homosexual. He remembered to say darling a great deal, and dabbled in drugs for the sake of his image. He was bound to know the very thing.

The telephone was answered on the first ring. Venice often thought that the telephone had been invented especially for Oliver.

'Oliver!' she shrieked. He tended not to listen unless one shrieked.

'Darling heart,' he cried. 'The utter heaven of hearing your voice. Where have you been? I haven't seen you for at least a month.'

'Working,' said Venice, in the quizzical voice she reserved for things which couldn't really be true but were. 'Don't laugh, it's absolute gospel.'

'How positively droll,' said Oliver. 'Do tell me, what is it like?'

'Quite the most drack thing imaginable,' said Venice. 'I couldn't even begin to tell you, you'd have to go and lie in a dark room for quite an hour. Really not even the smallest bit amusing.'

'I knew it,' said Oliver in triumph. 'You poor angel, my heart bleeds.'

'Well, so did mine,' said Venice. 'So I gave it up. Or rather, it gave me up. There was disenchantment on both sides.'

'Quite the most sensible thing to do,' said Oliver in approval. 'I mean really darling, some things are just TOO much.'

'So you see,' said Venice, 'I rang to ask you which of the older men are available at the moment. I knew you would know.'

Oliver gave a little cry of delight. Nothing pleased him more than arrangements.

'Darling, you should have come to me sooner. I've got just the very thing for you, as it happens. Only fifty, would you believe, money simply burning the poor man's fingers, and bored to death with his wife. Mind you,' he added pensively, 'if you saw the wife, you would understand why. I believe she's very rich, but apart from that, there's no excuse for her at all.'

'So,' said Venice, getting right to the bottom line, 'he's just waiting for me to come and brighten up his unbearably drab life?'

'But crying OUT for you, my sweet. It's charity, it's philanthropy, it's virtually a sainthood, that's all. Why don't you come round to dinner this evening and we can discuss it? Do say you're free.'

'Nothing I can't cancel,' said Venice, mindful of her priorities. Besides, she believed in standing people up from time to time. It stopped them taking things for granted.

When she arrived at Oliver's flat, it was full, as usual. It was enormous, with great plate glass windows letting in the view, and hovered precariously just on the right side of vulgarity. It was decorated with flowers and erotic art and the kind of French novels that no one had ever read, but everyone pretended they had. For the rest, he filled it up with people, whom he collected like postage stamps and then arranged to their best advantage.

'Venice,' he cried from across the room, as she arrived. 'But just look at you.' Everyone did. 'A poem, a dream, I do declare.'

Venice kissed him on both cheeks.

'Love the jacket,' she said, knowing what was expected of her.

'Oh darling, do you really?' Oliver was on an oriental kick. After all, everyone, but EVERYONE, was going to the east this year. His jacket was high Thai, and the room stank of incense.

'It smells like a massage parlour in here,' said Venice kindly.

Oliver looked at her with love.

'My angel,' he said, 'you do say the sweetest things.'

Venice found herself placed on Oliver's new sofa ('Flown in from Milan, darling,'), with a glass of saki and a rock star. He was quite agreeable, if monosyllabic. He said, in a voice weary with the world and all its diversions, that he was having trouble with his manager. Venice looked sympathetic, and wondered why it was that all rock stars seemed to have trouble with their managers. Perhaps it was like marriage, which Venice always thought a great

13

deal more trouble than it was worth. She smiled on him from a great distance. He was rather attractive, in a gaunt kind of way, but he really wouldn't do. Not rich enough for a start, and all he really wanted in life was a page 3 girl and a water bed. Which, if one believed the tabloids, he got. Several times a night.

Venice left him looking for all the answers to life's questions in the bottom of his glass of saki. She only quite hoped that he found them. Her mind was on higher things.

She crossed the room, skirting one of those sharp ugly journalistic women who was discussing *Vogue* with a fey black girl, who was said to be London's answer to Nina Simone. Venice certainly didn't want to waste any time on them. She only liked reading *Vogue*, not talking about it, and she really couldn't see the point in those chippy female journalists, always talking about their first at Oxford, as if a degree made up for never getting a man. Further along, a perfect little group was lamenting the demise of the Mirabelle. The men were urbane and beautifully groomed, the women pampered and glossy.

'I could weep, that's all,' one of them cried. 'I can't tell you. My dear old Pa used to take me there, as a treat, when I was a child. And now it's being made into some ghastly gambling hall, I could cry.'

Venice found Oliver by the window. He wasn't looking at the view.

'Of course,' he was saying seriously, 'she wasn't remotely interested until she went to Jamaica and saw the yachts and the houses and the cars. I believe gun running is very profitable. Then before you know it, all change, they're off to Asprey, you know that dear little man who has been there since time began, can't do enough for one, and the ring is on the finger, and

14

it's only going to be a short engagement. I ask you. Marriage! Only a year ago, she was smoking her way round India.'

'I went to the wedding,' said Venice, rather too offhand.

'No!' Oliver and his companion were bursting with indignant interest.

'So, tell all. What was it like?'

'Sit down lunch for three hundred,' said Venice. 'I went to sleep after the first course.'

Oliver gave a sigh of relief. 'Well,' he said happily, 'some people really do have NO idea.'

'Now then,' said Venice, capitalizing on his attention, 'what about this old man?'

Venice was exhausted by the time she got home. She had been caught by the woman journalist who wanted to use her for a piece on people who didn't work.

'You're a rarity in Thatcher's Britain, Venice,' she had said, her puffy eyes scornful. 'Everyone is so career orientated nowadays.'

Venice had been rather angry. She knew she was a rarity, but not for those reasons. She had stretched out her perfect neck, long and unmarked in contrast to the chicken-like object in front of her, and looked down her aquiline nose in ultimate disdain.

'Dear Carol,' she had said, in her most bored voice, 'I would love to help you, but you know I never talk to the press.'

Oliver, she had reflected as she turned her back, sometimes did make terrible mistakes when it came to his guest list. Carol Matthews should have been struck off years ago. Still, she had what she wanted. Oliver was going to organize a party for her. She could leave everything in his capable, conniving hands. Alabama might not approve, but enough was enough, after all.

15

While Venice settled down to the rigorous round of hairdressers, manicurists, masseurs, and all the other necessary preparations for catching a bank account on the wing, Alabama got to work on her new play. Each night, Venice would return to the house at two or three in the morning, only to find her sister hunched over the typewriter, surrounded by brimming ashtrays and cups of the blackest coffee, writing as if her life depended on it. Venice would avert her eyes and disappear to bed. She didn't like to look that kind of intensity in the face. It made her feel uncomfortable.

When Venice wasn't worrying about whether to have ash blonde streaks, or platinum, or both, she worried about Alabama. After years of protesting, she had finally come to accept the jeans, and the bourbon, and the shorn hair, and even the motorbike. But Alabama's way of life still bothered her.

After a week, Venice decided that she was well overdue for one of her regular homilies on the meaning of life. She had come home, flushed with champagne and compliments, only to find Alabama pounding away at the typewriter as if the devil were at her back. She steeled herself, longing really for her bed, but overcome with a sense of duty. Enough really was enough, after all.

'Here I am,' she said, by way of preamble.

'So you are,' said Alabama, looking up. Venice was the only girl she knew who looked almost better at the end of the evening than at the beginning. None of the smeared mascara and bleary eyes that characterized a hard evening's play for Venice, who looked as radiant as if she had just awoken from ten days' sleep.

'And here you are.' Venice gave her sister a look which was supposed to be searching, but which didn't quite come off under examination.

Alabama started to look fierce. She was in the middle of a particularly good scene. One of her characters had just revealed himself to be a woman, which had surprised no one more than Alabama, and delighted her, since it gave the plot, which she had feared was becoming dull, a whole new twist. Venice took no notice whatsoever of this fearsome look. Alabama had been trying it on her since they were babes in arms, and that was a lot of water under the bridge.

'OK, OK,' said Alabama, relenting. She pulled the piece of paper out of her typewriter with a resigned flourish, knowing that Venice would not give up so easily. 'Did you have a nice time?'

Venice smiled reminiscently. 'Heavenly. James was there, asking after you.'

'Well, he would.'

'He wants to have dinner with you, he says.' Venice smiled even wider, as if she was conferring some great honour. James after all did merit a very large paragraph in *Debrett*, and most of that was his seventeen titles.

'Do you know why he wants to have dinner with me?' said Alabama, thinking the time had come to defend herself.

'Why?'

'Because I don't want to.'

Venice sat down, and lit a cigarette. 'Elaborate,' she said, admiring her legs, since there was no one else there to enjoy them.

'Perversity of human nature, don't you know.'

'That sounds madly erotic,' said Venice, brightening. 'Rubber in the bedroom?'

'No. Sawdust in the brain.'

17

'Really, Alabama,' said Venice, in her most severe voice. 'You'll never make the right kind of friends if you go on talking like that.'

'But I so much prefer the wrong kind, thank you. Do you know what your eligible young friend tells me when I turn down his gallant invitations to the bedroom? He tells me not to be so silly. It's all I can do to stop myself saying "Up the feudal system", except I think that might be too much for the poor boy's overtaxed brain.'

'Oh dear,' said Venice. 'Most women love him.'

'Most women want to be the next duchess,' said Alabama dismissively. Most women in her opinion, were fools.

'He told me this evening that he had had a hundred and twenty seven women.'

'Errol Flynn, eat your heart out.'

'Is there nothing to be done for you,' said Venice, returning to the attack. 'I mean, really Al, you have four friends . . .'

'Three.'

'Three friends,' said Venice, undaunted. 'You own nine pairs of jeans and not much else, you cut your own hair in the bath. You hardly ever go out, you just sit here, night after night, drinking that filthy Jack Daniels or whatever he's called. When was the last time you went to bed with a man?'

'Earlier this evening, if you must know,' said Alabama, at her most insouciant.

'What?' Venice's perfect mouth fell wide open with amazement.

'Where did you meet him?'

'I don't know. Some bar.'

'But who was he?'

'I don't know. Some man.'

'Alabama! Even I don't do that.'

'No. You let a man take you to the Ritz first. I send out for pizza. That's the difference between us.'

Venice moved on to looking horrified.

'But you might have caught something.'

'I did.'

'What?'

'A number 19 bus. Couldn't get out quick enough.'

For the rest of the week, Venice went on muttering under her breath about bloody-mindedness in general, and misanthropy in particular, a new word of which she was inordinately proud and repeated lovingly at all opportunities. Alabama, used to Venice's little turns, took no notice whatsoever. She simply put Beethoven nice and loud on the record player, and carried on abusing her typewriter. A lesser woman than Venice might have admitted that she was no match for the choral symphony, but a girl with a name like Venice didn't give up that easily. Alabama was all of twenty-seven now, almost over the hill, and her biological clock was ticking away. It was high time she settled down with a nice firm husband who would keep her in order, and a handful of babies to occupy her. It worried Venice most that Alabama rarely went out. Venice couldn't imagine a life that wasn't social. Besides, how could a girl meet the man of her dreams if she sat at home all week? So, she persevered, utterly dogged in the face of adversity.

'I'm giving a dinner party,' she announced at six-thirty one night.

'Should I ring the *Tatler* and tell them?' said Alabama. 'Anyway, you can't cook,' she added, maddeningly prosaic.

'Quails' eggs and smoked salmon, I can,' said Venice triumphantly. 'Come on, admit you're tempted.'

'Sorry,' said Alabama, getting up from her desk and pulling on the leather jacket that always made Venice want to weep. 'I'm going to Croydon.'

'Where else?' said Venice crossly. 'I don't even know where Croydon is.'

'You don't have to. Have a nice evening.'

'Oh,' said Venice in frustration. She had been imagining a perfect evening, with Alabama meeting all her dashing friends and impressing them with her brilliance. There was the reflected glory to be considered besides. It never did Venice any harm at all, being Alabama's sister.

'I hope you crash your rotten old bike,' she flung at Alabama's swiftly departing back.

'BMW would have you for that.'

'You can stuff your bloody trades descriptions act where the sun doesn't shine.'

'Really Venice,' Alabama turned and gave her a nicely measured look. 'You should go and wash your mouth out with soap and water. So shocking.'

'So buy some.' Venice made a face at the retreating figure of her sister and wondered again how they could have come from the same genes. She supposed they must have done, since their mother simply didn't have the imagination to be unfaithful. This reflection only held her for a minute however, since she had rather more pressing things to think of. The quails' eggs that she had bought had had the indecency to be uncooked, and she had no idea how long to boil them for. She wondered which of her aquaintances knew how to cook. Quite apart from this, she had to worry about what to wear, and which lipstick to choose. Venice didn't believe in taking such things lightly. Not for her the unkempt hair and unpainted face of Alabama. Venice might not be able to write plays, or understand nihilism, or do *The Times* crossword, but she knew all about keeping the opposite sex enslaved, and whatever anyone said, it was no small matter.

While Venice went through her address book in the vain hope of finding someone who might know about quails' eggs, Max paced up and down the worn linoleum of his dressing room, mouthing his lines. A few minutes before curtain up there was a knock on the door and the stage manager, a peroxide neo-punk who had been a window cleaner before this job, jangled into the room.

'You'll never guess who's out front tonight,' she said belligerently.

'The Pope,' said Max, frowning moodily like he was taught at drama school.

'No lovey,' said Iona impatiently, 'Alabama Skye, that's all.'

'The playwright?' Max frowned more moodily than ever.

'No, the plumber. The lav's blocked again.' Iona adjusted her bracelets, which consisted of ten lengths of domestic chain bought cheap in a hardware store, and gave Max her least good sarcastic glance, which was pretty good by anyone's standards. 'Where have you been all your life?'

'Croydon,' said Max, not to be outdone.

'Yeah, well, it's better than Deptford,' said Iona with feeling. She knew all about the suburbs, and dreamt of waking up one morning and finding she lived in Soho. 'Anyways. Don't you think you ought to write her a note or something?'

'Great idea,' said Max, no mean hand at sarcasm himself. 'And what exactly do you suggest I put? Dear Miss Skye, do come round after the show, I'll give you a quick one, and you can write me into your next play?'

'Bad approach,' said Iona, shaking her nine earrings at him. 'Don't you read the papers? Never seen in public with a man.'

'She's never seen in public at all,' said Max.

'Well,' said Iona impatient to be gone, 'are you going to write a note or what? Come on, Einstein, stage managers have work to do.'

'Why should I?' said Max. 'What's the point?'

'Strings lovey,' said Iona, as if speaking to a slow child. 'How many famous playwrights do you meet in Croydon? It's not as if we get Harold Pinter in every night. Give yourself a break, why don't you?'

'Five minutes,' a voice yelled charitably.

'Shit,' said Max, moodier than ever.

Just before the lights went up, Alabama was handed a note by a peroxide blonde creation with three yards of lavatory chain about either arm.

'For you,' she said.

'Me?' said Alabama in surprise.

'Yeah.' Iona gave up her attempt to be charming. 'Read my lips.'

In the interval, Alabama bought herself a Miller Lite, and unfolded Max's note.

'Dear Miss Skye,' it said in a heavy black scrawl. 'I'm a great admirer of your work. I would be delighted (Max had almost put "honoured" but had thought that might be coming on a little too strong) if you would come backstage after the show for a drink. Yours sincerely, Max Charlton.'

In spite of herself, Alabama was interested. It was an unfamiliar emotion for her. The production itself would not be giving Richard Eyre any nervous breakdowns, although it was not bad. But Max, he was something altogether different. He made Alabama think of Brando when he was young. She knew it was a cliché now, but it was all she could think of when she watched him. Brando berating Vivien Leigh in *A Streetcar Named Desire*, backing her against the wall, allowing her no respite, smothering her with raw, naked, animal power. Max had that bruised, ill-used look that couldn't be taught. Alabama drank her beer with that little shudder she always felt when she saw pure talent on the wing.

She allowed him five minutes to change. The play had come to its brutal end, bodies littering the stage in the last minute afterthought of violence that the fringe seemed to demand these days, and the audience had dispersed, muttering about imagery and existentialism under its breath, comfortably looking forward to dinner and bed, too sensible of material comforts to be too stirred. Alabama leant against the brick wall outside Max's dressing room, smoking. Backstage was no worse and no better than she had expected. Peeling paint and strip lighting, a smell of old sweat and new greasepaint, and that certain unidentifiable mustiness that hung about all theatres. It was the same utilitarian arena where all young hopefuls started out, hitching their wagon to a star, dreaming almost impossible dreams. Alabama watched her smoke drift away down the corridor, and wondered what he would be like. Arrogant certainly, charming possibly. He had one of those cocky, truculent faces that said it demanded fame. She was prepared to admire his talent, but from his performance she didn't expect to like him. Still, she was intrigued. It made her feel vulnerable. For once in her life, she wished she had a mirror.

Max opened the door in jeans and not much else. His black hair flopped wet over his forehead, and his eyes still bore traces of make-up. Seeing Alabama, he smiled in amusement. To his surprise it was genuine.

'Is it so funny, or is it just the way I'm standing?' said Alabama conversationally.

'All this leather,' Max gestured helplessly. 'I didn't expect so much leather.' He wasn't quite sure what he had expected. Spectacles, perhaps, or a mackintosh. Certainly not this biking girl, all guns blazing.

'I give correction lessons,' said Alabama, quirking a near fatal eyebrow at him. 'For a fee.'

'What in?'

'French, Bulgarian, Serbo-Croat. Urdu is extra.'

'You must be a godsend to the foreign office.'

'Tell me about it. Might I come in, or do you want me to stand in the doorway all night?'

'I'd like to see you in chains,' said Max, letting her in.

'Don't worry, so would my agent. Have you got any whisky?'

'Bourbon.'

'Better and better.' Alabama let him pour her a drink, and tried to avert her eyes from the perfection of his bare torso. 'So,' she said, 'I suppose you want me to write you into my next play?'

'Of course not,' Max lied, opening his eyes as wide as they would do, as if in astonishment, as if the thought had never crossed his mind, for all the world as if he had simply asked her round to discuss Pinter and the state of the art. 'Like I said, I'm a great admirer of your work. It's not often I get the chance to meet a distinguished playwright.'

'It's all right,' said Alabama, draining her glass in patent disbelief, 'you don't have to put on the little boy blue act. It's very seventies. I've seen young actors on the make before.' She was good at being arrogant. It suited her.

'Yes?' said Max, at a loss. He wasn't quite sure what to say. Pointless to deny the make, since it was exactly what he was on.

'Yes.' Alabama looked him right in the eyes. 'You don't have to make a play for me. You interest me, so I'll think about it. We couldn't have you languishing in Croydon forever.'

'Thank you,' said Max, thrown even more off balance. He wasn't used to girls like this. Most of the girls he knew fainted every time he bought them a Campari and soda.

Alabama gave him a considering look. 'Come on,' she said, relenting a little. 'Get your clothes on. I'll buy you dinner.'

'No strings attached?' said Max, emboldened.

'As many as you can count.'

'I'm not sure my maths is up to it.'

'It's not your maths I'm interested in.'

Alabama took Max to an Italian restaurant she knew. It was small and dark and crowded, and the walls showed patches of damp. It was, like her, not at all what he had expected.

'So,' he said, lighting her cigarette before he could stop himself. He liked the way her eyebrows grew so straight and thick, almost meeting in the middle.

'So?' She gave him a searching look, giving nothing away.

Max grinned boyishly, deciding to go for charm. He knew his grin was irresistible. Girls had told him so.

'This is a treat,' he said, winningly.

Alabama laughed without mirth.

'Don't knock yourself out,' she said. 'I asked you here because you're good, and I shouldn't tell you that because you're cocky enough at it is.'

Max scowled, angry that she refused to play the game.

'You're so tough aren't you?' he said.

'My dear boy,' said Alabama, in her most irritating drawl, 'don't tell me you're worried about my feminity? Come back Miz Scarlett, all is forgiven?'

'Maybe you are a dyke,' said Max, crosser than ever.

'Is that what you think?' said Alabama.

'Never seen in public with a man,' Max intoned, remembering what Iona had said.

'Come along sunshine. I don't share the media's taste in restaurants, that's all. Grow up.'

'I'm twenty-two,' said Max huffily.

'And I'm twenty-seven, so that gives me the right to be as much of a bitch as I like. Now eat your spaghetti.'

Alabama wondered why she was being quite so aggressive. She wondered why she couldn't quite look at him, all of a sudden. She wished he would stop looking at her in that furious irresistible way. She wished he didn't look quite so much like a young Brando. She wondered just how long it was going to take her to succumb. Look at yourself, she thought in disdain. Alabama Skye, fearsome young playwright, world at your feet. Alabama Skye, pushover. Falling for a pretty face and a pair of dark eyes, at your age. Whoever said older meant wiser had been way off the mark.

'So,' she said briskly, trying to drag her mind away from such uncomfortable thoughts, 'they're casting a play of mine next week at the Royal Court. I can get them to see you, but after that you're on your own. They'll see you if I ask, because the director is a mate of mine.' She gave a twisted smile. 'He has to be, in case they need rewrites. It's been on in America, and it's a long way from New York to Sloane Square. So, what do you think?'

'Thanks,' Max growled, surly all over again. He wanted to say keep it, stuff it, I don't need your

charity, your gracious handouts, I don't need anyone swanning in and playing lady bountiful with me.
But he did need it. It annoyed the hell out of him.
This wasn't what being discovered was supposed to
be like, surely? Dark walls and harsh red wine and
a girl with a mean mouth? But with that startling
face, and legs that Cyd Charisse would have killed
for, he supposed that she could be as mean as she
pleased. He felt small and insignificant and cross and
out of his depth.

'Don't be too effusive,' said Alabama, who was starting to enjoy herself.

'I won't,' said Max. He was building up to a real
mood, but suddenly he caught Alabama grinning at
him, and he began to laugh instead.

'You really are a bitch, aren't you?' he said. 'Where
did you learn to be a bitch like that?'

'Too many Bette Davis films as a child. You must
admit I do it beautifully.'

'Oh sure. Poetry in motion.'

'Come on,' she said suddenly, standing up, oblivious
of everyone turning their heads to watch her go, 'I'll
give you a lift home.'

Outside, the BMW gleamed aristocratically in the darkness. It was big and black and looked as mean as
its mistress.

'Did you always ride a bike?' said Max.

Alabama laughed. 'What? Do you think the BMW
and I came out of the womb together? Who taught
you biology?'

'I was good at nuclear physics,' said Max, putting on
the spare helmet.

Halfway back, he realized something wasn't quite right.
He tapped Alabama on the shoulder.

'This isn't the way home,' he shouted.

'Glad to see you did better in geography than biology.'

'It still isn't the way home.'

'It is. My home.' Some things were just too good to pass up.

'I thought the casting couch was out?'

'It's making a comeback,' yelled Alabama recklessly as they jumped a red light.

Alabama had forgotten about Venice's dinner party.

'Shit,' she said tactfully, walking in to find the house packed with semi-recumbent forms.

'Al! You MADE it,' cried Venice joyfully, as if her sister had just returned from a particularly hazardous South Antarctic expedition.

'Not yet,' said Max dryly.

The young marquess was not there, much to Alabama's relief, but there were plenty of boys who would have been young marquesses, or viscounts at least, if they had been born a year or two earlier, which they all thought they deserved to be. They were the kind of boys who liked telling people who their great grandmother on their mother's side had been. One of them, who tried to look like Tyrone Power and just missed it every time, blocked Alabama's path. She tried to move past him, but he was swaying too much.

'Hello, Carlisle,' she said in resignation.

'I want you to meet a friend of mine,' he said with import. 'He's an actor.'

'Don't tell me,' said Alabama. 'Not Alec Guinness?'

'He's in *EastEnders*,' said Carlisle, not listening.

'Alan Bates?'

'At least, he's not in it yet, but they're negotiating a HUGE deal for him.'

'Not Albert Finney?'

'He's going to be huge,' persisted Carlisle. He always knew people who had once been huge, or who were about to be huge, but who were somehow never quite huge at the time of writing.

The man almost from *EastEnders* stared at Alabama with unfocused eyes and pin-point pupils and said hello affably. He was leaning against a wall as if the house depended on it.

'He's called Charlie,' said Carlisle sagely.

'Appropriate,' said Alabama, noticing the track marks on his arms.

'Must go to the loo,' said Carlisle suddenly. 'Want to come?'

'No thanks, sweet thing,' said Alabama. 'Mind you don't miss your nose.'

Further into the room, a large jocular man with a red face was holding court.

'Ask me what won the Gold Cup in 1921,' he said expansively.

'Whose gold cup?' asked Max, nonplussed.

Everyone shrieked with laughter at this sally.

'Where DID you find him?' Venice asked Alabama, opening her china blue eyes as wide as they would go.

'Croydon.'

'Where else? I don't even know where Croydon is.'

'You don't have to,' said Alabama firmly. 'He's with me.'

'Oh.' Venice pouted beatifically. 'Is he rich?'

'Come on, Ven. Does the Queen shit in the woods?'

'Ah.' Venice cheered visibly. 'And are you going to keep him in the style to which he is unaccustomed?'

'I don't know if I'm going to keep him at all yet. Ask me in the morning.'

'I shall expect a full report and marks out of ten,' said Venice.

A girl who looked like Madonna might after going six rounds with Mike Tyson was carefully laying out lines of cocaine on the table.

'Toot anyone?' she cried in the bright anyone-for-tennis voice of P.G. Wodehouse heroines.

'Get those Bolivians marching,' muttered Alabama, escaping into the kitchen.

In the fridge, she found a lone tin of Budweiser.

'Thought I heard the sound of corks popping,' said Max, coming up behind her.

Alabama turned in sudden relief. Even under the bright light, he still looked like Marlon wished he still did. His angry young man face was smooth and unmarked, and his eyes were shadowed blacker than ever.

'My sister . . .' said Alabama, all at once at a loss.

'Very nice,' said Max, getting his own back. 'Those eyes, those curves.' He gestured expressively, grinned a lascivious grin. 'Good enough to eat.'

'Feel free,' said Alabama sunnily, back on safer ground. 'I have plenty of good books.'

Max smiled at her, admitting defeat. She was still running rings about him.

'Actually,' he said, 'I was going to offer to take you away from all this.'

'How far?'

'Is upstairs far enough?'

'Yes,' said Alabama.

Much later, Alabama woke and looked down at the dark sleeping form beside her. Each time it happened, she was unprepared for how sweet it could be. She had no idea that going to Croydon could be so dangerous.

She smiled a twisted smile in the darkness and closed her troubled eyes to sleep.

In the next room, Venice stirred and muttered busily to herself as she slept. Beside her, one of the would-be young lords snored smugly. Downstairs, the man almost from *EastEnders* had crashed on the sofa, dreaming east to west end dreams. Carlisle, too wired to sleep, was trying to get through to Charlotte Lewis in LA.

'Of course she'll speak to me,' he told the operator haughtily, 'I discovered her.'

CHAPTER

2

Ten days later, Oliver gave his party. Max hadn't wanted to come. 'I'm not into all that society bullshit,' he had snarled. His snarl was not bad. He had modelled it on Humphrey Bogart in *The Petrified Forest*. He was rather proud of his snarl.

Alabama was not impressed. She never was.

'Listen sweetheart,' she had said, too offhand for words. 'You can take it or leave it, it's entirely up to you. If you want to go for mass exposure, I'd take it. You may not like it, but strings are the name of this particular game, so I wouldn't start developing too many artistic scruples, if I were you.'

'It stinks,' said Max ungratefully.

'Of course it does. But unless you want to spend the next five years in the provinces, you ought to bury your pride. There are a lot of actors out there who can't act their way out of a paper bag, scripts piled up on their desks, because they know the right people. Jump on the bandwagon, why don't you?'

Her investments, thought Alabama, sitting between them in the taxi. Venice, who could bleed any sugar daddy dry, and Max, who just might be able to convince

Oliver's influential friends that he was London's answer to Brando. She couldn't support them both on her own. At least, she reflected, in the light of the stock market crash that had sent all the poor yuppies scurrying about the Square Mile like so many decapitated chickens, her investments looked like a far better thing than BP shares.

They arrived a careful fifteen minutes later than everyone else's half hour. Venice liked to make an entrance.

Oliver swooped on them like some exotic bird of prey, uttering a sharp predatory cry of acquisition. He was *louche* tonight in red raw silk trousers, his hair slicked back off his face, his eyelashes dyed jet black for the occasion.

'The weird sisters,' he said dramatically. 'What utter heaven that we three meet again.' Oliver was proud of the fact that he went to serious plays. One could never get enough of the Bard, in his opinion. In the seventies, he had seriously considered changing his name by deed poll to Mustard Seed, but his father had threatened to disinherit him.

'Hello Oliver,' said Venice, not bothering to look behind her as she shed her coat. There was always someone there to pick it up. As it fell, every eye in the room was drawn magnetically to her voluptuous figure, its curves lovingly outlined in bottle green organdy. Grown men rushed to get her a drink.

'Well,' said Alabama, wryly offering Oliver her cheek, 'I see you haven't changed.'

'Darling!' Oliver gave her a skittish smile. 'As if I knew how.' His eyes moved restlessly on.

'Ah,' he sighed in appreciation. 'So this is the boy wonder. Too butch, darling, too butch.' He did love a boy in a good old-fashioned biking jacket.

'Yes,' said Alabama, enjoying the sight of Max's shoulders hunching in impotent rage.

'Very *On The Waterfront*,' said Oliver, licking his lips. 'Clever, clever you, I say.' His cup was near to overflowing. He loved to see his cousins in his flat, both so tall and vital. He loved the way they stood in such contrast to each other: Venice, with her opulent figure, her extravagantly streaked hair, her wide smile; and Alabama, thin and straight as a die, with her fine bones, her thick eyebrows, her eyes hooded to hide her secrets. They were quite simply a poem to aesthetics. Oliver watched Venice sail into the fray, hogging the limelight effortlessly, the crowd flocking to her like poor helpless moths round a candle flame. Alabama hung back, letting her sister steal her thunder. Still, thought Oliver, Venice might be acknowledged as one of the great beauties of her age, but Alabama, once seen was never forgotten. What a perfectly delectable couple to serve up to his guests. And as for the boy wonder, well he was simply the icing on the cake.

'Where DID you find him, darling?' Oliver asked, savouring Max's long lean figure.

'Croydon,' said Alabama, 'but don't tell a soul.'

Oliver might be frivolous beyond belief, but he did come up with the goods, thought Alabama as she surveyed the room. Among the great vulgar swags of lilies and the French novels and the erotic sculptures, she noticed a gossip columnist, a film producer, two theatre critics, and a woman journalist, as well as the usual collection of immaculately groomed faces that she recognized vaguely from the society pages.

She decided to go for the producer first. She rather liked him, and besides, he was about to start casting for his new film.

'Roger,' she said, propelling Max forward.

'Hello Alabama,' he said, kissing her. 'How was America?'

'Oh you know. The usual. Neurotic method actors screaming that they can't say this line and that line. Everyone munching Valium. The director having a roaring affair with the leading man. You know how it is.'

'Not quite the home life of our dear Queen,' said Roger, twinkling at her appreciatively.

'They're all dear queens over there. I had to concentrate on calling a cigarette a cigarette.'

'Ah,' said Roger, twinkling more than ever, 'but a good fag is a smoke.'

'That's very naughty, Roger,' said Oliver, who was mingling frantically, just like his mother taught him.

'Have you met my New Discovery?' said Alabama, thinking it was time to include Max before he went off into a sulk. 'Max Charlton, Roger Middlemarch.'

She watched the two men shake hands, summing each other up. Roger, smooth, urbane, gracefully middle-aged, and Max, young and raw and rough about the edges.

'Where did you meet Alabama?' asked Roger politely.

'She met me,' said Max, surly and in over his head.

'I bearded him in his dressing room,' said Alabama. 'Do you call that brave? I felt quite like a groupie.' For all her dislike of society, she could speak its language fluently. She was not Venice's sister for nothing. 'He's quite frighteningly good,' she added, just a shade too loud, so that the woman journalist, who was lurking behind them, could hear.

'Well, Carol,' she said turning as if in surprise. Venice always said that Alabama had eyes in the back of her head, just like nanny. 'Are you queuing up to meet

Max? I could hardly blame you. I saw that nice Zeke in New York, he sent love.'

Carol Matthews looked sour. Until a month ago, she had been having a rather public affair with an unknown American rock singer, who still thought punk was hip. He had moved in with her while she did a series of profiles on him and his band and his younger sister who wanted to be an actress, and then he had upped sticks and returned to New York, where it turned out he had an under-age wife.

'Hello Alabama,' said Carol, ignoring the dig. 'I hear America was a riot.'

'Depends on your point of view.' Alabama gave her a small smile. She and Carol Matthews had been on spitting terms for years.

She decided to leave Max to get on with it. Carol was looking so beady that Alabama half expected her to produce a tape recorder from one pocket. She was glad that Oliver had said boy wonder quite loudly. Perhaps it was going to work.

She wandered across the room. On the Milanese sofa, Venice had bearded her prey. Alabama scrutinized him out of the corner of her eye, while pretending to examine a sculpture of a Rottweiler doing very strange things to a semi-clad youth. As far as bank accounts went, Alabama had to admit he was not bad. Nice expensive suit, Gucci shoes, very white teeth and cuffs, hair greying in a distinguished sort of way. He looked very well tended, as if someone remembered to water him every day. Definitely menopausal, he was taking the bait with the alacrity of a trout leaping for a fly. Venice was looking up at him with round soulful eyes.

'Don't you think,' she was saying, 'that one can feel so ALONE in a crowd.'

Alabama winced. Where did she get those lines? She must have been watching the afternoon matinée again.

'Alabama! You must have been looking at that sculpture for quite five minutes. Is there something you want to tell me?'

The gossip columnist stood laughing in front of her. He looked innocuous enough, with his sandy hair and disarming smile, but he wrote scurrilous prose, living on a knife-edge of litigation.

'Hello Nicholas,' said Alabama. 'Are you sluming? I can see at least two heiresses over the other side of the room.'

'Now now. You know you're always worth a paragraph or two. I know which side my bread is buttered.'

'Only buttered? I thought you never ate anything less than *foie gras* these days. So, have you come to wean some murky secrets out of me?'

'As if I could,' said Nicholas, laughing again. 'You know you make a clam look talkative.'

'I think someone's used that line before.'

'I know,' said Nicholas, carefully lighting a cigarette. 'But they'd never dare sue. Tell me,' he added, a shade too casual, 'who is that handsome young man you brought with you?'

Alabama laughed, deep in her throat. A couple of the more glamorous women looked up in surprise, unused to hearing any expression of mirth above a tinkle.

'Darling,' said Alabama, in her best Tallulah Bankhead, 'Haven't you HEARD? That's Max Charlton, my new discovery. Don't you think he's rather to die for? Doesn't he make you think of Brando when he was young? And talented. Certainly the most exciting thing I've seen since Ken Branagh came out of Ireland.'

'Well . . .' said Nicholas.

'And between you and I, my sweet, we're having a bit of a thing. You see how I couldn't resist. I'm surprised you haven't heard. Everyone's talking about him.' They would be by tomorrow, she thought to herself as she sailed blithely away.

'Food anyone?' Oliver cried, ever the perfect host.

Alabama caught him on the wing.

'Where in hell have you hidden the whisky?' she said.

'Oh darling, since it's you. In the kitchen, but don't tell a soul. Someone has got to drink these filthy champagne cocktails.'

People were eating now. Two pretty boys were feeding each other slivers of smoked salmon. The glamorous women picked at their food disdainfully, wary of their calorie count. It was so unchic to be hungry. Roger and Nicholas tucked in greedily.

'The condemned men ate a hearty breakfast,' Nicholas said. He really did corner the market in universal truths.

Alabama decided to rescue Max, who was looking rather green about the gills after half an hour with Carol.

'Come along, my angel,' she said, taking his arm. 'Chow time. Do excuse us Carol.'

'Thanks,' said Max. 'That woman . . . And I thought you were bad.'

'That's what I love most about you,' said Alabama sweetly, 'your old-fashioned charm.'

'I thought you only loved me for my body?'

'That too.'

On the sofa, Venice was now popping quails' eggs into the bank account's mouth with delicious kitten-like laughs of joy. It was, thought Alabama, the most barn-storming début since Vivien Leigh in *Gone with the Wind*.

Max was picking at his food with even more disdain than the glamorous women.

'You call this food?' he said in disbelief.

'DESIGNER food, my angel,' corrected Alabama. 'You'd better get used to it.'

'This fish is raw,' said Max in disgust. He wasn't to know about the utter desirability of sushi. 'I don't understand a word of it. Designer food, society talk, and that.' He pointed at the Rottweiler, curling his lip with rather impressive disdain. 'I mean, what the hell is that?'

'Some people call it art.'

'The only thing I know about art,' said one of the pretty boys, passing them by, 'is that it's short for Arthur.'

'Oh Eugene,' said his companion in delight, 'you do make me SCREAM, that's all.'

'I bet you do,' said Alabama drily.

Alabama gave it another hour. She abandoned Max to the glamorous women, who received him with open arms and small sophisticated cries of joy, while she went to be particularly charming to one of the critics, who had had the temerity to give her last play an indifferent review.

'Milford,' she cooed, stretching out her hand, and enjoying the look of dread on his face, 'how ARE you?'

She was glad to see that Max was such a hit. They were all talking about him, but pretending not to.

'What a joy to meet someone so unashamedly heterosexual,' she heard one woman say. 'We've lost more men to homosexuality than we have in two world wars.'

Just at the moment when she felt that everyone had had a really good look at Max, but was still hungering for more, Alabama decided that it was time to go. She went up and took his hand.

'Let's go,' she whispered in his ear.

He turned in relief.

'Can we really?'

'I think we've done our bit. Besides, I've finished the whisky.'

Hand in hand, like fellow conspirators, they slipped out into the night, followed faintly by the roar of the party. Venice's voice, higher than the rest, rose pure and clear as the ringing of cash registers.

'Oh David,' she was saying, 'I do believe you're quite a flirt.'

Telephones were burning up all over London for days after Oliver's party. He was quite beside himself with delight. He hadn't had such a success in weeks.

The glamorous women rang him, ostensibly to thank for the party, and ask him where he got his flowers done ('We could tell at a glance they weren't Pullbrook and Gould darling, you are clever,'), really to dig for dirt on Max and get his telephone number. Oliver gladly passed it on, and agreed wholeheartedly that Max was the most delicious thing anyone had seen in years.

Venice rang Alabama to say that she wouldn't be home for a few days.

Roger rang his business associates to say that he thought they could have a hot new property on their hands if they moved fast enough. 'Like the class of '54 all over again,' he said. 'Remember Bates and Finney when they were young.'

Max rang Alabama to say that he wouldn't be able to make dinner.

The business associates then rang the glamorous women, who always knew everything, to see what they had heard. The glamorous women confirmed that the hot new property was to die for, and could be seen at Drones, Cecconi's, Langan's and the Ritz in the following week. 'Aren't we clever to have discovered him first?' they said.

Roger rang Max to ask him to audition for his next film.

Nicholas rang Oliver to see if it was true about Max and the glamorous women. Oliver confirmed everything. 'I introduced them,' he said in delight.

Nicholas's arch-rival rang Oliver to see if it was true about Max and Roger Middlemarch. 'Of course it is,' said Oliver in ecstasy, 'I introduced them.'

Alabama, incensed by Nicholas's reports in the paper, rang Carol Matthews to give her an interview on what it was like having an affair with one's protégé. 'The problem with these green actors,' she said darkly, 'is that they let a little success go to their heads.'

David Maxwell rang John D. Wood to ask them to find him a discreet mews house, in Belgravia for preference.

It was the next week that Roger sat with his under-age mistress in a seedy drinking club off the wrong end of the Tottenham Court Road. It was the kind of place where port, out of tea cups naturally, could be had until nine in the morning. Kiki insisted that Rod Stewart was a regular customer.

'It was raided by the police last week,' she said, lighting a Sobranie and sniffing laconically. 'The management fell behind on its protection money. You never saw such a fuss. One of those snooker players broke his ankle jumping out of the loo window.'

Roger felt a little *frisson* of pleasure. He loved the low life, and it didn't come much lower than this. The dim light couldn't quite conceal the hookers practising their trade. Kiki said that they came here in droves, their last port of call after a long night, making unsuspecting punters buy them bottles of Krug at £100 a throw, and collecting a large kick back from the management. Roger often wondered quite how Kiki knew these things, but he didn't like to ask. Kiki didn't care overmuch for questions.

At about three o'clock, as the nightclubs started to close, the overflow started to spill in, unwilling to go home. Henrys, trying desperately to pretend they weren't hooray, came in with upfront society girls, who called everyone, including the waiters, darling. Scions of the aristocracy could be seen necking with Greek shipping heiresses. Sharp-suited music executives arrived with interchangeable blonde girlfriends who all asked for Malibu and coke. A pair of Norwegian ship captains came in, looking very nordic and self-conscious, and were immediately pounced on by the hookers. At least Kiki said they were Norwegian ship captains, but by this time of night Roger was past questioning her pearls of wisdom. The snooker player was nowhere to be seen. Obviously at home, nursing his ankle.

'Kiki,' said Roger, 'have you ever heard of someone called Max Charlton?'

'Max Charlton.' Kiki put her head on one side, so as to think better. 'Rings a bell.' She frowned. 'Oh yeah.

A mate of mine is into all that fringe stuff, you know, dead alternative. She said she'd seen him in one of those plays they do upstairs at pubs. Drop dead gorgeous, she said.' She looked immensely pleased with herself after this effort of brainpower. 'He can't be that big though,' she added as an afterthought. 'I've never met him around the clubs.' Roger decided it wasn't worth the effort to try and explain to Kiki that there were perfectly legitimate forms of humanity outside the club circuit. The world ended for her with Bill Wyman. Roger rather suspected that she had never forgiven Mandy Smith for getting there first.

Back in Chelsea, Alabama lit another cigarette and stared blankly at her typewriter. It was very quiet in the house. Max still hadn't called. That made it more than a week. She sighed, poured herself a large shot of Jack Daniels, and started to write.

At the beginning of the next week, Nicholas arrived in his favourite Mayfair drinking haunt, only to find Oliver halfway through a bottle of Stolichnaya with the Bolshoi's latest offering.

'My dear,' said Nicholas, 'my congratulations. What a triumph.'

Oliver looked dreamily at his Russian friend.

'He is rather, isn't he?'

'Actually,' said Nicholas sternly, 'I was referring to your party.'

'Oh yes,' said Oliver, trying not to look smug and failing. 'That was rather a success. Telephones hot all over London.'

'A godsend to British Telecom. That dinner kept me in copy for days.'

'Talking of which,' said Oliver, suddenly conspiratorial, 'don't put anything in about darling Boris here,

43

I beg. All his Bolshie chums get frantically uptight if they see him consorting with the Other Side, you do see.'

Nicholas quite saw. 'I suppose you're corrupting him with your vicked vestern vays?'

'I do my humble best,' said Oliver.

'Oliver!' Venice as usual stilled the room. 'I knew I'd find you here.'

'Well,' said Oliver unnecessarily, 'would you look at that.'

Venice dwelt a moment at the top of the steps, letting the room take her in. She was reminiscent of the long gone movie queens of the golden days of Hollywood. She made one think of Constance Bennet, and Ava Gardner, and Norma Shearer. She gleamed all over. Sheer stockings clung possessively to her perfectly turned ankles, her shoes were softest calf-skin, and rubies encircled her tiny wrists and her slim neck. Her dress was a heavy red silk, St Laurent at his clever French best, and the coat she so care-lessly dropped behind her was a good long sable. ('In this weather!' said Nicholas under his breath.) In the midst of all this finery, her face, which she took religiously to Elizabeth Arden every day, glowed alabaster smooth.

She erupted down the steps, and pressed her scarlet lips against Oliver's cheek.

'Darling,' she said. 'How pleased I am to see you.'

Nicholas straightened his tie.

'Venice,' he said seriously, 'what would you say to a younger older man?'

'Now Nicholas,' said Venice, with that dazzling smile, 'that's very naughty. You know you never took any notice of me until I was in your column.'

44

'Nicholas judges everyone by the amount of print they command,' said Oliver. 'Where have you BEEN, angel? We haven't seen you for all of two weeks.'

'Oh, busy, you know.' Venice waved an airy hand. 'David is rather demanding, but tonight I managed to escape, isn't it clever?'

'Brilliant,' agreed Oliver. 'And are we to presume it is all a grand success?'

'Well, don't you think?' Venice preened herself for their delection. 'Doesn't being rich suit?'

'Down to the utter ground,' said Oliver, delighted with this new vision, and all his doing. 'Steady, Boris,' he said fondly to the Russian, who was swaying slightly, but still standing remarkably upright for a man who has recently ingested most of a bottle of vodka.

'So,' said Venice, accepting a drink, 'tell me the news.'

The wonderful thing about Oliver and Nicholas was not only that they knew everything worth knowing, but that they were always dying to tell.

'Where to start?' said Oliver, concentrating. 'Well, Carlisle had a tiff with his buddy almost from *EastEnders* over a few unpaid bills.'

'That was inevitable,' said Venice.

'He's consoling himself with a rather nubile graduate,' said Nicholas. 'One of those brewing heiresses.'

'Money and brains,' said Venice. 'That doesn't sound like Carlisle.'

'I've met her,' said Oliver, 'and actually she's utter heaven. She's convinced she can reform him.'

'By picking up his bills in Tramp?' said Nicholas archly.

'Do look at that,' said Oliver in horrified tones, his attention diverted by Kiki coming in on the arm of Nicholas's arch-rival.

'The sheer gall of that girl.'

45

'What IS Kiki doing with Carlton?' asked Venice. 'God, I'm out of touch.'

'Selling her story again,' said Nicholas gloomily.

'What's she done this time?' said Venice. 'Eloped with Mick Jagger?'

'Close,' said Oliver. 'Very close.'

'Kiki,' said Nicholas severely, as she passed. 'You're not really married to a forty-five-year-old rough trade musician, are you?'

Kiki shrieked with delight. She was unquestionably the bimbo in the spotlight this week, and she had a centre page spread and £20,000 in the bank to prove it. All she needed now was a record deal, and she would be nicely set up.

'Really Nicky,' she said in reproof. 'You shouldn't believe everything you read in the papers. YOU should know that.' And she skipped away, her waving platinum hair and her microscopic skirt proclaiming her status.

'Christ,' said Nicholas crossly. He hated being called Nicky. 'I don't believe she's under age at all.'

'Don't fret,' said Oliver, pouring him another soothing glass of Stoli. 'Pieces like that are born with fifty-year-old souls. All I can say is that I hope Roger doesn't catch her cuddling up to Carlton. He's quite a bully boy under that smooth exterior.'

'Do look,' said Nicholas, perking up. 'Here's your sister. What a turn-up for the books. I didn't know she frequented dives like this.'

Alabama looked terrible. She was drawn and pale and had dark shadows under her eyes. Her jeans looked more ancient than ever, and her hair needed a wash. Compared to Venice's unabashed radiance, she looked waif-like and uncared for.

'You do look peaky,' said Venice charitably.

'Thanks,' said Alabama. 'How are you? Last time I saw you, you were living with me.'

'Well yes,' said Venice, 'but you see, David has got me this rather *bijou* little house in Belgravia, could you die? So now I'm a real *demi-monde*. Don't you think I look well on it?'

'Yes. My felicitations. So what are you doing consorting with these undesirables?'

'Always a pleasure to see you, Alabama,' said Nicholas wryly, kissing her.

'You know I don't like the press,' said Alabama.

'So,' said Oliver, 'how's that young actor friend of yours? Is he still giving you the runaround?'

'I really don't know,' said Alabama wearily. 'I only read about him in Nicholas's column these days.'

'I do call it unfair,' said Oliver, 'after all you've done for him. I hear he's got the part in your play, and Roger's snapped him up for that film of his, and he's flavour of the month at every restaurant in London, and really, darling. I call it positively shoddy.'

'I could think of better words for it,' said Alabama, 'but I won't go into them now, since we're still in family viewing time.'

'Oh dear,' said Venice. 'You ARE cross.'

'Have some vodka,' said Nicholas kindly. Contrary to rumour, he did have a heart somewhere, and he felt sorry for Alabama. He had always thought her the classiest woman he knew, and she deserved better than that tatty little thespian.

'Thanks,' she said, with her quick smile.

'Anyway,' said Oliver, reverting to the matter in hand, 'where were we? Oh yes, I hear the Fosters have split up. The word is it was a younger man.' He suddenly didn't want to dwell on Max, since he felt it was partly his fault for introducing him to all those glamorous women.

'Personally, I blame the menopause,' said Nicholas.

'Oh,' said Venice with pleasure. 'You just would.'

CHAPTER

3

Max stared at himself in the looking-glass. He really was a magnificent specimen. He really deserved to be photographed for *National Geographic*, or *GQ* at the very least. He lowered his eyebrows a little to give himself a faintly dangerous air, that Johnny-come-lately, life on the edge, utterly unpredictable look that audiences needed more of, in his opinion. He ran his fingers through the hair that would just fall over his forehead in that rather becoming way. He had to refrain from kissing his reflection. That would not be altogether butch, and he had a reputation to protect.

Watch my star rise, he said to himself, watch it soar into the blue horizon. A scant month on from lowly Croydon and he had the part in Roger's film, and the Royal Court in the bag besides. On top of which, he had just completed two commercials which had paid him £5,000 each, with royalties to come, and only this morning a husky-voiced woman journalist had called to ask him to give her an interview on what it was like being a new face. Just look at my new face, Max thought. Just give its perfection a minute's silence.

Now that his new face was constantly pictured in the papers and glossy magazines emerging from all the most fashionable restaurants and nightclubs, Max had decided that it was time to move on from his squat in Shepherd's Bush. Most of the women he went out with these days didn't even know where Shepherd's Bush was. He had moved into a smart new rented flat in Chelsea, all thick blue carpets and stippling and looking-glasses everywhere. He had ignored his bank manager's pleas to buy. Bricks and mortar might be sure-fire investments, but Max wasn't ready for a mortgage. Too bourgeois. As he had said, echoing Dorothy Parker, all he needed was room to lay a hat and a few friends. The bank manager had not been amused. He had shares in Eurotunnel but no sense of humour.

And, of course, besides the new face, and the new flat, with its appropriately king-sized bed, there were the glamorous women. Max loved the glamorous women. He loved the way they were so perfectly dressed and coiffed and scented. He loved the way they never carried cash, like the royal family. He loved the way they knew everything and everyone worth knowing. He loved their disdainful cut-glass voices and their smart cars and their gold American Express cards. He loved the way they wore mink in May. Most of all, he loved the fact that they loved him.

He gave himself a final lingering look in the glass, and went out to dinner. The thought of ringing Alabama had not even crossed his mind.

Not very far away, Alabama sat in another of those small dark Italian restaurants that she preferred, and stared sadly into her whisky.

'Look at me Milo,' she said pathetically. 'I'm a mess.'

Milo looked at her sorrowfully.

'Never a mess,' he said. 'Really, anything but a mess. A poem, perhaps. A sonnet.'

Milo was Alabama's oldest friend. They had met at Oxford. Rival scholars in their college, they had resented each other on sight, and made a point of ignoring each other at all times. The rest of their year had divided into camps around them, taking bets on which would be the first to crack. The smart money was on Milo. No one had seen cheekbones like Alabama's in Oxford since Zuleika Dobson was a girl. No man could hold out against those for long.

The smart money was right. Late one night in his second term, Milo had found himself upsides Alabama in one of those dim smoky bars that undergraduates like best, and bought her a drink before he could stop himself. Within minutes, the smart money had collected, and they were nose to nose, discussing sex, that great leveller. Alabama always said that it was when she had discovered that Milo had lost his virginity to an upstairs maid that she had fallen in love with him. He came from one of those old in-bred Irish families, who were still muttering about Ireland for the Irish and cursing Cromwell into their Guinness. His earliest memory was of sitting on the lawn watching the house burn down, while the butler served a 1949 Moët to the family and their assorted guests (most of whom were looking rather sheepish after being discovered fleeing from the wrong bedrooms).

'You could of course,' he said now, 'marry me.'

'Milo, you've been proposing to me since we were nineteen. Don't you think you should have grown out of it by now?'

'But not at all. Rejection is so good for the soul. Besides, I'm a creature of habit. Imagine how it would put me out if I had to find someone else to fall in love with.'

'What would you do if I said yes?'

Milo looked at her in reproof.

'Skip the country, of course. I do have some kind of reputation to protect. Bright young husband just doesn't have the same ring to it as bright young novelist.'

Milo was one of the newest of the young literary stars. His first novel had just been published to astonishingly good reviews, and his articles, which six months ago he could hardly give away, now commanded absurd amounts of money. He was even a member of the Groucho. Like Alabama though, he made few concessions to success, knowing how fickle the public could be. He had seen too many talented writers fade away into obscurity after an initial burst of fame. He knew that a man is only as good as his last press release.

'And how is the bright young novelist?' said Alabama. 'Still as bright as ever? Still slaving away on the next masterpiece?'

'Well, I did think about being a one-book wonder, but I can't help myself. The new one is almost finished. How can I help it if I simply am a genius? I didn't ask to be.'

'Of course you didn't. I really don't hold it against you.'

'*Harper's and Queen* rang me up today to ask if they could come and take pictures of my flat. I said to them, I said "really ducky, I'll be opening church fêtes next."'

'And quite right too. You don't do nearly enough for the church. You haven't been near Farm Street in months. Imagine all those poor Monsignors weeping into their port at the thought of your terrible defection from the fold.'

'Don't speak,' said Milo in horror. 'I've converted. All that guilt, really, it's more than a boy can stand. Anyway, when we get married we'll have to be the same denomination, and I can't quite see you saying forty-five Ave Maria's before breakfast.'

'No,' agreed Alabama. 'How could I fit it in with the forty-five strong men I eat for breakfast?'

'Exactly,' said Milo in satisfaction, glad to see shades of the old Alabama that he knew and worshipped returning.

His optimism was short-lived. Alabama suddenly turned her deep wounded eyes on him.

'Oh Milo,' she said, 'what am I going to do?'

A mile away, in one of the lush watering holes he now frequented, Max sat, happily oblivious of the grief he was causing, with the most persistent of the glamorous women, the one he dined with twice a week, who was instructing him in the delicate art of eating asparagus without getting butter on his chin. Max often thought that it was these kinds of pearls of wisdom which had got the glamorous women where they were today.

'You are coming along a treat,' said Sabine approvingly. She sounded rather like a farmer admiring his prize pig. 'Although of course, we mustn't groom away all those rough edges altogether. Those are part of your charm. Under those expensive clothes, lurks the jungle, as Letty Gordon told me the other day.'

Max snorted. 'Letty Gordon is an idiot,' he said ungratefully.

'But a very influential idiot,' said Sabine. 'Her family owns half of Worcestershire, and she married the other half. Rather a sharp move, really. Tell me angel,' she went on, hardly pausing for breath, her eyes running over him appraisingly, 'Who chose that coat?'

'My jacket?' said Max. 'Don't you like it?'

'Only potatoes have jackets my sweet, remember that. And no, I don't. It reeks of suburbia, that's all.'

Max had soon learnt that suburbia was the mark of absolute death with the glamorous women.

'Carola Markham chose it,' he said.

'Ah.' The light dawned all over Sabine's elegant features. 'Well, that explains everything. Poor Carola. She does try so hard, but every so often she makes a frightful error.'

'Error?' said Max, a little lost.

'Yes, darling,' said Sabine patiently. 'She was a shop girl before she married Freddy. Straight out of one of those extraordinary places on the end of the underground. Of course, she went off to one of those style consultants to be taught how to dress and get out of cars and address a duchess and which knife to use for fish, but you see, one always KNOWS.'

'Does one?' said Max, with that grin that brought grown women to their knees.

'Yes, one does,' said Sabine, not letting herself be carried away by it. 'I always say that nothing can replace a good nanny, not even these days, with all this equal opportunity.' Sabine deeply disapproved of equal opportunity, and frequently said so. Phrases such as 'undermining the social fabric' and 'keeping people in their place' tripped easily off her tongue. Max thought to himself that she would be the first to go, come the revolution, but he was quite glad that the tumbrels were not rattling through Belgravia just yet.

It was late when they left the restaurant. Sabine's Bentley glided discreetly to the door. It was old and green and had been owned by an ex-king, which gave Sabine an inordinate amount of pleasure.

'Well, darling,' she said. 'Thank you for a perfect evening.' She always thanked him, as if she hadn't paid for a thing.

'I don't suppose,' she said, fixing him with her amber eyes, 'that you would like to come back for a nightcap? My old husband is away on business, so I'm all alone, do you see?'

Max quite saw. He wondered if he could resist her. She was so lush and rich and tempting. He decided he couldn't.

'I'd like that,' he said.

Sabine's smile put the Cheshire cat to shame.

'I rather hoped you would,' she said.

As Max sat back in the well-sprung luxury of Sabine's car, heading for the Aubusson rugs and Venetian glass of her Eaton Square apartment, Milo was walking back to quite a different part of London. He liked to walk at night. It was a time when he felt the city was really his.

He was worried about Alabama. He had only seen her like this once before. That time, she had locked herself away with a crate of whisky and a typewriter, and emerged a month later with her first, and some argued, her most brilliant play. The episode had never been referred to again. But this time she wasn't writing, she was just drinking. It was so unlike Alabama to allow herself the luxury of letting go. It was too early for the menopause, and besides, Milo didn't believe in blaming hormones. Something would have to be done.

Milo was a man of decision. The next day, he woke up, made himself a cup of the soupy black coffee he affected, lit a cigarette, and called Venice.

'Well hello,' she said brightly. 'I haven't seen you for about a hundred years. How does it feel to be famous?'

'Just ducky. How about lunch?' Milo believed in getting to the bottom line.

'You are lucky,' said Venice, 'I've had a cancellation. How about the Caprice, your treat?'

'One o'clock,' said Milo, and disconnected.

Venice arrived ten minutes late. It would have been her customary half an hour, but she knew Milo wasn't impressed by that kind of thing. She paused in the doorway, letting the room take her in, and gave a little sigh of pleasure to see that she was far and away the most beautiful woman there.

Milo was sitting at the bar, nursing a Bullshot and a hangover. He was wearing very black Ray Bans and a T-shirt with a picture of the Pope on it. It was his last concession to his faith.

'Tough night?' said Venice, kissing him sympathetically. She had been having a few tough nights of her own lately.

'It's all your sister's fault. I keep forgetting that she's been drinking me under the table for the last seven years.'

'That's a lot of Jack Daniels under the bridge,' said Venice. 'Do let's sit down. I hate bar stools. So unaccommodating.'

They made a regal progress across the room to their table, where there was very nearly an unseemly squabble between two waiters over who was to pull out Venice's chair for her. Milo grinned to himself. He had forgotten about Venice.

'You do look a picture,' he said, as they settled themselves. 'I hear you've become the last of the great courtesans.'

'Yes,' said Venice happily. 'Isn't it rather to die for? I'm quite terrifyingly good at it too. I deserve a Nobel Prize for services to mankind at the very least.'

'You do.'

'Thank you.' Venice stretched her neck. 'Aren't I lucky to be me?' she added inconsequentially.

Milo laughed. Venice brought artlessness to a high art. Only she could get away with such rampant narcissism.

'So,' she said, turning her great blue eyes on him, 'what has brought all this on. I know you're never normally seen dead with girls like me. What would your public say?'

'That's the thing about you,' said Milo, 'one forgets that you're not a complete idiot.'

'Well darling,' said Venice, who thought feminism was a type of sanitary towel, 'I'll tell you something for free. It never did a girl any good to let on that she has more than half a brain. Men don't like it, that's all. It makes them feel threatened. I mean to say, look at Alabama.'

'Precisely.'

'Yes,' said Venice sapiently, 'I didn't think you'd brought me out to discuss the joys of the *demi-monde*. She's not awfully happy, is she?'

'Not awfully. What do you know about this Max character?'

'Well, to tell you the truth darling, I'm so busy with David at the moment that I don't have time for much else. Last time I saw Alabama, she said he wasn't behaving very well. Is he still a problem?'

'Hasn't called for a month.'

'Oh dear,' said Venice. 'Well, I'll tell you about him. He's all mean and moody, you know the ones. Rather went out of date in the fifties, but seem to be making a comeback. The strong silent type, not really my cup of tea, I've always found it rather too much like hard work,

56

but you do see how Alabama couldn't resist. And he is very pretty.'

'Yes.'

'So, anyway, Alabama goes and picks him up out of the gutter, or rather Croydon, but I think it's much the same thing. And now he's got the part in her play, and I hear from Oliver that he's going to be in Roger Middlemarch's new film, you must have read about it in the papers, and every time you turn on the television he's advertising aftershave. I saw him last week in the Ritz, dressed from head to foot in Armani, looking very cosy with Sabine Borromini.'

'Sabine who?'

'Borromini. One of those rather predatory women of a certain age, as the French put it. You know the ones. A nip here, a tuck there, (you can always tell, because they go away for a very long skiing holiday and come back with their smile rather stretched and the cheekbones very prominent). She does manage to look remarkably glamorous for her age, I must say.' From her lofty position of both youth and beauty, Venice could afford to be bountiful. 'I'm afraid if Max hasn't called Alabama for a month, I'd draw the obvious conclusion, wouldn't you?'

'Yes,' said Milo, frowning. What kind of man could drop Alabama for some terrible painted harridan held together with surgical tape?

'I'm afraid that's the only conclusion that can be drawn, men being what they are. Something will have to be done.'

'I'll think about it,' said Venice, taking for granted her position as expert on affairs of the heart. 'And now if you don't mind, I'd like to be fed.'

As Milo and Venice discussed him over lunch, Max walked into a church hall in an obscure street in South

London for the first readthrough of Alabama's play. He had arrived half an hour early, terrified of getting lost, and had to go and sit in the local greasy spoon, sipping thick tea and feeling nerves stir up sickness in his stomach.

Sitting there, in the stuffy little café, with its linoleum floors and steamed up windows, he had suddenly been assailed with doubt. What if he couldn't do it? What if he made a mess of it? He started to regret all the late nights, all the expensive dinners, all the socializing. He had almost forgotten what he really was. Now it came flooding back to him, sharp and metallic in his mouth. The terror of stripping yourself bare, for people to laugh at. He tried to concentrate. He was looking forward to this, after all. Olivier always said that the first readthrough was where you breathed life into a character and saw its heart begin to beat. What could be more exciting than that? But what if the heart didn't start to beat? What then? Max took another mouthful of tea in a vain attempt to fill the hole where his stomach should be. Dammit, he liked this character, this character was a real shit, he could do it on his head. He practised some of the exercises that he had picked up from the endless books of theory he had read. Those were the days when he was starting out, young and ardent and besotted with his profession. The days when he had sat up until the dawn filtered through his window, devouring Stanislavsky, Brook, anything he could get his hands on about the craft of acting. The days before Alabama, before the glamorous women, before he had become sought after. He thought back to his books, to his training. Start with the feet, he heard some far-off voice say. How would this character walk? How would he tie his shoe-laces?

At last, it was time to go. Max crossed the street, and pushed open the door of the hall. He paused for a moment on the threshold. He could always just turn and run. He could fly back to Sabine's accommodating arms, and lay his head on her capacious breasts, and go to sleep. Except he couldn't. He took a deep breath, like his last breath of freedom, and walked in.

Inside, the hall was dark and hot and musty. There were tables and chairs stacked in corners and the bare floor smelt of damp. Odd dust-filled rays of sunshine fell through the grimy barred windows, which struck Max as being a little too symbolic. Community notices were pinned to the walls. Mrs Pankhurst, he noted with interest, would be doing teas at the Sunday crèche. There was no one in sight, but voices could be heard in the back.

Wandering through another door, Max found a kitchen, where two men were busily making vast steel pots of tea.

'Hi,' said one of them, cheerfully sticking out a pudgy hand.

'Alex. Stage manager.'

'Max,' said Max. He felt reassured. Readthroughs always started with the stage manager making tea. At least he had come to the right place.

'Am I very early?' he added.

'Not really,' Alex said easily. 'The director's just gone for cigarettes. The others should be here soon. Tea?'

The other actors started to lurk in, looking uncomfortably as if they were crashing a party and were terrified of being accosted by the hostess. They nodded at Max, not knowing him, but aware of who he was. They all made straight for the tea, murmuring appreciatively 'Ah, tea,' as if it were life-saving nectar, grinning sheepishly at Alex, fumbling with handfuls of biscuits. Finally, the director arrived, a slight slim figure, dressed from head to foot in black, waving a carton of Marlboro.

'Hello everybody,' he cried. 'Here I am. Hello darling,' he said to the leading lady, kissing her fervently. 'Do we all know everybody? I think Max is the newest among us. Does everyone know Max?'

They all nodded at Max again, making mumbling noises through their biscuits. They moved into the main body of the hall, reforming into tight little groups, making desultory conversation. The director hopped on one foot, looking at his watch. Max stood a little apart, gulping nervously at his too-hot tea, trying not to look too terrified, listening to the snippets of talk.

'So, how WAS Mold? Michael Hordern is marvellous though, isn't he? I mean getting on now, but marvellous.'

'I can't tell you what it was like. I dried in the middle of my big speech. I couldn't look anyone else in the eye for days after.'

'He got four million for that ad, you know, and he only came out of his trailer twice the whole day.'

'So he told me to do the method. If Robert de Niro could do it, I could. You know, put on two stone, and smoke cuban cigars for a month. I said well, it's all very well, but my wife would leave me.'

'Hell, utter hell. The matinées were full of O-level students taking notes. There was so much rustling of paper we were all yelling by the end.'

'A real heart-throb now. He came out of the squash court the other day and found love notes all over the windscreen of his car.'

60

'I can't tell you what heaven it is, working with Johnny again. The last director I had was a sadist, my dear, but certifiable. I went home in tears every night.'

Then, the door swung open for the last time, and Alabama came through it. Max stiffened. He had forgotten she would be there.

'Johnny,' she said breathlessly, kissing the director. 'I am sorry. The bike wouldn't start.'

Johnny clapped his hands.

'Now people,' he said in his carrying voice, 'now that the delicious Alabama has graced us with her presence, we can start. What do you think? Round in a circle?'

Everyone went to fetch chairs, and drew them up with great scraping noises, like children at school.

'That's right,' said Johnny approvingly. 'Just a gentle readthrough then everyone.' He looked at them all imploringly, as if he had demanded that they scale Everest in bedroom slippers and no Sherpas.

'Let's all enjoy it. Now Sasha,' he nodded at the actor who had the first line, 'in your own time, lovey.'

They started, their voices sounding curiously muffled and dead at first in the dim hall. Max didn't take in too much of the first few pages, he was too busy waiting for his entrance. He was conscious of the others watching him out of the corners of their eyes. They must be wondering quite how he got this part. He felt like a new boy who has arrived a term after everyone else. As the reading progressed though, he lost his self-consciousness, aware only of a growing excitement as he heard the shape of the work for the first time, the real sense of it out loud, brought to life as the voices carried, clearer and more confident now, into the empty space. He was surprised to find himself struck

61

by the force of certain lines he had thought routine, and furious when he stuttered over his biggest speech. He tried not to look at Alabama. She just sat there, quite still, her eyes far away, her long legs stretched out in front of her in those familiar battered jeans, smoking. He wondered how he could have forgotten how beautiful she was. Compared to Sabine with her generous figure, and her opulent face, she looked ill-kempt and uncared for and undernourished, but she still had those startling bones, that fierce keen look that no money can buy.

At last, it was over. A great sigh of relief ran round the company, as if they had indeed scaled Everest, and everyone lit up and started to talk all at once.

'It's a dream of a part, really a dream. I only hope I can do it justice.'

'I can't tell you what a relief this is, after farce.'

'Heaven to be working with Johnny again . . .'

'I saw it in New York, when I was there. You never saw such reviews.'

The girl sitting next to Max looked up at him with laughing eyes.

'Not too desperate, was it?' she said. She had a curious gruff voice, full of gin and cigarettes. 'I'm Emmie.'

'Max.' Max smiled at her, grateful for her easy friendliness.

'I know.' She smiled even wider, seeing his surprise. 'I've seen you. At Croydon. Very impressive.'

Max looked at his feet. Used by now to the extravagant praise of the *beau monde*, and he found himself brought to blush by two wry words from a scrap of a girl hardly older than he was.

'Don't worry,' said Emmie. 'We're all terrified. Doesn't it show? Look at Johnny, the darling of the West End, more awards than you can shake a stick at, and he's shit-scared.'

'Do you ever wonder why we do it?' said Max.

'Nope,' said Emmie, shaking her head decisively. 'It beats an office block and a bowler hat, as dear Larry once said.'

'I read that book too,' said Max, grinning at her again. It was going to be all right.

'Now everyone,' said Johnny, claiming their attention again. 'I think you will all agree when I say that Alabama has written us a dream of a play. Any questions for her at this stage?'

There was a general shaking of heads and murmurs of wonderful, lovely, which Alabama acknowledged with her quick smile. The only voice of dissent came from the female lead, an actress whom Max recognized for her talent as well as for her reputation for having slept with every producer worth his salt in London.

'Alabama,' she said earnestly, 'darling. I love your work, you know I do, as if it were my own. And I love this play, I really love it, but there is just this tiny bit in the second act . . .'

Everyone laughed, obviously knowing the joke of old.

'Charlotta lovey,' said Johnny, 'haven't you grown out of this? There's ALWAYS some tiny thing that bothers you in the second act. We can sort it out at a later date. And now then, angels, I think we've said enough about the play. We've got a marvellous cast, if we can stop Charlotta talking, and I'm absolutely certain it's going to be a huge success. I have a feeling about this one. And now I think we should all go and have a look at the set, and then have a word with Concepcion.'

Everyone dutifully moved over to have a look at the model of the set, which the designer explained in great detail.

'I never know why they bother with this, do you?' Emmie whispered to Max. 'How can you tell what the set is going to look like from a model? I don't understand a word of it.'

The others were making appreciative noises, and looking comprehending.

'I tell you what,' said Emmie, 'a few of us are going out to dinner afterwards. Want to come?'

'Yes,' said Max with pleasure. Sabine would be livid, but somehow he didn't feel like the high life this evening, and besides, this was work. Anyway, thought Max heartlessly, it would do her good to be stood up.

Finally, they all had to discuss their costumes with Concepcion, which posed rather a problem, since she had a scanty grasp of English. Charlotta's well-trained voice rose higher than the rest.

'No synthetic fabrics, darling, I beg of you. You've no idea what they do to me.'

It was only when Max turned to leave that he realized that Alabama had gone.

'What do you mean, you can't make dinner?' Sabine, her voice unbecomingly sharp, made it sound as if Max had just discovered that he had a particularly virulent case of herpes. 'One has to book weeks ahead, and then you tell me you can't make it.'

'It's work,' said Max. 'Sorry, but there's nothing I can do. I'm going now, I've run out of coins.'

'Sod you,' said Sabine to the dead mouthpiece.

Emmie took Max to a pizza restaurant with smiling harassed waiters and a juke box. How odd, Max reflected, as he and Emmie walked in, to be going to a regular kind of place to eat. He had found it so seductively easy to slip into the world of linen tablecloths and fawning head waiters and famous faces that he had almost forgotten what it felt like. How odd that the room didn't instantly look one over, noticing if one's coat was Ralph Lauren or Armani. How odd that all the other diners didn't instantly look up, to see who one was with, which table one was given. It was just a regular kind of place, with a lot of people gathered round painted tables, talking and eating and drinking as hard as they could. They weren't agonizing over whether to have the monkfish or the langoustine ('What a choice, darling. How can they do this to me?') They weren't wondering whether to choose a St Emilion or a Château Margaux. They weren't bothered about who was who and who wasn't.

Max and Emmie were late. Emmie had insisted on going via a tobacconist in some side street, which she swore sold the only decent Turkish cigarettes to be had in London.

'We're late, shoot us,' she said as they arrived. She brandished her cigarettes by way of explanation. 'I've brought Max.' She smiled triumphantly, as if she had just produced Anthony Sher from one pocket. 'Say hello nicely.'

They said hello nicely. Most of the cast were there, except Charlotta and the other lead, an older ex-RSC actor. There were four of them, three boys and a girl, instantly recognizable to Max, all secure in their status as the cream of the new generation. Max had seen their names in lights along Shaftesbury Avenue. He had seen them interviewed in the papers, read their views of the world. He had seen them act. They had made it, and he was fresh out of two miserable weeks at Croydon. When they appeared in the national press, it was in the arts pages. When he appeared in the national press, it was in the gossip columns. 'The boy wonder,' said one of them, who obviously read the gossip columns. Max winced, trying to maintain an insouciant front. They had come up the hard way, in the provinces, working their hearts out for no money in rep, and he dined at the Ritz. They must be looking at him, knowing him for a phony, wondering just how many strings he had pulled. He wondered if they knew he had been sleeping with Alabama. He wondered if Alabama knew he was sleeping with Sabine.

He started to look shifty, but then he saw that they were all laughing.

'Don't mind Sasha,' said the girl, who was called Minna, 'he can't help it if he's addicted to the gutter press. Do tell me, what is Roger Middlemarch really like? I've always harboured a secret passion for him.'

Max relaxed. It was going to be all right.

If Max had stopped to think about it, he might have marvelled at their lack of resentment. He was shooting to stardom the easy way, straight in through the side door. But as it was, he didn't dwell on it. His fatalistic view of life, easy come, easy go, stopped him from pausing to reflect. He simply accepted their acceptance, as he accepted everything, as his due. As for the others, they knew how difficult the road could be, and they didn't begrudge him his good fortune. They had all had their fair share of luck along the way, and they knew that they needed all they could get. And Max had the talent to justify his rise. They had seen him act, and they had heard him read, and he would do. He was no imposter, he was the real thing. So they settled down to enjoy their dinner, and everyone ordered four seasons pizzas with extra pepperoni, and a great deal of red wine, and Max coasted through it as he coasted through everything without a second thought.

At home in her bedroom, Alabama sat in front of the looking-glass and contemplated life, the universe, and her reflection. She was not as beautiful as Venice, but she had a certain something. She tried to work out what that certain something was. Striking bones, that was what she had. 'I love my bones,' she said without conviction. It wasn't any good having striking bones if they didn't work. Damn Max.

She poured herself another shot of bourbon. He hadn't even had the grace to acknowledge her. Perhaps she was slipping. She had never really considered her power to attract men. She always had, one way or another. She had never much cared for them when they appeared enslaved, but she supposed she had quite liked having them there. And now, the one man she did want to notice her had looked the other way. 'I'm getting senile,' she told herself furiously. 'Or perhaps I'm getting late adolescence.' She cried a few bitter tears, told herself not to be such a fool, and went out.

'I'm a fool' she told Oliver, whom she found in his usual Mayfair bar with a bottle of champagne and a French film star.

'Darling,' said Oliver, buying another bottle. He could see Alabama was in need. 'Your problem is that you won't allow yourself to be human. If I think of all the times I've had my heart broken. Simply smashed, darling, I mean absolute smithereens. Admit it, my sweet, you've finally joined the human race.'

'It stinks,' said Alabama gloomily.

'What does?' said Nicholas, breezing in with a large bunch of flowers and a hangover. 'Has Kiki sold her story again? Who's she married this time? Jack Nicholson?'

'No,' said Oliver with dignity. 'We were discussing the human race. Flowers? For me? Oh Nicholas, I didn't know you cared.'

'Actually,' said Nicholas, 'they were for a girl.'

'How droll,' said Oliver. 'Are you courting?'

'I was. We were supposed to be having dinner this evening, but she seems to have eloped to Mexico with her stepfather.'

'How Freudian,' said Oliver. 'Still, lovely roses.'

'I think I'll give them to Alabama. She deserves them more than you do.'

'I'm desolate,' said Oliver. 'I love roses. I need roses. It's all that makes life worth living, apart from lilies.'

'Thank you Nicholas,' said Alabama, accepting the flowers with as much grace as she could muster. 'Although a wreath would have been more appropriate.'

'Still in mourning?' Nicholas looked sympathetic.

'For her life, like Masha in *The Seagull*,' said Oliver, showing off. 'Of course, being such a philistine you wouldn't know about Chekhov, but there, you have your redeeming features.'

'Such as?'

'Oh don't put me on the spot like that, I beg. I expect I could think of some if you gave me a week and utter quiet.'

Alabama laughed. She couldn't help it. Her cousin might be frivolous beyond the bounds of decency, but sometimes a girl could take life too seriously. If she couldn't have Max, she might as well let herself be fed champagne and the ridiculous badinage that passed for conversation with Oliver. She tried a smile.

'That's better,' said Nicholas comfortably. He liked to see Alabama smile. It made him feel warm inside.

The French film star, who so far had not said a word, lit a Gitane and stared moodily into the middle distance.

'Don't mind him,' said Oliver, 'he reads too much Sartre, that's all. I never met someone so existential. And of course, he doesn't speak a word of English.'

'Not a word?' said Alabama.

'Well, apart from your place or mine,' Oliver conceded.

Nicholas laughed. 'There's something very reassuring about you, Oliver,' he said. 'The Government may fall, we could be struck by fire and flood, but you'd still be found in bars with the strong silent type.'

'Have a little respect, my dear,' said Oliver, lifting his chin as high as it would go, and looking down his aquiline nose. 'THEY would be found with ME.'

Max and Emmie left the restaurant late, full of pizza and wine, and decided to share a taxi home.

'My place or yours?' said Emmie boldly.

'Yours,' said Max. He couldn't remember if he'd cleared up after Sabine. Only yesterday, his daily woman, her mouth pursed up in a disapproving line, had presented him with a pair of black lace knickers which were obviously not designed for a man.

'After all,' said Emmie reasonably, 'if we are supposed to be having an affair in this play, it's only right that we should do plenty of rehearsing. Anything for Art.'

'Quite,' said Max. 'After all, we do believe in the Method.'

'Of course.'

'The only thing is, I'm also supposed to be having affairs with Charlotta and Minna.'

'That's all right,' said Emmie, who was a practical girl, 'you can do them next week.'

Max wondered what Sabine would say. He wondered what Alabama would say. Emmie laughed up at him, wanton and unconcerned. He decided not to think about it.

Eventually Oliver took the French film star, who still hadn't said anything, home. 'You can see the poor boy's exhausted,' he said unconvincingly. Alabama and Nicholas stayed behind. Someone had to finish the champagne after all. Alabama wondered at herself. She had never liked champagne and she had never liked Nicholas. She disapproved of both, and here she was, betraying her principles in an old-fashioned Mayfair dive. But at least Nicholas was solicitous and sympathetic, and if she was going to be miserable, she might as well be miserable with someone.

'Were you courting seriously?' she asked.

'Of course not,' said Nicholas indignantly. 'What do you take me for?'

'An incurable romantic.'

'Very witty. She was very attractive though, and very rich, and very willing.'

'Not that willing.'

'Until she ran off. It must be something to do with all those Oedipus complexes.'

'Must be.' Alabama couldn't help laughing at him.

'Oh don't. How can I help it if I only got one O level?'

'What in? Needlework?' said Alabama, laughing even more.

'Divinity actually,' said Nicholas, attempting to get on his dignity and missing.

'Don't tell me you were destined for a career in the church.'

'God no,' said Nicholas in horror, 'the only time I go to church is for weddings, and that's a strain.'

'Shall we get another bottle?'

'Let's. What else can one do?'

'Well, I did think of putting my head in the oven, only I've got electricity.'

70

Max was so busy kissing Emmie in the back of the taxi, that he didn't notice Nicholas' arch-rival observing him with interest from a neighbouring car as they stopped at a traffic light.

'Well,' said Carlton to his companion, who was a bottle blonde with an accommodating manner, 'how deeply interesting. The boy wonder in the back of a cab. It's worse than the back row of the movies.'

CHAPTER

4

Alabama decided to take a pull. It was all very well joining the human race, but she had to get her new play finished or her agent would kill her and she would have left the human race before her membership ran out. Besides, if she was going to go to the odd rehearsal, she would have to find something to take her mind off Max. She didn't want him knowing that she cared.

He was in the papers again this morning. Caught kissing some blonde in the back of a taxi, just like a teenager after his first grown up dance. Really, thought Alabama with scorn, couldn't he show a little more style. If he was going to set himself up as a philanderer, he was going to have to learn to do it properly.

She wondered what she should do. There must be some cure for heartache. She had tried whisky, but it wasn't working as well as it should. She had tried writing it away, but that hadn't been a great success either. Perhaps she should find another man and make Max jealous. That was rather crude for Alabama's taste, but it might work. Perhaps she should write him into her new play, and give him a real bitch of a part, and watch the critics tear him apart. That would be a Pyrrhic victory though,

since it would ruin her play. Alabama loved her plays
with the fierce possession of a mother for her young. She
always felt a terrible wrench when they were finished,
perfected, polished, and she had to give them away to
be performed, when she no longer had any control, and
she had to stand by and watch, helpless, as some actor
strutted and fretted his hour upon the stage, with her
material entirely at his whim. She couldn't ruin a play for
the sake of a man. No man was worth that. Perhaps she
should just ring up Venice. Venice would know what
to do. She might not be clever like Alabama, but she
was the past mistress when it came to men, everyone
knew that. Alabama felt herself becoming more human
by the minute. She didn't like it at all.

'I AM glad you rang,' said Venice, her temptress voice
carrying strongly down the line, somehow reassuring
in its eternal promise of sex and good times. 'Shall we
have lunch? Have you seen the Monster? Have you read
the papers?'

'Yes, no and yes,' said Alabama.

'Park Walk at one then?'

'All right.'

Venice stretched her perfect limbs between her linen
sheets. She was pleased that Alabama had rung. She
loved her new house, tucked in its little mews between
Belgravia's great white mansions, and she loved her new
possessions, all the jewels and clothes and hats and the
little bibelots that littered the house. She loved going
on shopping trips, charging everything, and returning
home, exhausted, arms full of flowers and hat boxes
and shiny bags, just like a real mistress, the kind they
don't make any more. And David was awfully sweet,
the way he just GAVE her everything, insisting there
were no strings attached, but he wasn't a whole bundle

of fun, and he did so love to tie her to the bedpost, which Venice found rather uncomfortable and quite dull. It wasn't all hearts and flowers being a mistress, she reflected, watching the sun work its way round to her window. It was quite like graft. Still, she supposed it was worth it. It was, after all, what she had longed for. It would be nice to see Alabama though. Alabama might take life too seriously, but Venice missed her.

Milo rang up Alabama to see how she was. He liked to call her most days.

'How about marriage?' he said cheerfully.

'Too early.' Alabama was heartless. 'I haven't had breakfast yet.'

'Pity.'

'You are a disgraceful liar. It's like a disease with you.'

'Not at all. It's charming. Never tell the truth if you can help it, it's terribly overrated. It's so . . . so . . . LUMPY. Like suet pudding.'

'Semolina.'

'That too. So, are you still heartbroken, or did you give it up as a bad job.'

'I'm desolate. I keep seeing articles in magazines about today being the first day of the rest of your life. So if today is the first day of the rest of my life, what happens tomorrow?'

'I see your point. Are you quite sure you don't want to nip up the aisle? It would give you something to do, anyway.'

'No. I want revenge.'

'You really want him back, after all this?'

'Of course I do. I'm a woman.'

'Alabama! What an admission. I think you ought to have some breakfast. Never try to think on an empty stomach.'

'I suppose I could marry you,' said Alabama doubtfully, 'and then Max could come storming up the aisle
at the last minute like Dustin Hoffman, and I could run
away with him on a Greyhound bus.'

'I don't think you should run away with Dustin
Hoffman, he's far too small. Besides, where are you
going to find a Greyhound bus in the middle of Par-
liament Square?'

'Oh. Do we have to be married at St Margaret's? I'm
rather taken by the idea of St James Piccadilly.'

'You're even less likely to find a Greyhound in
Piccadilly. And how do you know he would turn up?'

'Of course he would. He's an actor. No actor could
resist a scene like that. It would make his career.'

'That's being far too easy on him. You don't want to
make his career, you want to break it.'

'Problem is,' said Alabama ruefully, 'I've already
made him.'

'And like Frankenstein's monster, he's way out of
control. Have you read the papers?'

Venice arrived for lunch late, as usual. She looked
stunning, as usual. And, as usual, she stilled the room.

'Nice to see you haven't lost your touch,' said
Alabama. 'At least there is still one constant in the
world. While life crumbles about our ears, something
in the universe is still as it should be.'

Venice looked at her sister curiously.

'Alabama,' she said gravely, 'have you been drinking?'

'Not nearly enough,' said Alabama. 'Don't mind me.
I'm in love.'

'Don't be silly,' said Venice, 'you don't know how.'

'Don't underestimate me. I'm getting awfully good
at it. I sit up nights drinking whisky and listening to
Leonard Cohen and watching myself being unhappy
in the glass.'

'Do you really?' said Venice, enchanted by this idea. 'How positively droll.'

'It's not that funny,' said Alabama haughtily. 'I'm auditioning for the tragic heroine. *Dumped By A Monster*.'

'Makes a change from *Tough and Terrible*,' said Venice. 'Do you think you might grow your hair again?'

'It's not that bad,' said Alabama in reproof.

Venice looked at Alabama suspiciously.

'I think you're rather enjoying the whole thing,' she said. 'Are you collecting material for your new play?'

'I might be. I don't know yet. I don't know anything any more.'

They ordered a little food and a lot of wine. The waiters looked at Venice with love, but skirted round Alabama, with her threatening eyebrows drawn fiercely together.

'I never understand about people who work,' said Venice. 'How do they manage lunch?' Venice couldn't imagine life without lunch.

'It's a problem.'

'So, do you want to hear about David?' said Venice, thinking it was time to distract Alabama and make her smile.

'Do you want to tell me? Nicholas says he's into pain.'

'How does he know that?' said Venice indignantly. 'And what have you been doing with Nicholas? He's not exactly your cup of tea.'

'I don't know,' said Alabama. 'I rather like him, these days. It's so restful going out with a man with no brain.'

'David is very clever,' said Venice proudly. 'He can count up to twenty million.'

'Is that what he's worth?'

'Yes. Isn't it too *bijou* for words?'

'And what about the pain.'

'Well, to tell you the utter truth, I was slightly put out when he first asked me to pretend he was a naughty dog, and to spank him if he didn't eat up all his pudding like a good boy, and of course, one's arms do get rather sore from being tied to the bedpost, but at least it makes a change from the missionary position, do admit.'

'And,' said Alabama, who didn't miss that many tricks, even if her mind was somewhat *distrait*, 'he does load you with material goods.'

'But that was the whole point,' said Venice, at her most prosaic. 'I can't help it, you know I can't. I simply am a consumer at heart, I can't fight it. I think I love my Harrods charge card more than life itself.'

'I wish I did,' said Alabama, gloomy again. 'A Harrods charge card can't go to bed with Sabine Borromini.'

'I should hope,' said Venice with dignity, 'that it had more taste.'

'Max doesn't.'

'How on earth did you find out about that?' Venice was surprised. Alabama usually never knew who was having who.

'Nicholas told me.'

'Oh. Well, I'll tell you one thing for nothing. Max should have a care. She's had every man under twenty-five in London, and then some. He might catch something if he doesn't watch out. And who's the girl in the back of the cab?'

'One of the girls in the play, apparently.'

'Really,' said Venice, 'I'm shocked.'

'Careful where you throw your stones.'

'And glass houses to you too. At least I only do one at a time.'

'So,' said Alabama, 'what do I do?'

'Do?'

'Yes, do,' said Alabama with a touch of impatience. Venice was being a little slow today. 'I've got to do something.'

'I should go away for a nice long sea cruise and come back a new woman.'

'I hate water.'

Venice suddenly realized that her sister was serious. She gave Alabama a piercing look.

'You don't really want him back, after all this, do you?' she asked, echoing Milo.

'It's either that or marriage.'

'Marriage?' Venice almost stumbled over the alien word. Alabama married, there must be something very seriously wrong. 'To whom, pray?'

'To Milo, of course.'

'But that's a perfectly wonderful idea. He couldn't be better. Talented, handsome, rich, lovely house in Wicklow. You simply can't go wrong. I wonder you didn't think of it before. Can I be a bridesmaid?'

'Venice! Could you think like a human being for just a moment?'

'A human being?' Venice looked at her sister in horror. 'You really have got it badly, haven't you?'

'Yes,' said Alabama, settling the point once and for all. 'Now, what do I do? If you don't know, no one will.'

Venice accepted this as her due, and put her head on one side to think. She exchanged a surreptitious burning glance with an oil magnate from out of town whom she had spotted on the other side of the room behind a potted plant. Nothing like fiddling while the town burnt. The oil magnate looked as if he were about to spontaneously combust. No one knew quite how to look like Venice.

'Well,' she said, having the grace to return to the matter in hand, 'you won't like this, but I think you should play him at his own game. I think that you should go public.'

Alabama snorted. 'Like British Gas?'

'No. Like me.'

'There is only one you.'

'I know,' said Venice simply. 'Isn't it lucky?'

'Venice, concentrate. I'm in trouble.'

'All right, all right. Don't eat me, I beg. You really won't like it, that's all. First,' Venice took on the earnest tones of a lecturer, 'you should get some proper clothes.'

Alabama made a face. Venice ignored it.

'You should be seen in the right places,' she continued. 'You should then go to bed, very publicly, with someone very high profile, a prince for preference, or someone in films. You should make it patently clear that you don't need a shoddy little gigolo. You should let it be known that you are way above that kind of thing.'

'You don't really think that that would work?'

'I do, actually. Anyway, it's worth a try. It will make him livid at least. And you might even enjoy it.'

'Can I still ride the bike?'

Venice looked stern.

'Only in the privacy of your own bedroom.'

In blissful ignorance of these machinations, Max was enjoying himself. Rehearsals were hard work, and what with juggling Sabine and Emmie at night, he had his hands full. But he was delighted to be working again. The play was a dream. The cast was a dream, real professionals. And Johnny was a dream, the last word in directors.

79

'Darling,' he would say, 'I love you. I love the way you played that scene, but we're not playing a game of charades here lovey, we're looking for the Truth.'

Truth was a byword with Johnny. It was his religion, his faith, his *raison d'etre*. His entire life was one long search for the eternal verity.

Alabama went home thoughtful, and, mindful of Venice's advice, decided to ring up Oliver. Alabama had never followed Venice's advice in her life. But then, she had never chased after a man in her life. She supposed that twenty-seven was as good a time as any for firsts.

'Darling heart,' Oliver cried down the telephone. 'How are you? Tell me EVERYTHING. Are you still in love? Is your heart still broken? Do you weep in the still watches of the night? Is your life over?' Oliver had been to see some Chekhov the week before, and had been in the tragic mode ever since.

'Oliver,' said Alabama, getting to the point, 'do you know any princes?' She supposed if she was going to do something, she might as well do it properly. And it would give Oliver so much pleasure.

'Oh darling,' he said wearily, 'only three. Why?'

'I want one.'

'How positively touching. Do you want him just to look at, or did you have something else in mind?' Say what you like about the Skye sisters, Oliver thought to himself, but they did provide such an interest in one's life.

'I think,' said Alabama judiciously, 'that we should have lunch.'

'What heaven,' said Oliver. 'I long for lunch. Where would you like to go?'

'Anywhere smart.'

'All right, my sweet. You can count on me, I am your utter slave. I'll pick you up at half past one tomorrow.'

Oliver had decided some years ago that he was past the age of astonishment. He had seen so much in his peripatetic life. He had watched rabbits appear out of impossible hats from the Aegean to the Atlantic, and taken it all in his stride. He had learnt to expect the unexpected at a young age, but when he came to fetch Alabama the next day, even he had to admit that he was astounded. He circled round and round her in awe. Alabama stood quite still, letting him take it all in.

'Darling,' he said at last, with a kind of reverential respect, 'I could die, that's all.'

'Good,' said Alabama. 'Let's go.'

They arrived at the restaurant at a quarter to two, just when everyone had ordered their first course and settled down to drink their chablis and discuss the events of the week. There was a lull in the general conversation as Alabama walked in.

'Christ,' said Nicholas, who was lunching with Carol Matthews. 'Would you take a look at that. What a turn-up for the books.'

No one had seen Alabama in anything but her jeans for seven years. Now she stood tall, dwelling in the doorway for a moment as she had seen Venice do, just to let everyone appreciate the difference. She wore a perfectly cut, perfectly simple black coat and skirt, St Laurent's latest creation as only he knew how, the one that every woman worth her salt in London had been lusting after for the last month. Its lines were a poem of design, moulded to Alabama's slender form, swooping daringly low at the neck to suggest the cleavage, its short skirt skimming the thighs. Instead of her normal shock of hair, Alabama had taken her platinum locks off her face, to reveal her dangerous eyes, outlined in kohl. Her mouth was a wanton red, perfectly painted, setting off those startling bones. Her endless legs were clothed in sheer black stockings, and her shoes were suede. She looked glamorous and langorous, and more unobtainable than ever. Look, but don't touch.

'Who IS that?' said Roger to Kiki. 'I wonder if she can act.'

'Who?' said Kiki, not interested. She was rather too busy to notice, being in the throes of an ill-disguised flirtation with the waiter.

'Good God,' said Roger putting on the spectacles that he was too vain to wear in public, 'it's Alabama. I wouldn't have recognized her.'

'Well,' said Sabine to Max, who was having a day off, 'look at that. Alabama Skye. And in that St Laurent I've been wanting. Her plays MUST be doing well.' There was a distinct edge to her carefully modulated voice. For all her nips and tucks, she knew she could never look as perfect in it as Alabama did.

Max looked round, expecting the jeans, the muddled hair, the unpainted face. 'Where?'

'Just there,' said Sabine sharply. 'In front of you.'

'Jesus,' said Max, 'I didn't recognize her.'

'Hardly surprising, my sweet,' said Sabine. 'She was the worst dressed woman in London.'

'Of course she wasn't,' snapped Max. 'If you look like that you can wear sackcloth and still look good.'

Good enough to eat, he thought in spite of himself. He couldn't stop looking at her. Was this really the girl who had bitched at him, and bullied him, and taken him into her bed? He turned back to Sabine, and suddenly thought that she looked rather too done up, with all her powders and paints carefully disguising the wrinkles, and artfully applied rouge to give her cheekbones she didn't really have.

Alabama smiled a careful little smile to herself, and allowed herself to be seated. Suddenly all the waiters in the room seemed to be around her table, opening napkins, fighting to give her a menu, a drink, some bread, tickets for Michael Jackson at Wembley.

'Now I know how Venice feels,' she said to Oliver.

'Darling,' he said in real awe, feeling his prestige grow minute by minute, knowing that his telephone was going to be engaged for days, 'I could die, that's all. I could simply lie down and die.'

'You said that already.'

'I'll say it again.' Oliver was defiant. 'I could die. Why did it take you so long? You really should have come out of the closet sooner.'

'Perhaps I should,' said Alabama, surprised to find herself rather enjoying the alien experience of being stared at.

'I did always think it a terrible waste,' said Oliver, having a ball. 'That face could launch the entire navy.'

'After all,' said Alabama, laughing, 'they do say all the nice girls like a sailor.'

'Don't speak, angel. Sailors are my undying passion.'

As they finished lunch, apparently oblivious of being the centre of everyone's attention, and ordered coffee, a tall dark prince walked into the restaurant.

'Ah good,' said Oliver in satisfaction, 'here's Sergei. He's the Russian one. The most suitable, I think.' Oliver had given this matter quite considerable thought. He didn't believe in taking crowned heads lightly, even if they weren't crowned any longer. 'The Italian one is too Catholic,' he continued, 'and really rather serious, and the French one is still making up his mind whether to go for girls or boys. Besides, he seems to spend his life at the Crillon at the moment, so he's rather inaccessible. Sergei is nice and rich, goes back all the way, and his family features prominently in *War and Peace*.' If Oliver couldn't have Chekhov, he'd take Tolstoy any day. 'I think he'll do perfectly. Sergei,' he cooed, pronouncing it Sair-GAY. 'What heaven that you could come. Sit down and have some brandy, we're going to. Have you met my cousin, Alabama Skye?'

Sergei bowed over Alabama's hand and let loose a gracious smile. Alabama wouldn't have been surprised if he had kissed it.

'I don't believe I've had the pleasure,' he said in a rich Eton accent with European overtones. 'I have, of course, seen your plays. I am a great admirer of your work.'

Alabama looked involuntarily to where Max sat. He had said that too.

'Thank you,' she said, smiling back into Sergei's dark grey eyes.

The prince sat down. Brandy was bought with much bowing and your highnesses. Oliver looked ecstatic. He did so love being seen with the right people. He especially liked being seen with the right people by the right people. And the restaurant was full of the right people, with Sergei the most right of all. It couldn't have been better.

'Well,' said Sergei, 'what an unexpected pleasure. How is it that you have never introduced me to your cousin before now, Oliver?'

'Well my dear, to tell you the truth, she's always been rather disdainful about society.' Oliver gave Alabama an indulgent smile, as if she were a child who had just grown out of biting its nails. 'I've only just been able to tempt her out into the *monde*.'

'It has been our loss,' said Sergei, looking at Alabama again. His charm was grave and old-fashioned, definitely foreign, almost studied. Alabama, for all her better judgement, found herself rather liking it. Out of the corner of her eye, she could see Max staring at them with that furious brooding look that she knew so well of old. Perhaps it was going to work.

'Well,' said Nicholas to Carol, 'Alabama with Sergei Kolitsyn. Stranger and stranger. I must tempt her out for a drink and get her to tell me all.'

Carol looked sour.

'Since when have you been so chummy with Alabama?' she said scornfully. She had been nursing a secret love for Nicholas for years, but he only took her out when he wanted confirmation for a story.

'Oh,' said Nicholas, 'for a while, you know. I like her.'

'She's a bitch,' said Carol crossly.

'Well, they do say it takes one to know one.'

'Who's that?' Kiki asked Roger. She rather liked the look of Sergei, so tall and graceful. 'He looks like Mel Gibson.'

'He's a Russian prince,' said Roger. 'The last of the old-time playboys. Fast cars, yachts, racehorses, houses in the South of France. A real collector's item. They don't make them like that any more.'

'Oh,' said Kiki, in disappointment. 'I thought he might have been in the music business.'

Roger sighed with pleasure. Kiki really was the dregs.

On the other side of the restaurant, Sabine sat, grinding her perfectly capped teeth.

'Well,' she said, putting at least three syllables into the word, 'Alabama with Sergei Kolitsyn. Fancy that. I didn't know that they knew each other.'

She was feeling more piqued than ever. Not only did Alabama arrive looking as if she had just stepped out of *Vogue*, not only could Max not tear his eyes off her, but now, there she was, drinking brandy with the most eligible man in the Western Hemisphere. It worried Sabine. She had always relied on old-fashioned men being attracted by old-fashioned things, like curves and charm and a little artifice. To see a man like Sergei being captivated by a blue stocking upset an entire world order.

'Sergei who?' said Max, who couldn't be expected to know about such things.

'He's a prince, darling,' said Sabine carelessly, as if it couldn't matter less. 'A little above your touch. Astronomically rich, a first at Oxford, lives in state in Belgravia, every girl's dream.'

There was a note of ill-concealed bitterness in Sabine's otherwise perfect voice. Sergei was one of the few men worth having who had successfully resisted her advances.

Sergei, meanwhile, oblivious to all these character sketches, was busy telling Alabama about his horses. Oliver looked on benignly. It was affording him great amusement to see one of the world's most famous seducers so instantly captivated. He fitted a cigarette carefully into his ebony holder, and sighed with satisfaction.

'I have a horse running at Ascot tomorrow,' Sergei was saying. 'Perhaps you would care to come and watch her.'

'I've never been to the races,' said Alabama. It really wasn't her, but she wasn't going to tell Sergei that.

'It would be a delight to take you,' said Sergei, as if nothing could give him greater pleasure. Whichever charm school he had attended, Alabama thought to herself, it had done a perfectly splendid job.

'I'd like that,' she said. She smiled. Sergei smiled. Oliver smiled. Away across the room, Max ground his teeth.

Alabama went straight home and rang up Venice.

'Lucky to catch me,' said Venice, 'I was about to go shopping.'

'What the hell do I wear to the races?' said Alabama.

'Alabama! The races? Is this really you? Who are you going with?'

'Sergei Kolitsyn,' said Alabama, artless as a summer breeze.

'No!' Venice almost dropped the telephone. 'Don't tell me! Where on earth did you pick him up?'

'Don't be crude, Venice,' said Alabama haughtily. 'I met him at lunch with Oliver.' Alabama was matter of fact, for all the world as if this were the most natural thing imaginable for a girl who only a week ago never went out.

'Clever you, I say.' Venice was clearly impressed. 'Half the women in the land would give their eye teeth to be seen with him. I hear he's a veritable lady killer. What's he like in the flesh?'

'Ravishing,' said Alabama, just to annoy her sister.

'But darling,' said Venice, in concern, 'do you think this is wise? Out of the frying pan and all that. Have you got a bullet proof vest?'

'Don't be silly. He's charming. And Max was there, looking livid.'

'Ah,' said Venice, as the light dawned. 'Well. That's quite a different matter.' She was glad to see Alabama was taking her advice at last. After all, she was the past mistress when it came to men, everyone knew that.

'As you say,' said Alabama. 'Now, then. What do I wear?'

'Well,' said Venice, putting her mind to the matter in hand, 'it's Ascot, I suppose?' Venice didn't expect Sergei to be seen dead at Wolverhampton, which was the other meeting tomorrow. 'A smart little coat and skirt will be the thing. Have you got anything in cream linen? Or dark blue might be nice.'

'I can have by tomorrow.'

'I saw just the very thing in Jasper's new shop only yesterday.' Venice was fast coming to first name terms with all her favourite designers, Alabama noticed. 'And flattish shoes, or they dig into the grass. And perhaps a chic little hat.'

'No,' said Alabama, revolted. 'I may be selling my soul, but I do draw the line at a hat.'

'All right,' said Venice, soothingly. 'It won't matter, as it's not the royal meeting. And I should get some binoculars, it makes you look less of an amateur.'

'I'm taking notes.'

'Good. Now, whatever you do, don't talk about HORSE racing, it's just racing, and the male horses are called colts, not stallions, and the female ones are called fillies, and they never look pretty, they look well. What else? Oh yes, if you want to make some intelligent remarks in the paddock, you can say they look a bit trained, if they're looking rather thin, or if they're jumping about all over the place, you say they're on their toes.'

Alabama snorted. 'Like a ballerina?'

'Just so. Punting has nothing to do with undergraduates in boats, it means placing a bet. And getting the trip doesn't mean a day out to Bournemouth, it means they will be able to run over the distance. Talking of which, distances are measured in miles, and there are eight furlongs to a mile. Alabama, are you paying attention?'

'Yes, yes. How do you know all this, anyway?'

'Oh,' said Venice, airily, 'I had a bit of a walk out with a bloodstock agent once.'

'Of course you did,' said Alabama.

'Well angel, Chanel beckons. Have a nice time. I'm almost jealous. I shall expect a full report.'

The next day, Alabama, looking a picture of under-stated elegance in cream linen, descended graciously into Sergei's dark green Aston Martin.

'Would you mind if we had the roof down?' he asked tentatively, looking at her hair.

'Not at all,' said Alabama blithely. 'I shall just say that the tousled look is in.'

Sergei smiled. Most women made the most frightful fuss about the wind ruining their £90 hair cuts. But then, he wasn't to know that Alabama cut her own hair, in the bath.

They roared away down the M4, leaving London talking nineteen to the dozen in their wake. Whenever Sergei was seen with a new woman it was an event. Whenever Alabama was seen at all it was even more of an event. But for both of them to be seen together, that was almost too much. The summer was looking up. Max, sweltering in his church hall, thought angry thoughts, and forgot to concentrate. 'Are you with us, lovey?' said Johnny, in the nearest he ever came to a snap.

Alabama was rather fascinated by the races. She hadn't expected the course to be so pretty, so essentially English, with its great sweeps of lovingly mown lawn, and its pristine white railings. She stared boldly at all the women in their Sunday best, and the men, elegant in lightweight suits and panama hats. The atmosphere was tense with business and pleasure, the wandering crowds interspersed with people who had places to go, with little huddles of earnest talk, with boys leading their horses out, telling everyone to mind their backs. Sergei had a box, of course.

Up in the box, a long table was laid for lunch, and hennaed waitresses stood to attention, ready to meet every request. Smart women with suave escorts drank champagne without a second thought, and discussed the prospects for the first race, concentrating on their race cards and copies of the *Sporting Life*, looking up only for a moment to turn dazzling smiles of greeting on Sergei.

Alabama was introduced to various trainers, owners, racing journalists, and a bloodstock agent. She wondered if he was the one that Venice had walked out with. He looked rakish enough.

She wandered across the room, not yet quite sure of her ground. None of these people had ever heard of her. She caught snatches of conversation in the air.

'Got left, and had to run round the whole field . . .'

'Always likes to come from behind, has to be covered up, you can't let him see daylight . . .'

'Ran an absolute blinder first time out, but won't do a thing at home . . .'

'He won't pay more than fifteen grand for a yearling, and then insists I enter the bloody animal at Goodwood so he can show off to all his corporate clients. I said to him, a selling plate at Warwick evening would be more the mark . . .'

'Well you know Gay, every time I see him, he tells me he's about to win eighty grand on an accumulator, or a yankee, or I don't know what . . .'

'Did you see Tony's left his wife . . .'

'I don't care what price he is, he won't get the trip, not on this ground . . .'

'Well, you know Gay, he's the only man to have resigned from White's, Annabel's, and the Jockey club all in the same year . . .'

Sergei came up behind her.

'Are you enjoying yourself?' he asked.

'I don't understand a word of it,' she said, laughing up at him. 'All this coming from behind. It sounds very suspect to me.'

'Would you like me to explain?' said Sergei, smiling back at her in appreciation.

'No, no. I think a discreet veil is best drawn, don't you? Never forget, I'm a gently reared girl.'

Sergei wasn't to know any different.

'Well then,' he said, 'why don't we have another glass of champagne?'

Following Sergei's advice, and throwing caution to the winds in good time-honoured fashion, Alabama won £500 on the first two races, which would just cover the cost of her coat and skirt.

'Well,' she said, trying not to show that she was impressed, 'if I come racing with you much more often, I won't have to write any more plays.'

'The theatrical world would mourn,' said Sergei gravely.

'Oh really,' said Alabama. 'Did anyone ever tell you that you are the master of the overstatement?'

'Yes.'

'Who?'

'My mother.'

Alabama laughed. She couldn't help it. She was really having a shamingly nice time. She felt like a traitor. Sergei was everything that she had always despised, and then some. Ah well, she said to herself fatalistically, a girl only lived once, after all.

They went down to watch Sergei's horse saddled. She was a grey filly, and quite obviously the light of Sergei's ravishing eye. Her trainer was a stick-thin six foot five, and didn't look a day over seventeen. Sergei had told her with amusement that he had emerged from an expensive public school education without an exam to his name, but with a bank balance swelled with the illegal proceeds of a very successful bookmaking exercise. People who knew said that he was going straight to the top. Alabama watched his long thin fingers nimbly doing up buckles, straightening the saddle and the weight cloth, helped by his assistant.

'I can give you a couple of holes this side,' he said.

The filly tossed her head in a nicely judged little show of temperament, and lashed out as her girth was tightened.

'Steady girl,' said the lad. 'Steady old lady.'

Alabama hoped that she would still look like that when she was an old lady.

'It's all right gov'ner,' said the lad. 'I've got her.'

The filly was led out into the paddock, followed at a safe distance by Alabama and Sergei. They stood in the middle of the long grass ring, where other small groups were already assembled, owners and trainers in serious talk, watching their charges stalk round, with so many hopes resting on their aristocratic backs. The jockeys came in in a tight smiling bunch, tiny in their gaudy silks, whips tucked under their arms. Sergei's jockey came up and tipped his hat to them. Alabama thought the whole thing was too feudal for words.

'Jockeys please mount,' said the loudspeaker.

The jockeys were tossed up into their saddles, gathering up their reins, utterly businesslike, sitting steady as rocks, as the horses bucketed beneath them.

'Come along,' said Sergei, suddenly imperious, his interest all for his horse. Alabama followed him up into the stand. On every side, men with serious faces nodded at Sergei, and told him how well his filly looked.

'Do you fancy yours in this?' said one of them.

Alabama thought she would never understand this strange racing talk. Down by the rails, bookmakers called out their odds like market traders as the horses streamed past them, on their way to the start. People hurried and jostled to place their bets.

Alabama caught the high pitch of excitement in the air. These horses were some of the best of their generation, thoroughbred in every sense of the word, lining up to go out and do what they were bred for. Judge all on pure speed, no prizes for second place. The herd instinct brought to a finely tuned peak. She lifted her binoculars to watch.

'They're under starter's orders,' said the commentator, 'and . . . they're off.'

The horses surged out of the stalls in a tight bunch, from nought to thirty in a moment that would leave a Porsche standing. They swept over the undulating turf, jockeying for position. Sergei's knuckles were quite white where he held his binoculars. Alabama could see the filly, her colour distinctive against the chestnuts and bays of the others, lying in third place, moving in an easy rhythmic gallop, delicate legs stretching out, cutting through the air, her jockey poised, perfectly balanced over her neck. Into the straight they came, their riders starting to push them now. Alabama could hear the swift thud of steel-tipped hooves pounding the grass. The crowd stirred and shifted, murmuring under its breath, full of tense expectation. Out on the track, the final effort was starting, necks extended, strides flattened, heads down, and the murmur swelled to a roar. For a terrifying moment, it seemed as if all were lost. The filly dwelt for a second, seemed beaten, with nothing more to give, then found another gear, and at the last moment, with an astonishing burst of speed, she passed her rivals, stretching every sinew, every muscle, and flashed past the post, with her elegant nose held defiantly an inch in front of the nearest challenger.

Sergei and Alabama lowered their glasses and looked at each other.

'Well,' said Alabama, smiling in pure pleasure. 'Well.'

They went down to the winner's enclosure to greet the returning heroine. She came in off the course with her head held high in victory, snorting disdainfully at the waiting masses who let out a great cheer. The jockey slid off her back, grinning a wide, gap-toothed grin.

'I just had to ask her the question,' he said.

The press gathered round, scenting a star, notebooks at the ready, asking the trainer where he would send her next.

'We'll have to see how she comes out of this,' he said, calm as you please. 'No definite plans as yet.'

Much later, they drove back. There had been a great deal of champagne and celebration and backslapping. Sergei had taken it all in his urbane stride, but Alabama could sense how delighted he was. She kicked her shoes off and leant back in the luxury of the Aston. The wind was in her hair and she was still smiling. She could get used to this.

'Where would you like to have dinner?' said Sergei, pretending diffidence.

'Anywhere you like.' Alabama smiled wider than ever, devil may care. She should go home and work, but champagne and good times wouldn't do her any harm for a little longer. Some things were just too good to pass up.

CHAPTER

5

As Alabama and Sergei lingered over their brandy, Venice stepped out into the streets of Soho and climbed into her red Alpha Spider, another present from David. She had been dining with Nicholas and Oliver in a restaurant much frequented by the literary crowd. Nicholas liked going there, although he was treated with a rather touching disdain by its more high-brow patrons.

'If I'm going to be despised,' he said, 'I might as well be despised by the right people.'

Venice rather suspected that Nicholas had a sneaking desire to be a serious political journalist, although he would never admit to it.

She started the car, put David Bowie on the stereo, where he belonged, and settled down to drive back to Belgravia. Soho was still buzzing, even at this late hour. The punters were out, queuing for the Wag, exercising their street credibility. Some people seemed to queue there all night, even though they never got in, just to be seen. What shall we do tonight? Go and have a good queue. They all wore black, and tried to look like George Michael. Some of them almost succeeded. Further along, a pair of tramps were bothering late night diners for the price of a cup of tea, loose translation for a bottle of meths. From Ronnie

Scotts, the sound of hot south American jazz floated out into the warm night air. Venice loved Soho. She loved its association with drunks and decadence and flashes of genius. She loved it most of all at night.

Along Conduit Street, she noticed a policeman waving at her. She smiled at him, and waved kindly back. How touching, she thought to herself, checking her reflection in the driving mirror.

Regent Street was wide and quiet, except for the distant wail of sirens. Seeing the flashing blue lights behind her, Venice pulled over like a good citizen to let them past, wondering vaguely what heinous criminal they could be chasing. To her astonishment, the police van, its sirens flashing furiously, pulled up across her bows, and six brawny policemen leapt out. Venice surreptitiously rearranged her hair.

'Hello darling,' she said to the nearest. 'What a noise.'

'Would you step out of the car, madam?' he said politely.

Venice looked amazed. This was not quite what she was used to.

'Well,' she said, with an artistic touch of hauteur, 'of course.'

She emerged from the Spider, silken legs first as a lady should, and stood ravishing in the street.

'What IS going on?' she asked.

The six strong men and true hung back, trying to pretend they weren't mesmerized.

'Well,' said their leader, who had a wife and five children in Hackney and suddenly wished he didn't, 'a colleague of ours has informed us that he attempted to flag you down. If you don't mind waiting, he will be here in a minute.'

Venice looked about her. Sure enough, the colleague, accompanied by a mousey policewoman, rounded the corner and strode purposefully towards them.

'Oh yes,' said Venice in recognition. 'He waved at me. I did wave back.'

She wondered what he wanted. She hoped he wasn't going to ask her out. That would be tricky, with David as attentive as he was.

'Hello sweetheart,' she said to the newly arrived policeman. She supposed it had been a bit foolish to lead him on by waving like that. She wondered how she was going to soften the blow. She gave him her most sympathetic smile. He looked quite unimpressed.

'Madam,' he said, seriously and with meaning, 'did you see me flagging you down?'

'Well yes darling,' said Venice reasonably. 'Didn't you see me wave back?'

The policeman ignored this question. He looked more unimpressed than ever. Venice wondered if she ought to change her hairdresser.

'And yet,' he continued with portent, 'you made no attempt to stop.'

'Well,' said Venice, who decided she was rather tired of this conversation and wanted to go to bed, 'I'm not a taxi, you know.'

Significant looks were exchanged between the officers of the law, and an unseemly scuffle ensued as they all tried to produce a breathalyser at once.

'One at a time darlings,' said Venice. 'Who taught you boys manners?'

Finally they sorted themselves out, and the lucky winner asked Venice to blow.

'Do you know the procedure, madam?'

'Of course not,' said Venice, in reproof. 'Do you think I make it a habit to stand about on the street at two in the morning with perfect strangers blowing into tubes? It's not quite me, you know.'

'One long blow until I say stop,' said her persecutor, not to be deflected. 'Do you understand?'

'I'm not an intellectual, my sweet,' said Venice, 'but I do have a certain native wit.'

She blew. The policemen watched in consternation, desperately hoping it would be positive. A creature like this in the station would brighten up the evening no end.

'I'm afraid I'm going to have to take you in,' said their leader, looking at the breathalyser. A great sigh of relief went round the troops.

'Take me in?' said Venice, not understanding. 'In where? My number is in the book.'

'Do you know your rights, Madam?'

'Darling really,' said Venice with a touch of impatience. 'This sounds like a bad film. Do you mean to tell me that you are arresting me?'

'Yes, madam. I'm afraid so.'

'But what on earth for?'

'Drinking and driving, madam. Driving a motor vehicle with excess alcohol in your bloodstream.'

'Oh really,' said Venice. 'Everyone does that. You don't really want to arrest me do you? Wouldn't you be more gainfully employed arresting some real criminals, like the great train robbers or someone?'

'I'm going to have to ask you to come with me, madam,' said the policeman doggedly.

Venice knew when she was beaten.

'Oh well,' she said, 'if you insist.'

The mousey policewoman looked smugly at Venice as she got into the van.

'You smell like a brewery,' she said.

'Oh darling,' said Venice, carelessly, 'how sweet. Which one?'

The police station was bare and brightly lit. The smell of linoleum reminded Venice of prep school.

'Really darlings,' she said, staring in horror at the strip lighting, the walls adorned with posters warning against the perils of drugs and hardened criminals, 'I don't know HOW you stand it. Who is your decorator?'

Venice sat patiently while her bag was searched, her rights were read, and endless questions were asked. Policemen kept appearing in the doorway, staring at her for a moment, and melting open-mouthed away.

'What is your profession?' she was asked.

She looked astonished. 'Profession?' she repeated, as if it were a word that only boys knew. 'What do you think I am? I don't have a profession. I suppose you could put courtesan if you like, or does that count?'

Endless forms had to be filled in, in triplicate.

'Really,' said Venice, in admiration, 'I do think you are brave. I can't fill in a form to save my life.'

At last she was let go.

'See you in court,' she cried, waving to the police, who had lined up to see her off. 'Don't pine. It's only the day after tomorrow.'

The next morning, Venice woke up with a nasty little mother of a hangover, rang David to apologize for being out all night, and asked him to send his valet to collect her car from Regent Street. Then she called Alabama.

'You'll never guess,' she said, 'I've been arrested. Isn't it too droll?'

'What for?' said Alabama. 'Soliciting?'

'Really, Alabama,' said Venice in reproof. 'You know I never do anything in the street that might frighten the horses. Talking of which, how was your day at the races?'

'Spiffing,' said Alabama, in her best county voice.

'I die to hear more. I've got the most deathly hangover. Do you want to go swimming? It's the only cure I know.'

'All right,' said Alabama. 'I'll meet you at the health club in an hour.'

Venice's one concession to the current craze for fitness was that she was a member of the most fashionable of the health clubs. What Venice really approved of was the French way of doing things, where the beautiful women took themselves off to Guerlain or Estée Lauder, and had any incipient signs of flab or the dread cellulite smoothed away by friendly electric shocks combined with arcane herbal treatments which had to be religiously smoothed on to the offending parts of the body. They kept their richly curvaceous figures well into their fifties, without ever having to move off the salon couch. That, to Venice, was chic: that was sexy. Looking earnest in a leotard was not. Nothing, to Venice's mind was less sexy than jogging, nothing more barbaric than the Jane Fonda workout. In America, the god of fitness was so worshipped that a personal exercise instructor had become more of a status symbol than a stretch limo. No good having a stretch limo if you had stretch marks to go with it. These instructors, more priceless than Fabergé eggs, were always reported to be utter sadists, the contemporary Hitlers of life in the fat lane. Venice couldn't think of anything worse than being berated by a beefcake in a singlet. Still, she supposed each to each is what we teach, but she still couldn't bring herself to go near the gym. Occasionally, she looked in, watching with horrified fascination as the earnest disciples punished their bodies for not being perfect on machines that tested each muscle. Venice would stare at their red faces, dripping sweat, contorted in agony, and quickly look away again. As for the exercise classes, their very names were enough to put Venice off. The temptations of the 'Attila Circuit' with Steve, 'Fast and fizz' with Gabrielle, or 'Shape up' with Kelly, held no lure for Venice. Once or twice a fortnight, she went swimming, a dignified breast-stroke with her head held well out of the water, and that was that. As she pointed out, it was an even better cure for a hangover than a Bloody Mary.

Alabama was already in the pool when Venice arrived, showing off her crawl.

'Al!' cried Venice, as her sister paused for breath.

The other swimmers looked up in surprise. Strict silence was always observed in the pool area, as any noise tended to make the dedicated ladies lose count of their laps. It was more than their lives were worth to do less than fifty a day. Venice looked back at them disdainfully, as she stood tall in her Norma Kamali bathing suit, cut away to show hip bones that were born beautiful.

'Hello Venice,' said Alabama. 'My, don't you look fine. I thought you were suffering.'

'I am, I am. You can't imagine what a night I've had. Three hours in a police station, my dear, and they didn't even offer me a drink.'

The swimming ladies, desperately concentrating on their lap count against all the odds, looked shocked to their puritanical souls.

'What were you done for?' said Alabama with interest.

'Drunken driving,' said Venice. 'If you could call it driving. Couldn't you die? It's so seventies.'

'Well,' said Alabama, 'I could think of other words for it. Are you coming in?'

Venice descended graciously into the water, as if she were conferring on it a great honour.

'So,' she said, 'let me tell you. You wouldn't believe how long it all took. Half a hundredweight of forms to fill in, all in triplicate, because they didn't have any carbon paper, or some such nonsense. And they asked me the most personal questions. Where was I educated, did I have a mortgage, what was my profession. I told them to put courtesan if they liked, but I don't think they knew how to spell it.'

'Really, Ven,' said Alabama in reproof.

'Yes, well, but I was becoming a little impatient. Savile Row police station may be many things, but it's not exactly the Ritz. A girl can't even get a drink. Still, one of the policemen was rather attractive, which made it a bit better. And they were all very polite, I'll say that for them. They would insist on calling me madam, I felt like Cynthia Payne by the end.'

'I can imagine,' said Alabama dryly.

'But the boredom of it, I can't tell you. And I have to go to court tomorrow. I mean, what on earth does one wear for court? How am I supposed to know? As I said to the police, I said I'm not Joan Collins, ducky.'

'Would you like me to come with you?' said Alabama.

Venice looked at her with relief. 'Oh darling, would you ever? I hate to admit it, but I'm rather fazed by the whole thing.'

They swam gently for a while. Most of the swimming ladies, rigid with shock, had gone to recover themselves in the steam room so Alabama and Venice had the pool to themselves. Alabama did a slow breaststroke to keep Venice company. Venice had never mastered the art of crawl. She said that all the water went up her nose, and she couldn't see why people bothered, and that was an end to it.

'So,' she said, when they stopped to rest, 'what about your day with the to-die-for prince? I want to hear everything. I'm so glad you've stopped disapproving of the aristocracy. Did he seduce you?'

'Not at all,' said Alabama. 'Not even close. He was everything of the most charming. The perfect gentleman. It was very difficult for me. I wanted to despise him, but I couldn't.'

Alabama had been more taken with Sergei than she cared to admit, and had been shocked at quite how pleased she was when he had rung her that morning from his bed to see how she was.

'Oh Alabama,' said Venice in her infinite wisdom. 'What a lot you have to learn. All those people whom you affect to despise are quite irresistible in the flesh. Look at me.'

'Yes,' Alabama admitted. 'Just do.'

'You may think that I'm good for nothing,' said Venice with dignity, 'but it's terribly hard work being irresistible.'

'You were born that way.'

'Perhaps,' said Venice, looking pleased. 'But not everyone is as lucky. Most people devote their lives to it. That's why they don't work. No time, you see. Sergei wouldn't be anything like as alluring if he were something in the City.'

'Perhaps.' Alabama wasn't going to let herself be convinced so easily. She did have some principles left to defend, after all.

'It's quite true,' said Venice firmly. 'Remember that City boyfriend I had? Quite ravishing, all long and lean with those green eyes? I really did think that he was the last word. And he was charming after a fashion, but it all turned to dust when he started making me leave dinner early so that we could get back in time to listen to the *Financial World at Night* on Radio Four. And then it was the *Money Programme* in bed, and he couldn't speak in the morning until he had read the *Financial Times*, or I don't know what. You can imagine I didn't understand a word of it. And suddenly he didn't think it was so amusing when I made jokes about all the City types playing Footsie, or whatever it is that they do. He kept telling me how irresponsible I was. I said of course I'm irresponsible, all the best women are. So, of course then he saw that there was no hope for me at all, and he went running back to his ex, who was an awfully solid type, frantically successful on Wall Street, and didn't mind at all if he treated her like hell, and who fitted in with all his solid friends who talked about money all the time, and spent their spare time going to every wedding in Hampshire they could find, or taking dinky little trips to the Isle of Wight of a weekend. Well, the Isle of Wight may be many things, but it's not quite my idea of glamour, you do see.'

'I quite see,' said Alabama, who did.

'We've lost more men to the City than we have in two world wars,' said Venice, in her most weary voice, as if she had seen quite enough of the real world and wanted to get back to her own version. 'So really, when you meet someone like Sergei,' (here her tone softened, with infinite indulgence, and a touch of longing), 'I think you should hang out more flags. It's such a relief. I know SOMEONE has to do all those important jobs to do with money, but it doesn't mean that a girl has to spend any time with them. Life is too short, don't you think?'

Alabama listened to this touching lecture on the Meaning of Life According to Venice with a grave face. There was a small pause, and then Alabama tried to say something, but started to laugh instead.

'Oh Venice,' she said, in genuine appreciation, 'don't go changing, to please me.'

'Darling,' said Venice, as dignified as you please, 'I never change. I'm the one constant in a shifting universe, remember?'

'I remember.'

'And you must admit I'm right.'

'I admit,' said Alabama, who almost did. 'But does it ever occur to you that there is something beside the City type and the playboy?'

'Not much,' said Venice with conviction. 'Precious little. I should stick to the latter, and count your blessings.' And Venice, having said her piece, having done her duty by her sister, sailed off up the swimming pool, leaving Alabama laughing in her wake.

Venice went home to David and Alabama went home to get ready for Sergei, who somehow seemed to be taking her out to dinner. She hadn't really meant to go out, she had been convinced that she would spend the evening working on her play, but inspiration had deserted her, and when Sergei called and suggested they dined, she had given in, thinking that a girl has to eat, after all. Besides, if she was going to do something, she might as well do it properly. So she dressed up in her glad rags, and painted her lips and teased her hair, and even admired herself in the glass, and went out. She told herself that it wouldn't last long, and allowed herself the luxury of being appreciated, of having her cigarette lit, of being royally fed, of being paid for. It made a change anyway, and, she told herself firmly, it didn't do to get stuck in a rut. There was no harm in enjoying oneself. Venice could have told her this a long time ago, but the puritan in Alabama wouldn't have believed her.

'So,' said Oliver the next day, 'I want you to tell me all. I mean the last detail. I simply die to know. I've always had a secret love of policemen. You see how one couldn't resist. I mean to say darling, so BUTCH.'

After the infamous court appearance, Sergei had picked up Venice and Alabama in the 1965 soft top Mercedes which he referred to as his second car, and taken them to the bar of their choice, since they had declared that they needed a drink. The press had been beside themselves. Not only the Skye sisters in court, but a prince to take them out of it. It could have been made for the gossip columns.

It seemed almost inevitable that they should arrive at the bar only to find Oliver and Nicholas drinking Dom Perignon with Oliver's latest acquisition, who turned out to be a South American bongo player.

'Whatever happened to the French film star?' said Alabama.

'Well darling,' said Oliver seriously, 'it was getting just a fraction too existential, even for me. And after all, one can get bored of the smell of Gitanes, you know how it is. Carlos here is divine, no English of course, but a tremendous sense of rhythm. I found him in Ronnie Scotts, standing room only, would you believe?'

Carlos looked bemused and tapped out a salsa beat on the bar.

'Hello Alabama,' said Nicholas, kissing her fondly. 'I have to say I'm very taken with this new look.'

'Not only talented, but now showing herself to be one of the chicest women in London?' said Alabama quizzically, quoting from Nicholas's column from the day before. 'I do declare, I was positively touched.'

'Don't tease,' said Nicholas, blushing. He wondered if Alabama would ever settle for a man with no brain. He didn't think that his chances were looking too promising with Sergei around, but a man could always dream. It wasn't really fair when people were not only extremely handsome, vastly rich, but clever as well. Nicholas stifled a sigh, and shook Sergei's hand. 'Hello Sergei, we don't see you in this neck of the woods very often. Are you slumming?'

'Alabama is introducing me to her taste in drinking holes.'

'Well,' said Venice reasonably, 'you must admit it makes a change from the Ritz.'

Sergei looked about, taking in the long bar, the crowded tables, the fog of cigarette smoke hanging blue in the air, the starling chatter, and nodded.

'It certainly does,' he said.

'Now come on,' said Oliver, who was fast growing impatient. 'I want to hear all about your arrest. Shall we just eat here? Do you want a bourbon, Alabama? So? I can't bear the suspense. Did they use handcuffs?'

'Oh no,' said Venice mistily. 'David is the only one who uses handcuffs.'

Always ready to oblige, she dutifully recounted the story of her arrest. Oliver gasped and stretched his eyes, and licked his lips when it got to the part about the handsome policeman.

'Oh tell me do,' he said breathlessly, 'did he man-handle you? Did you get his telephone number?'

'As for the court,' said Venice, who was well into her stride and quite above such base interruptions, 'well, angels, it was too killing. There was the illegal alien, the token minor public school drug smuggler . . .'

'Fifty pounds' worth of hash cunningly concealed in a Jimi Hendrix album,' put in Alabama.

'The ducky little Italian shoplifter,' Venice continued, 'who had an interpreter with him who was best friends with every single policeman in the place, you never saw so much backslapping. And then there was an absolutely dotty African, who had done a spot of armed robbery on the Underground, and whose solicitors sent a note saying they refused to represent him because he had appeared in their offices the day before in an inebriated condition and thrown a desk out of a fourth storey window, I ask you. And the judge was rather a duck, he looked just like Rex Harrison, I kept expecting him to burst into song, and ask why can't a woman be more like a man.'

'All we needed,' said Alabama, 'was Audrey Hepburn, and we would have had a party.'

'Do go on, Venice,' said Oliver impatiently. Nicholas was busy taking notes. Carlos, looking more bemused than ever, seemed to have found a bug in his beard, and was scratching it.

'So,' said Venice, drinking her champagne, 'you can imagine, by the time it got to me, after all these terrifying criminals, the magistrate was so relieved to find a civilized person, that he quite forgot to give me a lecture.'

'It must have been the hat,' said Oliver. Venice was wearing a particularly fetching Beatonesque creation with a vast black bow on the back. Hats such as that, Oliver often felt, must have been the reason that the human race came out of the stone age. 'So what did he say?'

'Well, he looked at my name on his little sheet, asked me how my father was, as if I would know, asked me where I got the hat, and said that I would have to have my licence confiscated for a year, but I could always take cabs. And that was it. I must say the public prosecutor was a bit of a dish, but I didn't really have time to go into that, although he was making rather a lot of eyes at Alabama.'

Alabama went rather pink and avoided Sergei's eye. She still hadn't quite got used to people staring wherever she went.

'Well,' said Oliver, utterly replete. 'Well. Imagine the

magistrate looking like Rex Harrison, or should I say Sir Rex. Whatever next?'

Somehow, it was early evening by the time they dispersed. They hadn't bothered to move from the bar, so Oliver had ordered club sandwiches and olives and potato chips and tiny pickled onions, which was all the food the place had, and they had rounded it off with brandy and small bitter cups of espresso, and Venice had had to tell her story all over again. By the time they left, the first shift of early evening drinkers were arriving for pre-dinner Martinis, eyes firmly fixed on the barman to make sure he didn't use too much vermouth.

Venice went back to Belgravia to tend to David. Oliver took Nicholas and the South American bongo player off to a private view of the latest word in erotic art. 'The artist is a particular friend of mine,' he said dreamily. 'I couldn't let him down.' Alabama went home to change for the opera. Sergei, being a cultivated man, liked to go to the opera. Alabama only quite liked it, but she had accepted his invitation, supposing that it was good for her.

Back in the quiet of her bedroom, she watched herself dress in the great roccoco glass that covered most of one wall. Slipping into a little red silk number that had cost three weeks' worth of royalties, she wondered quite what Sergei's intentions were. In three short days, he seemed to have assumed the position of her official escort, and so far he seemed quite contented to drop her home at night with no more than a gentlemanly kiss on the cheek. If Alabama didn't know about his reputation, she would have been lulled into a delicious sense of security, but she wasn't a cynic for nothing. Men who bowled over fair maidens all the way from

Mayfair to Monte Carlo were not the type to spend fortunes on restaurant bills without hope of reward. Besides, Sergei didn't strike her as the kind of man who took girls out purely for the sake of their conversation. He was obviously playing the waiting game. Alabama wondered if she was being rash, if her lovely prince in shining armour might not turn out to be more of a rattlesnake on horseback. She wasn't quite sure what she was going to do when he did decide to make his move. She wasn't altogether used to dealing with experienced seducers. Still, she would deal with that hurdle when she came to it. She was having fun. She felt rather like a child rifling through the dressing-up box, with all her strange new clothes. They hung in her wardrobe, dresses for every occasion, no more than an everyday vamp's working clothes. And it did seem to be working. By some happy chance, they had bumped into Max again last night, and Alabama couldn't help noticing him noticing her all the way through dinner, grinding his teeth and casting angry longing glances in her direction. It couldn't be long before he called. No man could have that much self-control. She was purposely staying away from rehearsals, making duty telephone calls to Johnny to make sure he didn't need her for any last-minute script changes. Quite soon, she thought, the time might be nigh for a strategic entrance, stage left. It wouldn't do any harm to turn the temperature up, just a little. And, she told herself, falling back on time-honoured cliché, if Max couldn't stand the heat, he could get out of the kitchen.

She put the last touches to her face, and stood up to admire her reflection. She looked quite a different girl. She did miss the bike, but she had to admit she was rather enjoying the glamour kick. She was already coming to expect the heads turning wherever she went, and she was uncomfortably aware that she rather liked it. She blamed her genes. After all, look at Venice.

Back in his church hall, Max wiped the sweat off his face, and tried to concentrate on his lines. It was only two weeks until they opened, and he had the uncomfortable feeling that his character was dying on him.

'Come along, my sweet,' said Johnny patiently. 'Let's take it again, from your entrance. Places, everyone.'

He sounded just like Venice, Max thought. He had seen the evening paper, splashed with pictures of Venice and Alabama emerging from the Marlborough Street Magistrates Court, shading their eyes against the flash-bulbs, but still somehow managing to look as if they were posing for a Cecil Beaton photograph. Only Venice could go to court in a hat like that and get away with it. There had been the usual blurb about Alabama Skye, celebrated young playwright, and her beautiful sister, society girl, Venice Skye, arrested on a drink driving charge. Venice, when asked for comment, reported the paper, had said, 'They were all heaven, and now I'd like my lunch,' which seemed to have baffled the journalist somewhat. And there was Alabama, dressed to kill in a short skirt and a little nipped-in coat, with those ridiculous legs for the entire press corps to lust over, with her Ray Bans firmly in place, saying 'No comment,' and looking like a film star. What had happened to her? You couldn't open a paper these days without seeing her picture, usually on the arm of that bogus Russian, and more often than not accompanied by a ridiculously extravagant piece of prose from Nicholas, usually so waspish, so cutting, but strangely indulgent when it came to the beautiful, the talented, the chic, Alabama. If Max ground his teeth much more, he wouldn't have any left, and whoever heard of a romantic lead with dentures? He didn't stop to wonder why it all made him quite so cross.

'Come along, lovey,' said Johnny, more sharply than usual. 'Are you with us?'

Max grunted, and tried to drag his mind back to the matter in hand. From across the room, Emmie grinned heartlessly at him. And that was another thing. Emmie seemed to have transferred her rather liberal affections to Sasha. When Max had taxed her with it she had smiled sunnily at him without a hint of shame and blithely suggested that he move on to Minna. 'After all,' she had said, with maddening logic, 'you ARE supposed to be having an affair with her too. It's all in the script. I thought you were serious about the Method.' And that was all he could get out of her on the subject. She and Sasha had taken to going off into little huddles in the corner, giggling and sharing cigarettes and gossiping about the rest of the cast, whenever they weren't on. Max couldn't think why Johnny allowed it, but he seemed to have a soft spot for Emmie. As for Sabine, her husband was back in town, and she was rarely available. 'Sorry darling,' she would coo down the telephone, 'silly old marriage, you do see.' Moreover, Nicholas, not content with turning into Alabama's number one fan, had taken to writing bitchy pieces in his column about arrogant young actors, and Oliver had blatantly cut Max at a party the week before, in full view of the whole room. Max sighed heavily. It simply wasn't his day.

In Belgravia, Venice found a note propped against the mantelpiece. 'Darling,' she read, 'Moira has found out about us.' How corny, Venice thought, and who could really have a wife called Moira anyway? She must have made it up. 'I am going to have to stop seeing you for a while, until things calm down.' Of course, Venice remembered, Moira was a major shareholder in David's company. Mustn't do anything to upset the little missus.

Venice wondered that he dared have a mistress at all. 'Of course you must keep the house and the car and the jewels. They are yours whatever happens. I shall be in touch when I can.'

At this point whimsy and self-pity had obviously overcome the man, the fearsome businessman who could strike terror into the hearts of his entire board of directors. 'Please say you'll wait for me.' Venice snorted in utter derision, tore up the note, and poured herself a large brandy. What to do now? Here she sat in Belgravia, with her nice house and her nice car and her nice jewels. Not to mention the clothes, and the Matisse sketch, and the shares in Eurotunnel that David had insisted on giving her for a rainy day. She was, in fact, very nicely set up, the queen of all she surveyed and the envy of her peers. But what was she going to do this evening? It was all very well cancelling all engagements, but with David off soothing the ruffled feathers of the irate Moira, Venice was left with a spare night. She could just hear him now, insisting that it meant nothing darling, nothing at all, it's you I love, don't leave me now, I couldn't live without you, I'll give her up, I swear it. Venice snorted again, and looked at her glass which seemed to be empty. She filled it up, and wandered aimlessly about the room, touching her possessions with little smoothing gestures of love. It didn't help. Even the Matisse looked rather insubstantial, somehow. Venice was not the kind of girl who sighed with relief at the thought of a quiet night in with the television and a cup of hot milk. The very idea made her want to go and put her head in the oven. Only she had electricity.

Just as she was getting really angry, the doorbell went. Venice looked up in delight, her sulks forgotten. The doorbell to her was akin to the call to battle, even more exciting than the telephone. She hurried to answer it, a martial light in her eye, wondering who it could be. The boy at the door looked to be about twenty, tall, and thin as a whiplash. He was very brown, with bright tow-coloured hair, and those green eyes that Venice liked most on a man. She smiled, all at once a picture of radiance. Perhaps the evening was not such a wash-out after all.

'Hello,' said this vision, inclining its head in an odd little gesture of greeting. 'I'm looking for my father.'

Venice wondered if he had the wrong address.

'This is number six,' she explained kindly. 'There's only me,' she added, with that devastating simplicity that had brought most of the male population of London to its knees, at one time or another. 'Why don't you come in anyway? I'm quite alone, and rather bored.'

The boy looked at her consideringly, summing her up. Venice looked back in surprise. He wasn't displaying any of the usual symptoms. His eyes were quite unglazed, almost quizzical, and his knees looked quite disappointingly strong. He seemed to be making up his mind whether to accept, or not. Venice thought that she really would have to change her hairdresser.

'Thank you,' said the boy at last. 'That would be nice. I could do with a drink, if you have one. My name is Sebastian Maxwell. You must be Venice.'

Venice took a small step backwards. No wonder he was looking for his father.

'Yes,' she said, valiantly trying to take all this in her stride. 'I am Venice. How did you know?'

'Quite a place, you've got here,' said Sebastian, walking into the drawing room and looking about him with a perfectly indecorous lack of concern for one who has just been confronted with his father's mistress. Venice wondered quite what the correct form was. She supposed they wouldn't quite have a chapter on it in *Debrett*.

'Thank you,' she said faintly. Really, court and this all in one day was more than a girl could stand. Why did he have to be so ridiculously good-looking? Why hadn't David told her that he had a son? What WAS going on?

'How did I know?' said Sebastian, still with that maddening calm. He headed for the drinks tray and poured himself a stiff measure of whisky. 'Do you mind if I help myself? My father told me about you. He suggested I might like to come and visit you myself, to improve my game, so to speak. I do rather draw the line at sharing my father's mistress, but then he does have some rather odd ideas. That's a pretty sketch, Matisse no?'

Sebastian said all this in a bland flat tone, for all the world as if he were discussing the weather in St Moritz or the state of the stock market. Venice felt her astonishment grow to heroic proportions.

'Do you really mean to say,' she managed at last, 'that David suggested that we, we . . . I mean, you and I . . .'

'Exactly.' Sebastian sat down on the sofa in a peculiarly graceful gesture, took a crumpled packet of Lucky Strike out of one pocket, lit one, and drew the smoke in appreciatively. 'I think he must have thought I needed some sort of initiation into the noble art, as they say in the old country.'

'And do you?' Venice was verging on the incredulous now, rooted to her Aubusson rug in disbelief. With the part of her mind that was still working, she rather wished that Alabama had been there, to write it all down. No one would believe it otherwise.

'I like to think that I'm doing quite well enough. Although,' he added, looking at her with narrowed eyes through his cigarette smoke, 'I should imagine that you are boulevards ahead. Still, one learns. Practice makes perfect, someone once said, I forget who. What exactly do you see in my father? I had no idea that he had netted such a spectacular fish.' This should have been a compliment, but Venice had the niggling feeling that it wasn't, quite. Not the ones that she was used to, anyway.

'See?' she managed, wondering how much more off-balance she could be taken. How could this strip of a boy walk into her house, looking as if he had just stepped out of a Coward play, with his bottle green suit cut two sizes too large, and look at her with those bold unabashed eyes, and help himself to her whisky, and ask her what she saw in his father?

'Yes,' he said. 'I mean to say, that if I were a woman, especially one that looked like you, I can't imagine that he would be my number one pin-up. Was he the best that you could do?'

Venice tried to decide whether this was deeply insulting, or not. It was said in such tones of bland curiosity that she found it hard to take offence.

'Best?' she echoed hopelessly. She wondered if she was going to manage anything remotely approaching coherence. She felt some sympathy with goldfish.

'Well, yes,' said Sebastian reasonably. 'This is good whisky. Nothing like a good malt. He's rather a dull old stick, wouldn't you say?'

'Do you always talk this way about your father?' said Venice, in a sudden flash of speech.

'Don't you?'

'About my father? I don't talk about my father.'

'Oh well, I see now. My dear old dad is filling the parental void in your life. How slow of me. It's so Freudian, I didn't know it really happened.'

'It doesn't,' said Venice, feeling a welcome anger start to rise in her delightful breast. 'And, I might add, it has nothing whatsoever to do with you. My motives are my own.'

Sebastian laughed appreciatively. 'My apologies. I'd

forgotten about all the best women working in mysterious ways. Do forgive me. You must remember that I am young and know nothing. I was just curious.'

'What are you doing here anyway?' said Venice, feeling that it was time to pull rank. 'Shouldn't you be at school?'

'University,' Sebastian corrected, apparently not the least put out. 'Actually, I've just been sent down.'

'From where?'

'Oxford. That makes it rather better, doesn't it? No disgrace in being sacked from Eton or Christ Church. It's only bad if it's East Anglia.'

'It's not awfully clever, either way.'

'You sound just like my mother. How odd. Can I get you another drink?'

'No, you cannot get me another drink. You are insufferable. I think you should leave.'

Sebastian put out his cigarette, and looked at her again with those unimpressed eyes.

'Don't be a spoilsport. I was going to offer to take you out to dinner.'

Venice was only human.

'All right,' she said. 'Anything is better than a night in front of the television.'

So it was that Alabama and Sergei, after three gruelling hours of Verdi, found Venice ensconced on a red plush banquette with a boy young enough to be her brother, eating the best fish that Soho had to offer. And very pretty they looked too, thought Alabama, with their blond heads bent together, and the bloom of youth on their fine stretched skin.

'Well,' she said. 'What a surprise. I didn't know that you knew anyone under thirty-five, Venice.'

'This,' said Venice, giving Sebastian a resigned look, 'is my sister, Alabama Skye.'

118

'How do you do?' said Sebastian, standing up and shaking Alabama's hand. 'Won't you join us? I'm afraid I'm rather an admirer.'

Sergei rolled his eyes to the ceiling, which happened to be adorned with a rather fetching pastiche of French dancing girls showing too much knicker.

'How,' he said in resignation, 'am I supposed to compete with the younger generation?' He had been rather looking forward to a quiet dinner with Alabama, but it seemed that wherever he went, Alabama would have an admirer waiting to be captivated. He could hardly blame them, he supposed, being so taken himself. It was rather a novel experience for him. He couldn't remember being captivated by a woman in quite the same way since he was seventeen. That had been his housemaster's daughter, no mean blue-stocking herself, and it had all ended in tears. Sergei didn't like to dwell on it.

'Don't worry,' said Alabama, who was rather taken with Sebastian herself. 'You and Venice can console each other. Oh,' she added, remembering her manners, 'this is Sergei Kolitsyn. Might one know your name?'

'Oh yes,' said Sebastian, shaking Sergei's hand politely, 'my name is Sebastian Maxwell.'

'Any relation of David?'

'Son.'

There was an infinitesimal pause, as significant looks were exchanged around the table. Sebastian calmly ordered another bottle, as if he had been going out with princes and playwrights all his life.

'Don't say it,' said Venice. 'Just don't.'

Sergei started to laugh.

'No one,' he said with feeling, 'could ever accuse you sisters of being dull.'

'Well,' said Venice, as they finished dinner, 'I think that we should go drinking.'

She was in a mood to prolong the evening. Sebastian, who it turned out, had read English at Oxford, had involved Alabama in a long and lively discussion on the merits of various playwrights, most of whom Venice had never heard of, which seemed to have consisted entirely of comparing Alabama favourably with all of them. Venice had been left to talk to Sergei, which was not by any means disagreeable. In fact, she reflected, he would have done rather nicely for her, except he wasn't the keeping kind. Still, she was rather piqued by Sebastian's exclusive interest in Alabama. She loved her sister, but she wasn't quite sure that she liked her stealing her thunder. A move would be the thing.

'Have mercy on an old man,' said Sergei, who still hadn't become acclimatized to Alabama's drinking habits.

'Don't be silly Sergei,' said Venice firmly. 'You don't look a day over twenty-one.'

'Add fifteen, and you'd be on the right track,' said Sergei with a touch of gloom. It was his birthday next week, and for the first time in his life, he was aware of the years passing him by.

'Oh come on,' said Alabama, who was enjoying herself. 'I think we should corrupt the younger generation, don't you think?'

The younger generation looked at her appreciatively.

'Do corrupt me, I beg,' it said.

They went to the usual Mayfair drinking bar. It was full when they arrived, mostly because Oliver and his bongo player had decided to have a night out with the whole band.

'Soon,' said Venice, 'Oliver is going to have to buy a charabanc, so that he can transport his entourage in comfort.'

'Really,' said Alabama, 'I think he deserves an OBE at the very least.'

'What for darling?' said Oliver, swooping down on them in delight.

'Services to international relations,' said Alabama seriously. 'Have you met Sebastian Maxwell?'

'Sebastian WHO?' said Oliver in amazement, getting the connection at once, as usual.

'Don't say it,' said Venice fiercely. 'Just don't.'

Sebastian was looking about with interest. He had never been to a place quite like this before. How very clever he had been to get sent down, and with such impeccable timing.

'Darling,' Oliver was saying, 'my lips are sealed. You know I'm the utter soul of discretion.' He turned to Sebastian, his eyes alight with interest, taking in the eccentric green suit and the tall willowy figure in a glance. 'So tell me,' he said gravely, 'where do you spring from?'

Sebastian looked back, equally grave.

'Don't you want to ask me where my burrow is, so that you can come and f-f-ferret me out, like an old s-s-stoat?'

'Ah,' said Oliver, who didn't have that many flies on him, having read the book and seen the film. 'An undergraduate. Of course, how silly of me not to guess. Although I think I should be forgiven, since most of your ilk look like social workers, these days. And you, if I may say so, are simply glorious. Have a drink, do. Tell me, what do the bright young things at the House drink now?' Oliver had been at Christ Church himself, in those far-off golden days when one's tutor had doled out the green Chartreuse and dined with the Prime Minister once a week. 'I presume you are at Christ Church?'

'Was,' corrected Sebastian. 'Sent down.'

'No! When?'

'This afternoon, actually,' said Sebastian, with remarkable sang-froid in one so young.

'Well,' said Oliver, in his element. Trust Venice. 'This calls for a celebration I think, don't you. What shall we have, Crystal?'

'Oliver,' said Alabama, 'I love you to death, but get me a bourbon before I die of thirst, would you?'

'You see,' said Oliver to his South American troupe who were looking bemused but happy after seven Margharitas apiece, 'this is what I have to put up with, from my own flesh and blood too. Do you weep for me?'

Sebastian took Venice home. It had seemed only fitting.

'So,' he said, as the taxi pulled up outside the little mews house, 'might I call you?'

Venice smiled to herself in the darkness. It would just about serve David right if his son carried on where he had left off. And what a son, too. Venice couldn't help but be sorely tempted.

'Yes,' she said.

'I would like to see your sister again.'

Venice felt cross. She did love Alabama, really she did, but it had always been tacitly accepted that Venice was the one who enticed the men. This new state of affairs was going to take some getting used to. Could Sebastian be the only man in London who wanted a woman for her brain?

'Yes,' she said carelessly. 'I'm sure she would be delighted to see you again too. But I do advise you to step a little carefully. Sergei has been known to call people out.'

In Chelsea, Sergei dropped Alabama home. She turned to him as the car stopped, noticing again how noble his profile looked. Nobility or not, he was still the most famous playboy in the western world, and Alabama thought that it was high time that she investigated his intentions a little further. She didn't want to find herself caught on the hop.

'Don't you want me to ask you in for a drink?' she said.

He turned to look at her.

'Do you want to?'

'I'm not sure. You're confusing me, and I resent that in any man.'

Sergei laughed.

'You've been watching too many old Fred Astaire films. Let me park the car.'

As Alabama opened the door, she wondered if she was being a little foolish. Time, she supposed, would tell.

'What would you like?' she said, heading towards the kitchen. 'I've got some brandy, or there's vodka in the freezer, if you'd prefer it.'

'Vodka then. Thank you,' he said, with those formal manners back in full force. Alabama felt that he was laughing at her.

She poured them both a drink, and sat down on one end of the sofa. Sergei settled himself on the other end with perfect propriety, and looked at her over the rim of his glass. There was a small pause.

'So,' said Sergei, rather matter of fact, 'would you like me to seduce you now?'

'Do you want to?' Alabama couldn't quite look at him. She wondered if this was always the way that such practised womanizers worked. She thought it was rather blunt.

'It's usually expected of me. I don't like to let a lady down.'

Alabama looked up and saw that he really was laughing at her. She started to laugh herself.

'Oh you beast,' she said. 'This is absurd. You should have stopped me.'

Sergei laughed even more.

'Forgive me,' he said, 'but you did look so enchanting, offering yourself, so to speak.'

'I wasn't sure what to do,' said Alabama candidly. 'I do think it's rather unfair on a man to let him take one out to endless dinners and then send him home on the doorstep.'

'What extraordinary ideas you do have,' said Sergei gravely. 'You should learn a little from your sister. If a man wants to spend his money on you, you should take it and run.'

'Should I?' said Alabama curiously. 'It still doesn't seem quite fair. Besides, you don't strike me as the sort of man who is interested in women purely for the sake of dinner party conversation.'

'Don't underestimate me,' said Sergei, who could have taken offence at this, but knew Alabama well enough not to. 'Perhaps I simply know the wrong women.'

Alabama gave a quizzical smile.

'So now you've discovered me,' she said, 'you've decided that you love women for the sake of their minds?'

'Not all women,' said Sergei. 'I could, of course, seduce you now, if you would like, but I'm not used to being second best.'

Sergei had had a rather illuminating conversation with Venice, and knew all about Max. Venice, with her usual lack of any kind of discretion, had kindly explained about her advice to Alabama, and how Alabama was using Sergei to follow it. Sergei felt that he must be mellowing with age. Six months ago, he would have been furious, and set out to make Alabama fall in love with him in earnest, as revenge. But now, he thought the whole idea rather amusing. Besides, Alabama was so refreshing, with her utter lack of guile and her incomprehension of artifice and social graces, that he felt he could forgive her anything.

'Second best,' Alabama said. 'What do you mean?'

'Well, you are in love with that young actor, aren't you?'

'I'm not sure. I thought I was. Perhaps it's just bloody-mindedness. I don't really know.' Alabama didn't stop to wonder how he knew about Max. It was rather a relief that he did.

'I think you are. So you see, I think it best if I leave you for him, and not complicate things further.'

Alabama suddenly laughed again. It really was the most penny-novelettish situation, quite unlike her.

'Sergei,' she said, 'is this the transformation of the most notorious rake in Europe? Could you have become a philanthropist in your old age?'

'And what if I have?' said Sergei, with dignity. 'Do you think you should really offer yourself up to me in payment for a few dinners?'

'I am sorry,' said Alabama, suddenly contrite. 'I've offended you.'

'Alabama,' said Sergei, 'if you will forgive me, I must tell you that you have a lot to learn about men.'

'I quite forgive you,' said Alabama humbly. 'You're absolutely right.' She really did know nothing about men. She had never really needed to, unlike Venice who had made them her life's work from an early age. There had been her work, and Milo, who was her friend and her swain and beautifully uncomplicated, and the few hearts dropped at her feet along the way had been rather carelessly tossed aside without a second thought. So, until Max, she hadn't realized how little she did know. And here she was, twenty-seven years old, fearsome young playwright, worldly wise

125

and appropriately cynical, admitting to herself that the opposite sex were a closed book to her.

'Well then,' continued Sergei, 'if you will permit me, I shall make a small suggestion. First of all, I should like it very much if we could go on seeing each other, as friends you understand. It makes a change for me, to have a woman friend. An interesting change, for the better, I think.'

Alabama smiled to herself. Until she had met Sergei, she didn't believe such people really existed. If she had known Sergei a few short months ago, she would have smiled even more. If the glamorous women could have seen him now, they would have fainted away in astonishment. Sergei Kolitsyn, going platonic all of a sudden, at his age. It was too much to contemplate.

'You smile,' said Sergei, 'but it is true. I am used to mistresses, irate husbands, that kind of thing. You see how it is.'

'I quite see,' said Alabama. 'Go on.'

'Well, I think that you should concentrate your energies on this young man. He is obviously sowing his wild oats, now that he has a little success, a little publicity. It is so often the way. He is intoxicated with it all, with himself as this new figure, but it will pass. If you wait, he will come back. Think how it must be for him. You are successful, fêted in your field, beautiful, and not exactly what I believe is called a pushover. Don't laugh, it's true. So he must feel a little threatened, and when such accommodating ladies as Sabine Borromini beckon, it is an easier option for him. But he will tire of it. Men have been tiring of Sabine since I can remember. And of course, now that you have stopped hiding your light under a bushel, he will soon realize that you can give him the glamour he so obviously craves, as well as all the things that those other glamorous women do not have.'

'Such as?' said Alabama, who couldn't help but be fascinated.

'Intelligence, wit, a few still waters running deep. Women like Sabine are rushing rivers, all verve and hurry, but shallow. Wait, and make him jealous. There I can help you.'

Alabama grinned.

'It never did a girl any harm at all, being seen with you.'

'So they tell me,' said Sergei. 'And now I must go. Thank you for the drink.'

He made his curious little bow over her hand, and kissed her cheek. Alabama smiled up at him.

'I think,' she said, 'that it's your old world charm that gets me every time.'

'Well,' said Sergei reasonably, 'at least all that finishing in Switzerland served some purpose.'

Meanwhile, in Belgravia, Venice lay back in her lace pillows, and allowed herself a little dream of Sebastian, so clever and young and golden, so utterly irresistible after the prosaic greyness of his father. Venice thought it was quite a diverting little dream, until she tried to go to sleep, only to find that the vision of that blond head and those clever green eyes wouldn't go away however hard she tried. Finally, she gave up all thought of sleep, and went downstairs to get a cigarette. She sat smoking it, watching the first light filter through her window, listening to the birds start up, mingling with the clip of army horses on their way to exercise, and wondered at herself. Nothing had ever stopped her sleeping before.

CHAPTER

6

The next day dawned bright and sharp with sunshine. Venice and Alabama woke up in their respective residences, stretched in a contemplative kind of way, and went to work. Both had spent the night doing some serious thinking.

Alabama surveyed her wardrobe, shaking her head as if in sorrow. She had made the elementary mistake of thinking that glamour meant a great many sharp chic little suits. Those might work on Venice, with her open face and tumbling hair, but even she had to undo one crucial button to avoid severity. On Alabama, they simply looked frightening, power dressing for the Thatcher generation. She would have to start again. She bundled the lot over her arm, and took them to Oxfam, who almost fainted at the sight of half this season's Paris collections being dumped unceremoniously on their doorstep.

'Well,' said Alabama to the astonished assistant, 'that should feed a few babies, at least.'

Then she went shopping, boldly brandishing her credit card, once rusty with neglect, now bright and shining with use. She bought armfuls of silk and chiffon and fine linen, the kind of clothes that give little away, but always contrive to look as if they might just slip off. That was much more the thing. Everything guaranteed to entice, or your money back. She also bought a gallon of Floris bath oil, half a hundredweight of pot pourri, and a vast bunch of roses. She considered a hat, but couldn't quite bring herself to do it.

As Alabama went home, and started arranging all her new possessions, Venice entered Hatchards in search of knowledge. She didn't know a great deal about under-graduates, but she had a sneaking suspicion that they expected everyone to be as clever as they were them-selves. She would have to fake it. She bought the entire works of Scott Fitzgerald, Hemingway, Evelyn Waugh, Shakespeare, and Harold Pinter, whom Sebastian had said he admired. She also took two books on art history, one on eighteenth-century architecture, and a biography of Napoleon, whom Sebastian also admired. Unable to face carrying all this erudition, she asked for it to be sent. She then went to the newsagent, and manfully placed an order for the *Daily Telegraph* to be delivered every day instead of the *Daily Mail* (how she would miss seeing her face staring prettily at her from the paper over breakfast), and also for the *Spectator* weekly. She considered cancelling her subscription to *Vogue*, but decided that she had to draw the line somewhere. No man was worth missing *Vogue* for. Then she went to see Alabama.

When Milo dropped in later that afternoon, he found Alabama and Venice sitting on the sofa, swapping notes. The room was filled with flowers, and all the chaos of books and papers and ashtrays and bottles that surrounded Alabama when she worked were van-ished. Even the typewriter seemed to have disappeared.

They were watching a video of *To Have and Have Not* and Lauren Bacall was asking Humphrey Bogart if he knew how to whistle. Venice was reading a copy of *Pravda*.

'Well,' said Milo, not entirely sure what to make of all this. 'Have I come to the right house?'

'Sit down and don't mind us,' said Alabama, flapping a weary hand at him, 'we're just doing a touch of role reversal.'

Milo looked at her curiously. He still couldn't quite get used to this new Alabama, with her hair smooth and shining, and her face painted. She was wearing a rather old-fashioned swirl of peach today, the sort of thing that Isadora Duncan might have felt at home in, but Milo still missed the jeans. Next thing he knew, she'd be lying on a day bed, dripping langour.

'Forgive me if I sound obtuse,' he said, 'but could you elaborate just a fraction.'

'Well, Milo,' said Venice, taking pity on him, and speaking very clearly as one might to a slightly slow child, 'I am in love with a man who wants a brain, and Alabama is in love with a man who wants rather more body, do you see?'

Milo didn't really see at all. They had never been great girls for love, unlike most women.

'Am I supposed to think that you are going to swap men?' he asked.

'Not men, dummy,' said Venice. 'Characters. I shall become Alabama, and she shall become me. Could you die?'

'Seems a very complicated way of doing things,' said Milo. He put it down to the fact that they had lacked any parental guidance from such a young age.

'It is rather,' Venice admitted. 'But we think it's worth it. Faint heart, and all that.'

'When I think,' said Milo sorrowfully, 'that you were set up for life with your sugar daddy, and Alabama was well on her way to becoming a princess, I do wonder. I do.'

'Some girls are never satisfied,' said Venice happily.

'And do these paragons know what's in store for them?'

'Not yet,' said Alabama. 'I have to watch some more Lauren Bacall films first, and Venice is trying to work her way through two years' worth of back copies of the *Spectator*. Give us a week.'

'I think,' said Milo judiciously, 'that I need a drink.'

Venice insisted on giving Alabama tuition. Venice showed her sister how to get out of a cab, and use her eyes, and lower her voice at the appropriate moment so that a man had to bend his head to hear.

'Now,' she would say seriously, 'there is only one way to let a man light your cigarette. Cast your eyes down to the flame, that's right. Draw in the smoke. Steady his hand for a moment with yours. And at the last minute, raise your eyes and look into his. Just for a second mind, we don't want to overdo it. Now try it again.'

'Christ,' said Alabama, 'it's hard work being a *femme fatale*. I think I might go back to writing plays.'

'Don't be silly,' said Venice, with a bracing smile. 'You're doing beautifully.'

Sebastian, true to his word, did call.

'Come to tea,' said Venice carelessly. 'I think Alabama is coming round, so you can discuss Pinter.'

'I'll see you at four then,' said Sebastian.

When Sebastian arrived, punctually at four o'clock, he found Venice stretched out on the sofa, reading a copy of the *New Statesman*, and drinking beer out of the can.

131

Her perfect legs were encased in Alabama's oldest pair of jeans, and her hair was held back in a red bandana. She had kicked her shoes off, and her feet were bare.

'Well,' said Sebastian, looking at her reading matter, 'I didn't think that girls who looked like you could read anything except the instructions on suntan lotion bottles.' Anyone but Venice might have taken exception to such a remark. However, being Venice, she took it as a compliment. She stood up and smiled kindly on him, noticing how deliciously *louche* he looked in one of those old fawn housecoats that butlers used to wear in hot climates.

'Have a little respect,' she said, 'some dumb blondes have hidden resources.'

'I'm impressed,' said Sebastian truthfully.

'Well. What would you like? Beer? There's some Miller Lite in the fridge.' The other thing Venice had heard about undergraduates was that they drank all day, heedless of whether the sun was anywhere near the yard arm. She didn't want to make a terrible *faux pas* and offer him anything as innocuous as tea.

'Thank you,' said Sebastian. He seemed a little lost for words.

'Beer would be fine.' Somehow he had been expecting Earl Grey out of paper-thin china cups. Venice looked like the kind of girl who got out the Crown Derby at the slightest provocation.

Just as they were staring at each other rather in the little pool of silence that had developed, there was a knock on the door and Alabama breezed in. She kissed them both breathlessly, dropping a Fortnums carrier bag as she went.

'Darlings,' she said, just as Venice had taught her, 'don't tell me I'm late. I couldn't get a cab to save my life. I brought you some Bath Olivers,' she said to

Venice. 'Hello,' she said to Sebastian, stressing the last syllable, 'what perfect heaven to see you again. Venice was clever to find you.'

Sebastian looked from one sister to the other. He might not be used to such exalted circles, but there was something going on here that he was missing.

'Well,' he said, most uncharacteristically at something of a loss, 'Well.'

'Isn't this cosy?' said Alabama, draping herself over the sofa as if she had been born graceful. She looked at Venice's magazine. 'Really, Ven, are you still reading this stuff? Doesn't it bore you to death? I don't know how you can stand it.'

Venice took on a look of utter hauteur, with a cunning touch of disdain.

'Someone has to take an interest in world affairs,' she said. 'We can't all spend our entire lives in St Laurent, you know.' Until the week before, Venice could have thought of nothing nicer than spending her life in St Laurent, but Sebastian wasn't to know that.

'Some of us can,' said Alabama, turning her head away to hide her laughter. Venice was surpassing herself. Alabama thought that her own performance was rather good as well, although it was a shame Max wasn't there to see it.

Sebastian sat himself down on the sofa rather abruptly. He concentrated on his beer, which at least was reassuringly familiar. He knew Alabama for the most fiercely intelligent playwright of her generation, her name was still legend in Christ Church, and here she was looking and sounding as if she had just stepped out of an old film. And as for Venice, the darling of the gossip columns, the *demi-monde*, the kept woman, here she sat, in a pair of jeans that looked as if they had come in with the ark, occupied with reading

133

matter that most self-respecting undergraduates didn't even consider. He had felt quite able to deal with her when she was just his father's mistress, put her down comfortably as eminently decorative and quite empty-headed, and allowed himself a little glow of superiority, but this, this was quite another Venice altogether. What was going on?

'What did you read at Oxford?' asked Venice, as if she were really interested.

'English,' said Sebastian.

'How fascinating,' said Venice carelessly. 'Of course I did think of going to Oxford, but I decided to go round the world instead.' Venice was never above a few strategic white lies. She had, in fact, only been to Oxford once in her life, for a party. She had thought it all vastly pretty, and rather romantic, and she had been captivated by all the young bloods dressed up in their delicious Bullingdon tails. The party itself had been rather fun too, although slightly marred by the fact that her escort, so attentive, so eligible, so charming, and with such an alluring trust fund, had turned out to be engaged to someone else.

'Round the world?' said Sebastian, rather idiotically.

'Well, yes darling,' said Venice patiently. 'I thought I'd like to learn about life first hand, do you see, rather than out of a book.' Venice opened her eyes so wide, and looked so earnest, that Sebastian could not possibly guess of her economy with the truth. Round the world in this case meant the South of France, where Venice had spent a very enjoyable season at the *Hôtel du Cap* once, at the expense of some old European white trash friends, who liked paying for everything. Venice loved people who liked paying for everything, and had always rather lamented the fact that the family had no sons of marriageable age. The world rather ended for her with Italy, so she supposed that going as far as the Riviera

134

was almost halfway round the world, and that wasn't so much of an exaggeration then. And she had learnt a great deal about life that summer, spending her time playing backgammon with professional gamblers, and tennis with professional playboys, and bridge with everyone else. So she really could hardly be said to be telling a lie, could she?

'I've never done much travelling,' said Sebastian, who had spent endless summers on the Riviera too, and in Rome and Naples and right down into the south, bandit country around Reggio, but who thought he couldn't quite count that as travelling compared to Venice's impressive trips.

'Oh but you should,' said Venice, more earnest than ever. 'It gives one a much clearer perspective on things. Take South Africa for instance.' This was the moment that Venice had been waiting for. She knew that everyone got terribly upset about South Africa almost all the time, that arguments about the pros and cons of the situation were constantly splitting up marriages and dividing families, so she had naturally thought that it must be the first thing that she should learn about. Luckily, the *Spectator* had a particularly long and dogmatic article on the subject this week, which Venice had learnt by heart and then paraphrased. Until this week, all she had known about South Africa was that it was where she got her peaches from. Listening to her talk, her beautiful face impassioned, words new to her, like terrorism and ANC and means justifying ends, dropping easily from her perfect lips, Sebastian was quite taken in. Alabama busied herself with lighting a cigarette to cover her absolute amusement. After about ten minutes, she decided that Venice should be rescued before she came to the end of her new-found knowledge. Alabama could see that the undergraduate was impressed. Faintly puzzled, and who could blame

135

him, but definitely impressed. Alabama was rather impressed herself. If she didn't know better, she would have thought that Venice really cared.

'Oh do stop,' she said, as if she were too bored by the whole thing. 'Really Venice.'

'But I was just getting started,' said Venice in utter indignation, giving Alabama a look of relief that Sebastian couldn't see.

'I know,' said Alabama, sounding resigned. 'And I for one am certainly not feeling strong enough for one of your three-hour lectures on putting the world to rights. That's what we pay the Government for.'

'They don't do a very good job at it, though,' said Sebastian.

'Well, what do you expect from a bunch of bourgeois civil servants?' said Alabama, her drawl more exaggerated than ever. 'They're all so dull, God save me from them is all I beg. Really, it makes me want to yawn, just thinking about this. Do let's talk about something more interesting.'

'Oh all right,' said Venice, graciousness herself descending from a pillar of pure intellect. 'If you absolutely insist. Tell us some Oxford stories Sebastian.'

While this tea was in progress, Oliver was ringing up Nicholas, to make a few arrangements. He did so love organizing things, and had so agreed with Sergei when he had rung and suggested that a little party might be the very thing. After all, look at the tearaway success of the last soirée he gave for the Skyes.

'Hello my dear,' said Nicholas, in a rather pleased-with-himself voice. He had just effected a most judicious coup in stealing a story from under Carlton's nose. Any more of this and his editor would give him a rise. 'I suppose you want a favour.'

'It's such a tiny thing,' said Oliver in his most caressing tones. 'And entirely to your own advantage. I know how you worry about filling up that *bijou* little column of yours day after day. Anyway, it's really for Alabama, not me at all.'

'Oh well,' said Nicholas, 'in that case, fire away. I am yours to command.'

'Nicholas,' said Oliver, who couldn't help but notice the uncharacteristic note of indulgence in Nicholas's voice every time Alabama's name was mentioned, 'have you designs on my cousin?'

'I'm only human,' said Nicholas. 'What do you want me to do?'

'Well,' said Oliver, settling back into his Milanese sofa, and taking a delicate sip of his Martini, 'what is called for at this stage is a tiny bit in your column to the effect that Alabama, the delicious talented Alabama, whose plays everyone adores, is contemplating matrimony to the oh-so-eligible prince, who, needless to say, is smitten in his turn. You can embroider a bit to the tune of rings from Cartier and perhaps a racehorse as a wedding present, you know the form. Sergei won't sue.'

'It's not true though, is it?' said Nicholas in alarm.

'Of course not,' said Oliver soothingly, although he rather thought it should be. If Sergei proposed to him, he wouldn't hesitate. 'I'm not dashing your hopes entirely. All we want is that nasty young actor to take the bait. We think he's had it rather too easy so far.'

'I see,' said Nicholas in relief. 'Does Sergei know that he's about to be compromised?'

'Of course, my dear,' said Oliver, with one of his coy little laughs. 'The divine *principe* suggested the idea. He doesn't like to see Alabama eating her heart out.'

Nicholas grunted crossly. 'I didn't know he was so big-hearted.' He had been chronicling Sergei's amorous adventures across five continents for years, and he didn't altogether trust this sudden burst of philanthropic behaviour. 'Isn't this rather odd coming from a man who has bowled over more women than I've had libel cases?'

Oliver laughed again, knowing exactly why Nicholas sounded so cross. The idea of the hard-boiled scourge of Fleet Street nursing this hopeless passion for Alabama was affording him so much amusement. Hours of fun for all the family. 'I think,' he said naughtily, 'that Alabama may have reformed him.'

'Hm,' said Nicholas, even more crossly. 'Old rakes don't reform, they just go to seed.'

'Well, darling, there we are. What can I tell you? Do you think you could just do this small thing? It's part of a bigger plan. And say you're free tomorrow night.'

'All right,' said Nicholas, with as much grace as he could muster. 'My heart is breaking, but I'll do it. You can take me to dinner next week though, and fill me with caviar. I don't put my neck on the line for free.'

'Of course you don't,' said Oliver caressingly. 'My ducky South American bongo player has deserted me, gone to Antwerp on the first leg of his world tour the beast, so I'm feeling rather spare.'

Nicholas noticed that since all the interest with Venice and Alabama had come into his life, Oliver had quite forgotten that he hadn't quite come out of the closet yet. He had always been rather discreet about his men friends, and now he was quite brazenly taking them everywhere. Nicholas found it rather a relief, since he didn't have to pretend not to know any more.

Meanwhile, back in Belgravia, Alabama was taking a well-timed leave, in a positive swirl of chiffon scarves.

Sebastian was starting to look at Venice in that old–fashioned way that made Alabama feel they would rather be alone.

'I have a date with my divine prince,' she said airily. 'Don't let Venice bore you to death, Sebastian. You have to be very firm with her.' She kissed Venice fondly. 'Lunch perhaps, darling,' she said, 'if you can tear yourself away from world affairs for five minutes. Call me.' And she was gone, leaving a faint whiff of Chanel No. 5 behind her.

Oliver, busy with his arrangements, had got as far as O in his telephone book. He rang Milo.

'My dear,' he said, 'I know it's late notice, and you're bound to be going to dinner with Antonia Fraser, or I don't know who, but do say you're free tomorrow night.'

'I could be,' said Milo cagily. 'As long as you're up to no good.'

'Of course I am,' said Oliver in delight. 'I'm teaching that actor a lesson. Long overdue, wouldn't you say?'

'I would,' said Milo firmly, although he didn't think that Oliver's idea of a lesson would be quite the same as his own. He knew that Oliver abhorred violence, and something told him that he wouldn't approve of castration. 'I'm free then.'

'Good,' said Oliver in deepest satisfaction. He liked Milo, and besides he was a crucial part of his plan. 'Now what I need is as many of those ravishing literary friends of yours as you can round up. I see a perfect vision of Alabama surrounded by a sea of handsome men, with Sergei the most handsome of all. What do you say?'

'Oliver,' said Milo sternly, 'isn't that just a little crude?'

'But my dear,' cried Oliver, almost overcome by his own cleverness, 'Max IS crude. There lies the whole point. The morning paper is going to make him cross, make sure you read Nicholas's column, but this is going to make him incandescent. Haven't you ever heard of dogs in the manger?'

'I think I was one once.'

'Well, there you are,' said Oliver, in the triumphant voice of one who has just discovered quantum physics. 'I'll expect you at eight.'

Oliver put down the telephone, and paused only to light one of the custom-made Turkish cigarettes that he felt sure Noel Coward must have smoked, before taking it up again. He had so many people to call. It was such a great piece of luck that his florist and his caterers knew him so well, or they would never have consented to do a party at such short notice. As it was they had been charmed, as if they could imagine nothing nicer than an impromtu soirée, when they normally required people to book months in advance, as Oliver very well knew. Now all he had to do was call up his accommodating wine merchant, and go through the rest of his address book, and then all that would be left would be the vital question of what to wear. Oliver knew it was Alabama's evening, but he still wanted to look his best. Old habits did, after all, die hard, so they told him.

Sergei had asked Alabama to dine, partly because he had to tell her about his fiendish plan, but mostly because he couldn't think of anyone else he would rather see. Sergei had a little black book that put *Who's Who* to shame, but suddenly it seemed rather obsolete.

'So,' he said, smiling to her, 'how does it feel to be engaged?'

'Like a public lavatory,' said Alabama gloomily. 'It's ridiculous.'

If the glamorous women had heard her, they would have fainted dead away. Engagement to such a catch was the kind of thing that they had dreamt of all their adult lives. But then, it was a well-known fact that Alabama was a mystery, a law unto herself.

'Genius,' said Sergei, not put out at all, 'is mostly an infinite capacity for taking pains.'

'So they say,' said Alabama, as if she couldn't think who they were, and cared rather less. She lit a cigarette and drew in the smoke as if it might make everything better. She wasn't at all sure about the fiendish plan, and there seemed something not quite right about dragging Sergei into it, although he did rather seem to have taken it upon himself. And what if it didn't work, and all these efforts were for nothing. She wasn't at all sure that she wanted the world to witness her defeat. She raised her chin, and tried to look on the bright side. 'It's just,' she said, 'that it all does seem rather much, for one man.'

'But why not?' said Sergei, who was rather enjoying himself.

'Even teenagers don't go to such lengths. It's silly.'

'But rather amusing, even you must admit. And think of Oliver, it's his *raison d'être*. He hasn't had so much fun since he discovered the canapé.'

'Oh well,' said Alabama, smiling despite herself. 'If you put it like that . . .'

'I do,' said Sergei firmly. 'Now have some more champagne, and count your blessings.'

'I have striking bones,' said Alabama.

In the interval at the Wyndham Theatre, Sebastian fought his way manfully through the crush to buy Venice a bottle of champagne. She had suggested that they go to the new Steven Berkoff, produced two tickets out of thin air, and borne him off in a cab, before he had time to be amazed. And now she stood, like a perfect little island in the sea of earnest theatre-goers, who knew how important it was not to look shocked by Berkoff's latest profanity, because it was Art after all, and everyone knew how important it was to be cultured, and he had to get her some champagne if he died in the attempt.

'Thank you,' she said, as he returned after five hard-fought minutes, bearing spoils that she could have got with a bat of her eyelashes. 'How lovely.'

Sebastian felt as if he had just mined the world's largest diamond. He tried not to grin idiotically.

'That's all right,' he said, as if it had been nothing.

'Are you enjoying it?' she asked, as if it were only his opinion that mattered. Personally, Venice thought the whole thing quite incomprehensible, but she supposed it must all be frightfully clever. Everyone always said how clever Berkoff was, and so who was she to argue. All the same, she rather felt she would take Coward any day, clever or not.

'Oh yes.'

'Good.' She smiled largely and drank her champagne.

Sebastian looked at her curiously. She was the most puzzling girl he had ever met. But then, he supposed he hadn't really met that many girls.

'You are surprising,' he said abruptly, although he had not really meant to.

'I am?' Venice was a picture of carelessness, as if she didn't care about what men thought of her, only of the things that really mattered, like world oppression and the poll tax.

'Well, yes,' said Sebastian doubtfully. 'I didn't expect anyone who could have an affair with my father to be like you. I thought you would be an idiot.'

'Have a little respect. Your father is a very powerful and interesting man. We can't all spend our lives going out with rock stars.' Venice conveniently ignored the fact that whenever David started talking about high finance, which he inevitably did whenever there was a pause in the conversation, she immediately switched off and started to plan her winter wardrobe. The new collections had just come out, and they really were to die for.

'I suppose so,' said Sebastian, frowning. Could she really be interested in the price index and the American trade figures in the same way that David was?

'He's taught me a great deal about the inner workings of the economy,' said Venice firmly.

'He has?' Sebastian looked quizzical. 'I can't stand economics.' He did hope that Venice wouldn't expect him to discuss commodity prices. For all his native wit, he didn't think he would be able to keep it up for long.

'Ah well,' said Venice kindly. 'Each to each, and all that.'

She finished her champagne, breathing a sigh of relief. At least she wouldn't have to bluff her way through an in-depth discussion of the budget. The Chancellor of the Exchequer looked so much like a common farmyard animal that the very thought made her feel quite faint and not herself at all.

In Chelsea, Max was having a quiet night in and sulking. Sabine was busy, at one of the charity evenings that her husband liked her to attend, Emmie was out with Sasha, and there was no party to go to. Max's invitations, once stacked like a pack of cards on his smart new marble chimneypiece, had rather fallen off of late. He knew that he should be thinking about his part, but he couldn't concentrate. He wandered about the flat, wondering what he could do. There didn't seem to be anyone he could call. He thought fleetingly of Alabama, of the newly glamorous Alabama, probably out with her bogus Russian, being wined and dined and paid fulsome compliments, letting the whole room stare at one of her shoulders, which was bound to be uncovered. He certainly couldn't call her. He could just hear her satirical voice answering the telephone. He had rather burnt his boats in that quarter. He went to get a beer from the fridge, and contemplated getting really drunk. He felt twitchy and uncertain. He was caught between two stools, still on the rise, not yet quite established either on the stage or in the salon. He suddenly envied Alabama and Venice and Oliver and Sabine and Emmie and Sasha, who moved so easily, with such confidence, carelessness even, in their respective spheres. They had done their apprenticeship, years before, when Max was still wet behind the ears and trying to rid himself of his accent. They were in, and he was still on the outside, hovering on the sidelines, not quite sure when he would be let in. Max had spent his life on the outside, looking in, aspiring always to more than he had. For all his success, he was still excluded. He was being judged, measured, and sometimes he wondered if he was going to come up to scratch. One false step, and he would be back at the bottom of the heap. His work at rehearsals lately had been average, and he was no longer invited everywhere. There was a new sensation on the rise, a young writer the glamorous ladies had taken up, on a whim, and fêted in their usual extravagant fashion. As far as they were concerned, Max was very nearly yesterday's news. Their memories had always been conveniently short, but Max wasn't to know that. If he had, he might have stepped a little more carefully, might have paused for a moment before he threw Alabama over and allowed himself to be taken up. If he didn't pull something out of the bag now he could just go back to being a nobody, and he wasn't sure he wanted to. He had had a taste of honey, and he liked it. He could just close his eyes and let himself drown in the sweetness of expensive restaurants and desirable addresses, and scented cheeks. He wanted to succeed so badly he could taste it in his mouth, sharp and metallic. He had to make it. If he got good reviews for this play, if he was a hit in Roger's film, if, if, if. He wanted to be able to walk into a room, and watch everyone watching him, not because of who he was with, but because he was Max Charlton. He wanted to hear people murmuring his name under their breath, pretending not to stare, feigning disinterest because they knew that it was not quite the thing to be impressed by stars, even though they were secretly impressed as hell. He would like that. He would like to feel that his future was assured. At the moment, he wasn't sure.

The telephone went, shrill into Max's introspection.

'Hello,' he growled.

'Well,' said Oliver brightly, 'you DO sound cross, ducky. Did you get out of the wrong side of bed this morning, or did you just have a tiff with one of your many girlfriends? There are so many of them now I can hardly keep up, I wish you'd tell me how you do it.'

'What do you want,' said Max, scarcely polite. He was damned if he was going to tell Oliver about his troubles. Although, knowing Oliver, he would probably know already. Oliver had a happy knack of knowing most people's secrets before they knew them themselves.

'Well my dear,' said Oliver, not at all put out by such an ungracious reception. 'I know it's terrifyingly late notice, but I'm having a little party tomorrow night. Might you drop by, if you're not too desperately busy?'

'I could,' said Max, more charmless than ever.

'Don't put yourself out,' said Oliver, smiling into his Martini, 'but Dent Ludlow is coming, so I thought you might be interested, that's all.'

That's all, thought Max, astounded by such understatement. That's all. Dent Ludlow was only the most important living American film director, that was all. To meet a man like that was the kind of opportunity Max would be dead and buried to miss, as Oliver very well knew.

'I'll be there,' said Max, taking the bait hook line and sinker, in the most old-fashioned way. Oliver always rather loved it when clichés came true.

'See you tomorrow then,' he cried, almost too pleased with himself for words. He knew that Max would come. Dent Ludlow would probably not be able to make it, since he was shooting in Mexico, but Oliver would leave a friendly message with his secretary anyway. Then he wouldn't be telling an utter lie. He was simply being economical with the truth. As far as verity went, Venice and Oliver had been taught in the same school.

CHAPTER

7

The party was quite organized. Milo was bringing all his bright young literary friends, Sebastian had been alerted, Sergei was coming with some of his more disreputable cronies, Roger was bringing Kiki, for a joke, Nicholas was bringing his pocket camera and a tape recorder, and Alabama and Venice had spent all day getting ready.

Oliver surveyed his flat. It did look like a slice of heaven, with the heavy orange evening sun slanting through the wide windows. The caterers had surpassed themselves. A great table was laden with the kind of food so avant-garde that most people didn't even know what it was called. Oliver hardly knew himself. All he knew was that it certainly looked far too pretty to eat, which was the point of food, in his mind. What he had hated most about school food was not so much that it tasted of old socks, but that it had looked so ugly. Mealtimes had been a torture to him all through his childhood.

In the bathroom, the bath was filled with ice and rows and rows of Dom Perignon in its elegant green bottles. Not for Oliver the ignominy of having champagne served with napkins carefully placed to obscure the label. There was nothing more shabby, in his opinion.

Enormous vases of lilies, pale half-open roses, and orchids were everywhere, their scent mingling with the heady smell of Floris lamp oil. Oliver put Mozart's piano concerto for two pianos on the record player. There was something almost unbearably decadent about a piano concerto for two pianos.

Oliver gave a great sigh of utter satisfaction. He did so love the moments before a party, when the room was quiet and still, ready to receive its babel of guests, and the anticipation of the night to come was a sharp excited thrill in the stomach. He looked about the room one last time, as if to reassure himself of its perfection, and went to give himself a final glance in the looking glass. It pleased him so much that the Crolla shirt he had chosen so carefully exactly matched the flowers. Really, he did show flashes of genius sometimes. He smoothed his hair unnecessarily with a supplicating little gesture. He looked a picture and he knew it. He smiled at himself with love.

'You are quite to die for,' he told his reflection with feeling. His reflection smiled graciously back, adept at accepting a compliment.

And now for the performance to begin. It was going to be quite a night.

Alabama sighed, tossed her head a little, frowned twice, and tried to start from the beginning. Her bed was littered with clothes. It was too hot for velvet, and the pale chiffon had a mark on it. The washed linen shirt was just too understated, and the crushed silk Bruce Oldfield was just too much. Alabama concentrated as hard as she could. There must be something that was just right. She sighed again, a little wistfully. She thought of the days when it had taken her five minutes to get dressed to go out. Those simple days when it was a matter of which pair of jeans was clean. She looked rather piteously at her old cowboy boots, scuffed from years of uncomplaining service, now consigned to the depths of the wardrobe. It was all very well turning herself into the latter day answer to Ava Gardner, but no one had warned her about all the work involved. She drew herself up tall, pausing to admire her silk underwear. She did look rather fine in it. She couldn't let a small thing like this defeat her. She was the best playwright of her generation. She had a double first. She was brilliant. She was not going to be thwarted by a tiny matter like what to wear. She took a deep breath, and started again.

Venice finished painting her lips and pouted at herself in the glass. She did have the best pout in London. She had much to be thankful for. She smoothed the perfection of her brow, which ached a little from all the knowledge that she had crammed into it in the last week. She was almost ashamed to admit that she found the *Daily Telegraph* rather amusing, and that she didn't miss the *Mail* nearly as much as she had expected. Perhaps she was a closet intellectual after all. That would be a thing. Imagine, after all these years, a Venice who minded about more than finding exactly the right dress to wear to a party. Life did throw up the most extraordinary surprises, just when one was least expecting them. Venice looked at her face again, something she never tired of. It looked rather strange with so little make-up on. Rather fine, really. Almost ethereal, in fact. Perhaps intellectual? Venice told herself to stop being fanciful. Enough was enough, after all.

It took her hardly a moment to dress. She had decided to strike a balance somewhere between glamour and utter carelessness. She still drew the line at wearing jeans to a party, whatever Alabama said, so she had settled on a little black dress. Venice knew all about little black dresses and their importance in the history of seduction. She knew that every girl should have at least one. This particular one was simple and short and made of material that clung lovingly to her figure. No jewels, Venice decided firmly, with hardly a backward glance at her box of baubles, the box which only a week ago had given her so much pleasure, the box which she could quite happily gaze at for an hour, when she had an hour to spare. No jewels, just sheer black stockings and a dash of Chanel No. 5, and that would do very nicely indeed. Venice looked at her wardrobe for a moment, with a faint look of longing, running her hand for a brief forbidden minute along the collection of silks and satins and rich organza. It was only for a minute. She turned back to her reflection, thinking that perhaps she looked rather young and slim and fine, and anyway, some things were more important than clothes.

Nicholas sighed heavily, and put one of his old Ella Fitzgerald records on, to accompany him while he dressed. It fitted his mood quite perfectly. He had no heart, everyone knew that. So what was all this, mooning about like a lovesick adolescent? And why was there a hole where his stomach used to be, even though he had eaten a whole lobster for lunch, and two helpings of summer pudding, every time he thought of Alabama? It was getting too ridiculous. He was the toughest nut in a street of very hard cases, he was the man who dared people to sue, he was the man who could make and break reputations and marriages, so what was the matter with him? He sighed again, and slapped on some of his best aftershave, with a vain attempt at carelessness. He looked at his collection of suits, said by some to be the most extensive in London, although he felt that Sergei might have the edge on him, and wondered which he should wear for maximum effect. The pin-stripes were too formal, the cream linen too cricket, the Anthony Price too reminiscent of a television personality. After some deliberation, he chose a double breasted Prince of Wales check which he had always been fond of. That should do, not too sharp, yet modern, with a hint of witty nostalgia that was so essential these days. Perfect. He brushed his hair, and shot his cuffs, and fitted his cigarettes into a silver cigarette case, and told himself for the sixty-fourth time not to be so ridiculous.

Milo worked on his book until late. He only needed five minutes to get ready anyway. He put his head under the tap, and then pulled on a pair of jeans and a white shirt and had done with it. He was fond of Oliver, in a wry kind of way, but not that fond. Besides, there was little point in dressing up. This was Alabama's night. He didn't want to steal any thunder at all.

Scattered across London, his literary friends were putting on much the same uniform. Most of them looked like Montgomery Clift anyway, so they didn't need any more adornment. That was why they had been invited, if only they knew it. As it was, they were looking forward to a good evening. Oliver's parties were famous, and the Skye sisters were fast becoming legendary, and there was bound to be an extraordinary amount of material for their next books.

Above an off-licence in the King's Road, Sebastian paused in front of the glass to accompany Eric Clapton in a particularly gruelling guitar riff. The least one could do for a sound like that was give it a little respect. Sebastian bowed extravagantly to an imaginary audience. Too kind, he thought. What a great crowd you are. Really, it was nothing. He wondered if he should dress up for this party. King of the social circuit in Oxford, Sebastian had never been to a really sophisticated London party before. All his parents' friends were serious financial wizards who occasionally gave drinks parties on Sunday mornings, and his own friends were still bringing bottles. What did really sophisticated London party goers wear? Should he dress up, or down? He didn't quite dare ring Venice to ask her. He would have to improvise. After some thought, a tin of Miller Lite, and a couple more guitar solos which sent the audience wild, he decided on a pair of red trousers belonging to some obscure military regiment, the 54th dragoons or some such, which Sebastian was particularly fond of since they were the only item of clothing he had ever bought in a street market, a white evening shirt with stick ups, and his leather jacket. This ensemble, he felt, rather cunningly mixed elements of smartness, street credibility, and wit. Anyway, it would have to do.

Max grunted crossly to himself, and wondered again why he had accepted Oliver's invitation. Curiosity, and ambition, he supposed. Besides, he hadn't been to a good party for quite a fortnight, and he rather missed it. How was he going to impress Dent Ludlow? Should he go for the raw Brando look that Alabama had preferred, or the smooth sophisticate that impressed the glamorous women? Perhaps he should simply capitalize on his dark looks. That would do. He pulled on some black trousers and a black shirt and slicked his hair back with the Brylcream that had so suddenly come back into fashion after twenty years of obsolescence. Everyone would keep saying that black was out, but it suited Max, and he was damned if he was going to be a slave to fashion. He looked cool in black, he looked dangerous and langorous and fierce. He wondered if the leather jacket might be overdoing it. He decided it was rather, so he compromised with a pair of suede boots instead. That way, he could at least step on a few toes, if all else failed.

Sergei dressed as he dressed for everything, with care and thought and just the right amount of concentration. He put on a dark grey suit, and a cream shirt and a blue tie. Everything was beautifully laundered and pressed, and laid out lovingly by his man. As usual, he looked immaculate. He looked like what he was, rich, pampered, tasteful. Of course, being Sergei, he didn't think that. He was too busy wondering quite what the evening had in store, and whether his fiendish plan was going to work. He couldn't help a sneaking desire that it would backfire, and the nasty young actor would run off with a bimbo, or just not turn up. He couldn't help feeling that Alabama was worth rather more. He gave himself the usual cursory glance in the glass, simply to make sure that everything was quite as it should be. It was. He smiled to himself. Whatever else, it was going to be an interesting evening.

* * *

Oliver slid sinuously through his guests, mingling just as his mother taught him, trying rather unsuccessfully to suppress what might be described by the less charitable of his acquaintances as a smirk. This was the kind of evening that seemed destined for the history books. There was Alabama, holding court shamelessly, just like Venice used to in the old days, looking an utter dream in a little raw silk number that would just keep slipping off one shoulder. Sergei, looking too much like old money and twice as noble, stood by her, showing just the right amount of proprietory interest, while the young literary bucks laughed delightedly at her sallies, and fought, in spite of themselves, to light her cigarette. Across the

room, Venice, looking more understated than Oliver
had ever seen her, and almost more beautiful than ever,
was talking to Milo. Oliver had to admit, that although
he rather missed the silks and satins and the jewels and
the furs, he was rather impressed with this new look.
Utter simplicity did have such a satisfying puritanical
aspect to it. Milo, with that pleasing clever look in his
light eyes, was bending his head to hear Venice: they
seemed to be having a frighteningly serious discussion.
That should impress the undergraduate. Milo was becoming rather a big fish these days, if one believed the
literary papers. Quite soon, he would be quotable.

In another corner, Sergei's cronies were discussing
racing and skiing and backgammon with those of the
glamorous women Oliver had allowed to attend. He
had chosen them carefully, asking only the cleverest, the
most witty, ruthlessly excluding the more predatory. He
had taken especial pleasure in not asking Sabine, whom
he knew would be quite mortified with pique. Soon the
two leading men would arrive, and the tableau would
be complete. Oliver had to stop himself rubbing his
hands together with glee. This was so much what he
needed to take his mind off the South American bongo
player, whom he missed more than he cared to admit.
Underneath it all, Oliver always liked to insist, he
was just an old-fashioned romantic. Talking of which,
there was Nicholas, looking soulful in a corner. Oliver
approached. If he didn't know Nicholas better, he would
almost feel sorry for him.

'Well,' he said, 'I do declare I've never seen anything
quite like it. What do we have here? Love?'

'Don't tease, I beg,' said Nicholas, toying hopelessly
with his drink, and wishing Alabama didn't look quite
so bewitching, draped in silk and enslaved admirers. 'It's
not the smallest bit amusing.'

Oliver decided to take matters in hand. He couldn't have one of his guests eating his heart out in a corner all evening, even if it was Nicholas.

'Come along,' he said kindly. He took Nicholas's arm and steered him gently across the room. 'Let me introduce you to someone who might cheer you up.'

He drew Nicholas across to where Carlisle was talking to a girl with short blonde hair and torn jeans.

'Hold on,' said Nicholas, baulking. 'Spare me Carlisle. Do you want to put me over the edge?'

'It's not Carlisle we're interested in. He's only here because I wanted the girl. She's my new discovery. Doesn't she make you think a little of Alabama?'

Nicholas looked again, considering.

'Not a patch on Alabama,' he said, shaking his head mournfully.

'Of course not,' said Oliver soothingly, realizing he had taken the wrong tack. 'But rather fetching in her own way. She'll amuse you.'

'Oh all right,' said Nicholas, with a deplorable lack of grace. 'If you insist. But I don't expect it will help.'

'Hello Carlisle,' said Oliver, in the special resigned voice he kept for Carlisle. He kissed the girl. 'My sweet,' he said fondly, 'I AM pleased you came. Nicholas, I want you to meet Arabella Vanbrugh.' The girl raised bright eyes to Nicholas's heavy ones.

'Hello,' she said, putting out her hand. 'Do call me Van. Isn't Arabella the most ghastly name? Debs and dances and guards officers, I could kill my parents.'

'Nicholas is a gossip columnist,' said Oliver. 'I brought him over here so that you could disapprove of him.'

'Should I?' said Van.

'But you must,' said Oliver. 'He likes nothing better. And be careful what you say, or it'll all be in tomorrow's paper. Now come along Carlisle, you can't monopolize

Van all evening, I want you to meet someone.'

Van and Nicholas looked at each other in the way that people do when they have just been introduced and left with the expectation that they will instantly burst into torrents of scintillating conversation. Van lit a cigarette and smiled faintly through the smoke.

'So,' she said, looking up at Nicholas with one eyebrow raised a little, as if she wouldn't presume to take him or the party or anything else too seriously.

'So,' said Nicholas, looking longingly at Alabama, 'what are you doing with a man like Carlisle? Has he told you how he discovered Charlotte Lewis yet?'

'Well yes,' said Van, who had been asked that question before. 'Several times. He's rather sweet in his own way.'

'Hm,' said Nicholas in patent disbelief. 'You're more charitable than I am.'

'But that's your job. Anyway, it's too easy to be rude about him. He's been very kind to me.'

'Are you having an affair?'

Van laughed. 'Actually,' she said in amusement, 'I'm the nubile graduate who is trying to reform him, if your column is to be believed. What is it I must say now? We're just good friends, or should it be a dignified no comment? I never know.'

Nicholas dragged his eyes away from Alabama, having the grace to look a little abashed.

'Oh dear,' he said.

Van laughed again. 'No really,' she said, 'I was positively flattered. Nubile, I mean to say . . .'

Nicholas looked at her. Perhaps there was some method in Oliver's madness. Van was no beauty, not in Alabama's league, but she did have rather good eyes, a sort of thick opaque blue with heavy eyelashes. She was looking at him with them now, a wry look of amusement on her face.

'Forgive me,' he said. 'I'm a little *distrait*.'

'So I see,' said Van dryly. 'Is it love, or are you going to put Alabama Skye in your column tomorrow?'

'I did that today.'

'Then it must be love.' Van tried to straighten her face. Nicholas looked so much like a faithful spaniel who can't take his eyes off his master for a moment lest he disappear. 'I didn't think gossip columnists ever fell in love. Won't you be prosecuted under the Trades Descriptions Act?'

'Quite possibly,' said Nicholas, looking more moony than ever.

'Oh dear,' said Van, still looking amused, but sympathetic. 'And think what a terrible end to such a brilliant career. Why don't you have another drink and tell me about it?'

Oliver, pleased to see that Nicholas was being so well looked after, looked at his watch. Sebastian should be arriving any moment. Max hadn't been asked until a little later. Oliver had wanted him to make his arrival with the stage set, Alabama and the admirers in place, and the party in full swing. Right on time, Sebastian walked in. Clever clever Venice, Oliver thought, as he went to greet the new arrival. He really was a dish, so young and tall and thin, and those eccentric clothes were so endearing. Perfectly delectable. Oliver was glad to see that there were some undergraduates left without spots and parkas. It gave him faith in the world.

'Sebastian!' he cried. 'Come in, do. Now what will you have to drink? Champagne? Let me see, who do you know?'

Sebastian looked about, impressed. Everyone seemed to be sparkling with clever conversation and *joie de vivre*. He wasn't to know about Oliver's parties.

157

'No one really,' he said. 'Never forget I'm only just out of the dreaming spires. A mere provincial in your terms.'

'Don't run yourself down, my dear,' said Oliver. 'Let me see. Well, here's Venice. You know her of course. And this is Milo Oranmore, our very own young novelist.'

'How do you do,' said Sebastian. 'I've read your book. I thought it was brilliant.'

'Thank you,' said Milo gravely. Out of the corner of his eye, he noticed that Venice was portraying a commendable lack of interest.

'Now,' said Oliver, 'don't let these two bore you to death. They've been through everything from James Joyce to Proust already this evening, or I don't know what.'

Oliver was extemporizing here. If only he knew that the serious discussion he had observed earlier had consisted entirely of Venice telling Milo how utterly wonderful Sebastian was, how he looked like a Greek God, how clever and brilliant he was, and how he had those green eyes that she liked most on a man. Milo, who was no slouch in the intellectual stakes himself, who had eyes that had driven at least one woman to drink, had listened to all this with touching attention. He disapproved of Venice, he always had, but he found himself rather taken with this new human Venice, this Venice who could no longer get whatever she wanted with a toss of her perfectly coiffed head, this Venice who was going to such unimaginable lengths to get her man. Strange things were going on with these sisters, and Milo couldn't help but be intrigued. Seeing Sebastian, he quite understood why Venice was so enchanted. All young and golden and arrogant, he was the obvious antidote to the jaded rich that Venice always used to devote her time to. He thought that it was definitely a change for the better. But still, Proust and Joyce, that was more than a man could stand.

'Oh for the old days,' he said, 'when all we were allowed to discuss was who was misbehaving with whom, and who had lost all their money at the gambling tables, and who had stolen whose mistress.'

Sebastian, who was rather a fan of the old days, was dying to know who was misbehaving with whom, but he didn't quite dare ask. Venice seemed to keep such exalted company. Playwrights and princes and spectacularly bright young novelists, no wonder she spent her life discussing Joyce. Personally, he wasn't a great fan. He always rather agreed with Evelyn Waugh, who had insisted that Joyce wrote gibberish, and said that you could hear him going mad, sentence by sentence. Part of the reason that Sebastian had been sent down was a long-running dispute he had had with his tutor, who always said that the world was divided into two camps: those who had read Ulysses, and those who hadn't. Sebastian hadn't.

'Hello Sebastian,' said Venice. She suddenly couldn't think of anything else to say. For the first time since 1974, she was lost for words.

Tripping across the room, admiring his guests, so witty and pretty, Oliver ran into Alabama, the wittiest and prettiest of all.

'Darling,' he said, bursting with pride, like an indulgent uncle, whose wayward niece has at last come good, 'I could die that's all. It's the last word. You're outdoing yourself.'

'I'm thinking of auditioning for the National after this,' said Alabama. 'Third spear carrier for a year would be more restful. Tell me you've got some whisky. I'm desperate.'

'All right darling,' said Oliver. 'You do deserve it. It's in the kitchen.'

'Thanks,' said Alabama with gratitude. 'When is Max going to arrive?'

Oliver checked his watch, which happened to be Piaget, a gift from the bongo player, whose album had been selling rather well of late.

'Ten minutes and counting,' he said.

But Max arrived early. As he walked into the crowd, unobserved by Oliver, he could hear the literary bucks crying mournfully 'Where IS Alabama? Where HAS she gone?' He saw Sergei, all bogus and Russian and perfectly dressed, consorting with his cronies, discussing the prospects for Goodwood. Over in one corner, he could see Nicholas talking earnestly to a girl he didn't recognize, a girl who looked just a little like Alabama used to, rather unkempt, with her jeans ripped. Further on, there was Venice, looking strangely subdued, with her face unpainted, talking to a ravishing and very young boy. Whatever happened to the sugar daddy, Max wondered. Roger was talking to the glamorous women. Max shied away from them, rather relieved that Sabine at least didn't seem to be there, and went to look for the whisky. He was going to need it to face this lot. He was certainly going to need it if he was going to face Dent Ludlow. And he was definitely going to need it if he was going to face Alabama. He had rather forgotten that she would be bound to be there. These days, he supposed that none of Oliver's parties would be complete without the newly glamorous Alabama.

Oliver left Alabama in the kitchen. He couldn't bear to leave his guests for long.

'Five minutes darling,' he said firmly, mindful of Max's impending arrival. 'It's all I can allow you, and that's generous.'

160

'It's your party and I'll drink whisky if I want to,' said Alabama. 'I'll be there.'

Max knew where the whisky was kept. He had a memory for such things. He headed purposefully for the kitchen.

'Oh,' he said, pausing on the threshold, unprepared for Alabama. Unprepared for her looking like this. He still thought of her, when he thought of her, in her jeans and her tough leather jacket, and her mussed hair, and her keen pale face. Why couldn't she wear something that didn't show her shoulder? Why couldn't she behave like a normal person and drink Dom Perignon like everyone else? Why couldn't she leave him to his shot of whisky in peace?

'Well hello,' said Alabama, attempting *sang froid*, as unprepared as he was. Why couldn't he arrive when he was supposed to, at the time he had been invited, and find her surrounded by the most handsome and brilliant men in London? Why was he twice as handsome as any of them, and infinitely more alluring?

'I was looking for the whisky.' Max stood his ground, rocking a little in his suede boots, attempting defiance.

'So I see.' Alabama was collecting herself fast. 'I got there first. Here.' She offered him the bottle. Jim Beam at his finest, a welcome sight for any man.

'Thanks.' Max took the bottle, turned to find a glass, glad of something to do, relieved to be able to avert his eyes and gather his wits. 'Half the men here are busy mourning your absence. You shouldn't neglect your public like this.'

At least he had taken in the admirers. Perhaps the evening was not ruined. Alabama drew herself up, and drew carefully on her cigarette.

'They can wait,' she said in her most careless voice, treacle poured over gravel, the one that Venice had

161

taught her, the one that could trace its roots back to Dietrich through Bacall. 'They always do.'

'Well,' said Max, knowing that this conversation was going nowhere. She was still getting the better of him. From the drawing room, the sounds of the party reached them, as if from a great distance. Oliver had put Mozart's requiem on the record player, just because he felt like it. The literary bucks could just be heard over the *dies irae*, their voices rising in harmony, getting rather heated over which of Alabama's plays were her best.

'Well,' echoed Alabama. 'So, tell me. How is the play?'

Max had the feeling that she didn't really want to know, that she was just making small talk, that she was remembering her manners, that she was humouring him, poor booby. He had the distinct impression that she would much rather be out there, discussing her plays with her admirers. This was good, since it was exactly the impression that Alabama wanted him to have.

'It's fine,' he said inadequately. 'It's fine.' All of a sudden, he wanted to tell her how worried he was about it, how he felt that he was losing the character, how he was terrified of not doing the work justice, how it was his big break and he was petrified of blowing it. She of all people must understand.

'That's good,' said Alabama, as if she didn't mean it, as if she couldn't really care less, as if she had asked him what the weather was like, and been told it was sunny. 'I'm looking forward to the first night.'

'Are you?' said Max. 'I thought the first night was always the worst if you wrote it.'

'Sometimes,' said Alabama, remembering that she had told him that, late one night, in the days when they had shared a bed. 'It depends how much confidence you have in the cast.'

'Oh.' Max wondered if this was a dig. 'And do you?'

'Shouldn't I?'

'Well yes.' Max was suddenly hearty. 'Everyone is terrific.' Everyone except me.

'Well, that's all right then, isn't it? I have nothing to worry about.'

'Yes. I suppose it's all right.'

'You don't sound altogether sure.' Alabama didn't quite stifle a yawn, but managed to give the impression that she was about to.

'I don't know,' said Max. 'I don't know if I am sure. I hope I can do you justice.'

Alabama looked at him consideringly.

'The only person,' she said slowly, 'to whom you must do justice, is yourself.'

She drained her whisky, put her glass down, gave him a vague fleeting smile, and was gone, leaving a faint smell of scent and roses behind her. Max was left alone, with the bottle of Jim Beam, and a terrible sense of his own inadequacy.

Back in the drawing room, the party roared on into the night. Venice had relented, deciding that she couldn't possibly go through a whole evening pretending to talk about *Remembrance of Things Past*, and was regaling Sebastian with scurrilous stories about her early days in London, aided and abetted by Milo, who had rather taken to Sebastian, and was very glad they didn't have to talk about Proust, for all their sakes. Nicholas, having told Van all about his undying passion for Alabama, how it had come upon him in such an unsuspected fashion, how he wasn't at all sure what to do with it, had perked up somewhat and was telling a long and astonishingly indiscreet story about a diplomat who had five mistresses in five different continents.

Carlisle had found a soulmate in the rock musician whom Oliver asked to all his parties for the token low-life element, and was busy telling him how Pete Townsend was his best friend. The fact that Carlisle had met Pete Townsend once in 1979 at a nightclub and offered to sell him some drugs, and the fact that everyone in London knew this, and teased him about it mercilessly, didn't seem to deter him in the least. The glamorous women, their voices rising a decibel each time they had another glass of champagne, were gathered about Roger, whom they loved because he made such clever successful films, and always invited them to the premières so that they could have their photograph taken with Jeremy Irons. They were telling him at length about the latest film festival that they had all attended, naturally, as they attended everything where their photograph might be taken. If they were to be believed, Robert Redford, whose *bijou* little film had had such critical acclaim, was in love with all of them now he had finally left his wife. Roger smiled urbanely, and pretended to believe every word.

Alabama rejoined her swains, and decided that if an oscar was worth winning, it was worth winning properly.

'So tell me boys,' she said, in her best Tallulah Bankhead, 'did you miss me?'

The literary bucks, who had had more champagne than perhaps was good for them, swore that they had almost died without her. Oliver, overhearing, smiled to himself, and thought privately that almost anyone would die without Alabama, these days. He glided past the smitten and wandered up to Sergei.

'Well,' said Oliver, 'what do you think?'

'I think she's doing very well,' said Sergei. 'I think the young actor might find himself a little impressed, don't you?'

'If he isn't,' said Oliver with feeling, 'he should be shot.'

'If you want my opinion,' said Sergei with unwonted frankness, 'he should be shot anyway.'

'At dawn?' said Oliver with interest. One simply never knew with these Russians, that was the heaven of them.

'At once,' said Sergei, 'but then, I may be wrong.'

'Oh what tangled webs,' said Oliver, with a little *frisson* of pleasure. This party was certainly coming up with the goods, in spades.

Max came out of the kitchen. He felt a little better after the whisky, but only a little. If it hadn't been for Dent Ludlow, he might just have turned and run, but he told himself that he was made of sterner stuff. He squared his shoulders manfully, and went out into the fray. 'Now,' cried Oliver, spotting him at once with those Argos eyes that missed nothing. 'You've arrived. Come and have a drink. I'm afraid that Dent cancelled at the last minute, something about dinner with various producers at Claridges, do you call that terrible manners? Really, these colonials do have no idea. No history, that's their problem, poor dears, so one mustn't mock. Not everyone has our advantages. Now, who do you know?'

Max, rather taken aback by this wave of chatter, felt his eyes go involuntarily to Alabama.

'Ah,' said Oliver, as casual as you please. 'The young playwright. She's rather busy, I never saw anyone so in demand to tell you the utter truth. I must tell those boys to stop monopolizing her. Bees round a honey pot, if I ever saw it. You'd think they'd all be far too busy winning the Booker Prize, or whatever it is they do. Come and meet Milo Oranmore. He's the latest literary sensation, you must have heard. He brought all these undesirables, I blame him utterly. They're all far too much the flavour of the month at Hamish Hamilton or Deutsch, or I don't know what. Too highbrow by half, I say. You'll like Milo.' Oliver propelled Max forward, without giving him time to argue.

'Milo, my dear,' he said. 'Have you met Max Charlton? He's to star in Alabama's play, so we must all be off to the Royal Court in about five minutes.'

'Hello,' said Milo, turning away from Venice and Sebastian, who he felt were now doing perfectly well without his help. So this was the great love. He was handsome enough, Milo could see that, but the obvious looks were marred by a cross and sulky look. Spoilt, thought Milo dismissively, summing him up instantly, as he did everyone. It stood out a mile. Couldn't Alabama see that? Milo could understand Venice's efforts utterly. Sebastian and she were perfect for each other, anyone could understand. But this furious fifties throwback, this was not worth a snap of Alabama's fingers, let alone this elaborate charade that she had embarked on so uncharacteristically. Milo was disappointed. He would give Alabama all the rope she wanted, but he had no time for people who didn't come up to the mark.

'Hello,' said Max moodily. He really wasn't in the mood to talk to a young literary sensation. The only sensation he was interested in was himself.

'I'm afraid I haven't seen you act,' said Milo blandly, 'but Alabama tells me you're very good.'

'Does she?' Max was unforthcoming, aware that this sounded like a compliment but clearly wasn't.

'Well, she should know after all,' said Milo inexorably. 'She did pick you up out of obscurity, didn't she? You must be very grateful to her.' No harm in rubbing his perfect nose in it.

'I am,' said Max, who had tried to forget. He had gone a long way to convincing himself that his rise had been entirely of his own making. He liked to think of himself as his own invention. He didn't like to feel encumbered. He didn't like to dwell on how much he owed Alabama.

'She really put her neck on the line for you,' mused Milo. 'Extraordinary really. She never does that. She doesn't have to, you see.'

Max quite saw. He wished that he hadn't come to this party. He should have known that it would have been like this. He decided to get very drunk indeed. He wasn't going to leave and let them all see that they had got the better of him. He was a young star on the rise, and he didn't need any of them.

The party wore on, unfolding inevitably into what people were to remember long after as one of the great successes of the year. The company was growing unsteadily more expansive, if that were possible. Kiki was necking in a corridor with the rock musician, who had left Carlisle in full flood with a potted plant. Carlisle hadn't even noticed his absence. Fortunately for Kiki, Roger was discussing business with one of Sergei's cronies. Venice, who had decided that a little diffusion of her charms was called for, was circulating among Milo's literary friends, who were only too enchanted to instruct her in the mysteries of iambic pentameter. They were all so handsome, and so accommodating, that Venice quite forgot to be bored. Alabama was sitting on the Milanese sofa, draped all over it in the most fetching manner, allowing one of Sergei's racing friends to make the most unsubtle passes at her. She was finding it rather restful. She didn't have to say anything, just sit and look bewitching, and he was so drunk that it didn't take much dexterity to deflect him. Van was amusing Nicholas, who was now too drunk to speak, by telling him stories about the 237 women her father had seduced. 'I never really know if I'm my mother's child,' she said. Sebastian had been pounced upon by the glamorous women, who were simply eating him up. 'Tell us more about Oxford,' they said again and again. 'Did your tutor really tell you that Louis XV wasn't safe in taxis?' 'I worship Louis XV,' cried Oliver in passing. 'The furniture, to die, really. Such a relief after the vulgarity of Louis XIV.' He was busy impressing people by offering them the kind of little pink pills that one could only get from a certain Manhattan doctor. Sergei and Milo, rather surprisingly, were closeted in a corner, having found a good bottle of Armagnac, and were talking Platonics, which Oliver said was very bad form. 'Honestly, darlings,' he told them sternly, 'philosophy is all very well, but there are limits. I read in the paper today that the philosopher's congress in Brighton is considering whether man really does exist. I ask you.'

'Well,' said Milo laughing, 'it's better than Fichte. He insisted that the world was his idea.'

'Really,' said Oliver. 'If the world was anyone's idea, it was mine. I feel sure I was terribly creative in my former lives.'

Alabama decided that enough was enough. The racing friend of Sergei's was in imminent danger of going to sleep with his head in her lap, and Max had been sulking in a corner most of the evening. The party was roaring along very nicely without her, and she was tired. She had played her piece to perfection, and it had certainly not gone unnoticed. She expected rave reviews in all the dailies the next morning. She could go home now, like a good girl, who deserves her bed. She went to the kitchen for a last slug of whisky.

'So,' said Max, coming up behind her. 'We seem destined to meet in the kitchen at parties.' His words were only slightly slurred.

'Yes,' said Alabama clearly. 'I was just leaving.'

'Don't go,' said Max abruptly, his voice thick with drink and cigarettes and the lateness of the hour.

'Why not?' Alabama turned to look at him, raising her eyebrows into two perfect arcs of disdain. 'A girl has to get her beauty sleep, after all.'

'I want to talk to you.' Max's eyes were lowered, hidden under his eyebrows, unable to meet her gaze. He looked like a surly fourth former, scuffing his feet on the floor, up on the carpet in front of the headmaster, caught smoking behind the bicycle shed.

'Well, my sweet,' said Alabama, in her sunniest voice, the one that was guaranteed to enrage, 'that's all very gratifying, but I really am rather exhausted, so if you'll excuse me . . .'

'I need to talk to you, dammit.' Max sounded almost desperate, pleading. Alabama paused, looking at him again, not used to hearing that note in his voice.

'What about?' She was still cool, untouchable, miles above him, condescending to his level only for a moment.

'That play,' Max said furiously. 'It's your bloody play, you wrote the bloody thing, you must know how it should be done.'

'I thought that was what Johnny was there for.' Alabama almost looked at her watch, but she thought that it might put him over the edge altogether.

'Please.' Max looked at her at last, his eyes black and desperate.

Alabama contemplated for a moment the pleasing irony of him having to come to her for help. She almost left him to it, but something made her give in. She felt angry, but she wasn't going to let him see. She maintained an imperturbably impregnable calm, just as all the best heroines always could.

'Very well. I'm rather busy at the moment, but if you give me a call, perhaps we could have lunch.'

'Tomorrow,' Max persisted, dogged with drink.

'Max, I'm busy for lunch tomorrow.'

'Cancel it.'

'Certainly not.'

'Why?'

'Because,' Alabama explained patiently, 'my life, luckily for me, does not revolve about you.'

'Who does it revolve about now? That bogus Russian? That fake remnant of the feudal system?'

'Look who's talking about bogus. You're drunk Max. Go home and sleep it off, and we'll talk about this some other time.'

'Are you really going to marry him?' Max laid his hand on her arm, gripping it tightly so the fingers dug into the flesh. 'Are you?'

So Nicholas's piece had not gone unnoticed, bless him.

'What if I am?' Alabama looked down at the hand on her arm, as if she could not imagine how it had got there, or what it was doing. Following her gaze, Max dropped it abruptly.

'He's a fraud, that's all. Old enough to be your father.'

'Not unless he was a very early starter. I think you overestimate him. You really should go home. You're starting to talk like a penny novel.'

'So what if I am? Don't marry him, come to lunch with me.'

'No.' Alabama looked at him swaying in front of her, his face flushed with anger and champagne, his eyes bright. He was so ridiculous, so full of fire and brimstone, so unreasonable and arrogant and selfish.

170

He was absurd. Alabama had never been very clever when it came to men.

'Tea then,' he said.

Alabama decided it was time for a tactical retreat. He was obviously not going to give up, and she didn't want to be reduced to the indignity of a fight. She rather thought that she had got what she wanted. It would be a shame to spoil her victory now, because of pride. Everybody knows that pride comes before a fall, and Alabama was riding too high for a fall now.

'All right,' she said, still in those dulcetly calm tones. 'Come round tomorrow afternoon. We can go over your part, if it's worrying you so much. Now I am going. Goodnight.' And she swept out, leaving Max looking after her, still with that baffled angry look on his face.

The day after the party saw everyone reaching for their telephones. Oliver rang Alabama as soon as he woke, which was lunchtime.

'Well,' he said breathlessly, positively bursting with interest, 'tell everything. If you leave anything out, I'll never speak to you again. I die to know.'

Alabama told.

'Well,' said Oliver, when she had finished. 'I do think we're getting there, don't you? I must hand it to you darling, you were an absolute dream, I mean really a dream, poetry in motion. I can tell that my telephone is going to be burning up for days with people asking for your number, that's why I had to ring you at once before I became engaged. All those literary types of Milo's (weren't they too pretty for words, the ducks?) were so desolate when you left that I hardly knew what to do to console them. I had to throw them out in the end, because they were starting to fight over whether your eyes were more beautiful than your nose. Isn't it deliciously old-fashioned? You and Venice make me think of the Gunning sisters, it's too eighteenth century for words.'

'I'm glad I did so well,' said Alabama dryly. It did always astonish her that Oliver could produce such torrents of conversation before he had even finished his first cup of coffee. It always took her at least an hour before she could speak in the morning, but Oliver seemed to wake in the middle of a conversation, and pick it up without thought.

'Don't knock it darling,' he said. 'I know it's not your *raison d'être*, so to speak, but it's not so bad to be going on with, is it? And you can always write your plays on the side. That's the joy of being an artist, I always think. Flexible hours.'

'I suppose it's not so bad,' said Alabama, laughing.

'Anyway,' Oliver continued, hardly pausing to take a sip of his coffee. It was a rather good new Brazilian blend that his bongo player had recommended, and one could only get it at Fortnum's, which Oliver thoroughly approved of. He hated having to do his shopping at an ordinary supermarket. The thought of Sainsbury's made him feel quite faint. 'I think you have your young actor by the nose now, by the sounds of things, so we've achieved our object. Sergei will be pleased.' Privately, Oliver didn't think that Sergei would be pleased at all. Whatever game Sergei was playing, it was a deep one, and Oliver had to admit that he didn't quite follow all the rules. That was the thing about these Russians, they were so inscrutable. 'And Sebastian was looking just a trifle forlorn when Venice made her exit, so it's two birds with one stone.'

Oliver then proceeded to regale Alabama with all the dramas she had missed. He knew that she would be dying to know. Apparently, after she had left, there had been such goings-on as had not been seen in one evening since the great parties of the sixties. Roger had caught Kiki with her hand well advanced into the trousers of the rock musician, who didn't seem to be protesting in any way, and had thrown him over the balcony. Fortunately, his fall had been broken by a strategically placed collection of dustbin bags, which, as Oliver pointed out, was very lucky for Roger, since the musician's guitar hand was insured for quarter of a million, and if anything had happened to it, he would have sued. Nicholas had been taken home by Van, who had taken a distinct shine to him. He had had no say in the matter, being comatose at the time. The literary bucks had obligingly carried him to the car for Van, whom they loved because she bought all their books, and understood them.

'Imagine what a shock he's going to get when he wakes up,' said Oliver in glee. 'I'm utterly certain that Van will try and reform him. I never met such a girl for lost causes. Imagine thinking that Carlisle wasn't past saving. She's given up on him, but only after three months of trying.'

One of the glamorous ladies was looking for a divorce lawyer ('Can you think of one? I can't remember who it is that one goes to these days, since old Lionel retired.') since her husband, in a rash gesture of marital goodwill, had come to collect her from the party, only to find her clasped in the arms of Sergei's drunken racing friend. Her protestations that she had been experimenting with a new cure for lumbago that she had read about that day were in vain.

'Don't you die?' said Oliver excitedly. 'Marriages breaking up under my own roof, what more could one ask?'

Meanwhile, as Oliver happily related, his bright voice piping eagerly down the line, as joyous as birds in springtime, Milo and Sergei were quite calmly finishing off a bottle of ten-year-old Armagnac, oblivious to all the excitement, and discussing Wittgenstein. Sebastian, equally calmly, missing Venice, but determined not to leave the party until the last drop had been weaned out of it, had settled himself in a corner with a bottle of champagne and a copy of *The Last Tycoon*. 'You never saw anything like it,' said Oliver wistfully. 'He looked so beautiful sitting there, all young and golden, and well-behaved as you please, like a little boy waiting for his mother to come and collect him from a tea party. At about five, he suddenly looked up, and realized that it was quite light and that everyone had gone home, so he smiled at me, shook my hand, and said he'd never enjoyed a party more, and wasn't it a shame everyone left so early, and could he take the book with him, because he had almost finished it and he had forgotten how beautiful it was. Could you believe it? So off he went, as happy as Larry, walking off down the street into the dawn, reading it as he went.'

Alabama laughed.

'Oliver,' she said, 'everyone knows you give the best parties.'

'Yes,' said Oliver with a sigh of pleasure at such an acute observation. 'Don't I just?'

Nicholas woke up painfully, opening first one eye, then the other, and finally, with an immense effort, both at once. He wondered if it wasn't a mistake. He wished the sun wasn't shining quite so brightly at him. That was odd. The sun didn't reach his bedroom until late afternoon. Surely he couldn't have slept that late? Steeling himself, he opened his eyes a fraction wider, only to find that someone had painted his walls dark green while he was asleep. It was rather an esoteric shade of green, but he hadn't really planned on redecorating. The curtains also seemed to have been changed to scarlet. Could it be a present from his mother? What was going on? Slowly, as consciousness crept back, he became aware that this was not his bedroom at all. He also became aware that it was not his bed. It was much more comfortable for one thing, and it was occupied. He turned his head a fraction, carefully so as not to jolt it, half dreading what he would find. He really ought to stop all this fast living.

'Hello,' said Van companionably. She was sitting up in bed reading a copy of *The Crack Up*, which Nicholas felt was a little too appropriate in his present condition. She looked rumpled and fresh faced and vaguely familiar. 'You do look peaky,' she continued in the same alarmingly friendly fashion. 'Would you like some Alka Seltzer? Or do you prefer a Fernet Branca?'

'Alka Seltzer,' said Nicholas faintly. 'Please.'

Van went to fetch them.

'Here,' she said, only laughing a little. She handed him a fizzing glass. 'I've given you six, do you think that's enough?'

'Plenty,' said Nicholas gratefully.

'Breakfast?' What a pragmatic girl she was. He wondered who she was, but this didn't seem like the right time to ask questions. It was a matter of priorities.

'Coffee, please.' Nicholas drained the glass, made a face, and sank back into the pillows, exhausted by the effort.

'Black, I suppose?'

How did she know that? Nicholas nodded his head weakly, and lay back to conserve his energies. He had been in worse situations before, and after all, the bed was very comfortable.

Venice rang up Alabama.

'Well?' she demanded.

'He's coming to tea,' said Alabama, as if it were the

175

most natural thing in the world, and she couldn't think why Venice would have to ask.

'Fancy that,' said Venice. 'You and I do seem to be going in for a lot of teas these days. Do you think we're trying to recapture our lost childhood? I'm sure there's something madly Freudian about cucumber sandwiches.'

'I'm sure you're right,' said Alabama. 'What about you, anyway?'

'Well, I'm feeling quite hopeful. Didn't you think I looked rather fine, all in black? We had a very comfortable chat, Milo came to my rescue to tell you the truth, saved me from Proust, are you sure you shouldn't just marry him? And then I did a bit of circulating, just to show I could, and flirted with a few of those pretty literary boys, and scintillated a few people, and then I left.'

'Oliver tells me he sat in a corner, after you'd gone, reading *The Last Tycoon*.'

'How enchanting,' said Venice, much taken with this idea. 'Do you think I'm in love?'

'Stranger things have happened.'

'But not before breakfast.'

'It's lunchtime.'

'Well, that's all right then,' said Venice, reassured. 'It is rather a novelty. Don't you think he is rather to die for?'

'Yes,' said Alabama truthfully. 'And a great improvement on his father.'

'Don't speak,' said Venice. 'I'd better go now. I'm having lunch with one of Milo's friends. He's going to tell me all about Pinter.'

'Rather you than me,' said Alabama.

'I shall expect a full report on this afternoon,' said Venice, and disconnected.

Sergei rang Alabama to ask her to lunch.

'He's coming to tea,' she said.

'Congratulations,' said Sergei. 'I'll pick you up in half an hour.'

'I think you need some lunch,' Van told Nicholas firmly, diagnosing his condition with a practised eye. It was nothing that a drink and a gallon of aspirin couldn't cure. 'Where would you like to go?'

'Where they have the best Bloody Marys,' said Nicholas, fainter than ever.

'All right then. We'll go there.'

Since there are very few places in London where they really know how to make a Bloody Mary (plenty of lemon juice and a dash of dry sherry) and since everyone who was at Oliver's party was in dire need of one, it was inevitable that Nicholas and Van should arrive only to find Alabama and Sergei already ensconced, with Venice and Oliver pleading with the waiter for more chairs.

'You can't make us sit at separate tables,' said Oliver piteously. 'We'd die, that's all.'

'Put me at one end,' said Venice firmly. 'Xan and I simply must have some time to ourselves to talk about Pinter.'

The waiter looked faintly bemused. Lunchtimes were usually so quiet. Venice gave him a reassuring smile, which helped restore quite a deal of his equilibrium. Of course chairs would not be a problem. Nothing could be easier. For such a vision, he would get dancing girls and trained elephants if necessary. After all, they said you could get anything at Harrods, these days.

'Hello Nicholas,' said Oliver with glee. 'I won't ask how you feel because I gave up sadism for Lent, lucky for you. I'm glad to see Van has you in hand.'

Nicholas gave a sigh of relief. Van, so that was her

name. Parts of last night started to filter back to him. He vaguely remembered telling her rather a lot of indiscreet stories, and explaining at length about the perfection of Alabama. Oh dear.

At last the table was arranged for nine. 'I know we look as if we're only seven,' Oliver told the waiter confidentially, 'but there are bound to be two more.'

He was right. Milo and Sebastian breezed in at that moment, looking far too well for everyone's liking, except of course, Venice's. She loved to see Sebastian looking like a young Greek God, even if he did have the mother and father of a hangover. She loved the way his hair was still wet at the back from the shower, and how his green trousers matched his eyes.

'I won't say it's a small world,' said Milo, who was looking *louche* in black Levis and a T-shirt with lust written on the back in capital letters, 'because it is, and it's getting ridiculous that one can't go out to lunch without meeting exactly the same people one saw the night before.'

'Don't complain Milo,' said Venice, allowing Sebastian a small but potent smile. 'You know you love us to death.'

'All I wanted to do was have a quiet Bloody and discuss the state of the art, and what do I find?' persisted Milo.

'All I wanted to do was talk to Xan about Pinter, but do you see me complaining,' demanded Venice, pretending not to notice Alabama laughing into her napkin. Xan, who was so hungover he could hardly speak, looked vastly relieved that help had come to him in his hour of need. At times like this he could hardly remember who Pinter was.

'Sit down Milo,' said Sergei smoothly. 'Let's all have a drink.'

As usual, when Sergei spoke, everyone did exactly as he asked. The Bloody Marys arrived in an instant, with just the right amount of tabasco, and Milo sat down and grinned sheepishly.

'Can I lay my head on your breast and go to sleep?' he said to Alabama.

'Certainly not,' said Alabama. 'I'm a well-brought up kind of girl.'

It was Venice's turn to laugh into her napkin.

'I do call it unfair,' said Milo, 'that I've been asking you to marry me for seven years and you always say no, and now I read that you and Sergei are tripping up the aisle.'

'But,' said Alabama reasonably, 'you know you never believe anything you read in the papers.'

'So I don't,' said Milo, reassured.

Venice was pretending to look at her menu, while looking at Sebastian through her eyelashes. He was laughing at something Van had said. She must gather her resources and say something clever and memorable. Her mind went immediately blank. Perhaps she could just remain silent and convince him that she was a woman of mystery. If she looked enigmatic enough it might work, at least until after the first course. Sergei, who was observing the assembled company with an amused and indulgent eye, decided to help her cause.

'Well, Venice,' he said, turning to her. 'I missed you last night.'

'Oh Sergei,' said Venice gratefully, thinking that if he wasn't a prince already he deserved a knighthood at the very least, 'I did say hello.'

'It's no consolation. You were far too busy discussing plays and playwrights with the literati to bother with me. I felt distinctly neglected.'

Sebastian was looking visibly impressed. Venice was not only one of the brightest girls he had met, but she also seemed capable of enslaving one of Europe's most famous seducers. Even Sebastian had heard of Sergei, who after fifteen years of being the most famous playboy in the western world, was just as much of a household name as Terry Wogan.

'Poor Sergei,' said Alabama, laughing. 'There you were, eating your heart out, while Xan was composing odes to Venice in heroic couplets.'

'Well,' said Sergei, 'it would appear that you were getting your fair share of odes as well.'

'Never let it be said that I let an ode go by,' said Alabama.

'Oh really,' said Oliver. 'Do let's order something to eat. All this talk of odes is making me hungry.'

They ordered some lunch, although everyone was rather more interested in their drinks than in food. However, being well-mannered they ate for form's sake, and so as not to offend the chef.

After the third Bloody Mary, Nicholas started to perk up. Out of the corner of his eye, he examined Van. He was glad to see that he hadn't made a bad choice. She certainly wasn't Alabama, but he had woken up to worse.

'Well,' she said, in that amused voice, 'marks out of ten?'

Even Nicholas had the grace to blush.

'I do beg your pardon,' he said humbly. 'The coffee was marvellous.'

'And the bed was very comfortable,' she reminded him.

'Yes, that too.'

She laughed, a deep salty laugh, taking pity on him.

'It's all right,' she said. 'You have every right to ask questions. You were comatose when I took you home.'

'Oh dear. How rude of me.'

'It's quite all right. You were rather fetching before you passed out.'

'Do you often take unconscious men home with you?' asked Nicholas with interest. What an extraordinary girl she was.

'Not often. I thought it might make a change.'

'But how did you get me home?'

'I have hidden strengths.'

'Obviously.' Nicholas looked at her slim arms, thinking that they didn't really look capable of tossing him over her shoulder, but then one never knew with women.

Oliver, who had been listening to this conversation with some interest, decided that Nicholas was now strong enough to take a little teasing. Who would have thought that Van would have taken it into her head to take him home like that? It really was too fascinating for words, and most unexpected.

'Well, darling,' he said, 'aren't you grateful to Van for taking pity on you? I don't know how you would have got home otherwise, no taxi driver would have been brave enough. You had to be carried away by six grown men.'

'I didn't really?' said Nicholas in horror.

'I'm afraid so. It was quite a picture. But don't fret, I shan't tell a soul.'

'Oliver,' said Van sternly, 'don't be bitchy. It doesn't become you.'

'Oh angel,' said Oliver, thinking that he really couldn't be more pleased with this new find, 'you are a regular Daniel in the lion's den. I apologize.'

'Quite right too,' said Van. 'What's the point of having a spare bedroom if you can't use it?'

She was damned if she was going to let Oliver

181

know that Nicholas had spent the night in her bed. It was humiliating enough suffering from an undying passion. Van had had a few undying passions of her own, and she knew. Besides, she rather liked Nicholas. She was sure that his soul was quite lost and in need of salvation.

Further down the table, Venice was trying to talk to Xan about an article she had read in the *TLS* about the letters of George Bernard Shaw. Xan shook his head in a pitiful attempt to clear it, and agreed with everything she said. He was utterly sure she was right. No girl could look like that and not be right. He wished they would bring him another drink. He sighed, and tried to focus his eyes and concentrate.

On the next table, a couple in matching his and hers striped shirts and Gucci shoes were talking house prices in Kensington.

'Really,' said one of them, 'ten years ago you could buy two bedrooms for £10,000, and now you won't get any change out of £150,000, and that would probably need doing up.'

'Peasants,' said Milo loudly, to no one in particular.

'Personally,' said Venice, trying not to laugh, 'I blame Mrs Thatcher.'

'Well darling,' said Oliver seriously, 'I could forgive her everything, really I could, if only it wasn't for that hair. God save me from the bouffant.'

Venice gave in and laughed. After all, a girl could only be serious for so long. 'Long live the blue rinse,' she said.

Sebastian looked rather surprised and laughed into his salmon fishcake.

'Bloody good fishcakes,' he said.

'Can we have another bottle?' asked Xan plaintively.

'Sergei,' said Oliver, 'you ask. I think that waiter is in love with you. You're the only person he listens to.'

'Jealousy ill becomes you, Oliver,' said Alabama wickedly.

'Don't mock darling. My heart is in Antwerp.'

'Extraordinary place for it,' said Milo.

'I didn't know salsa was so big in Antwerp,' said Nicholas, who had perked up no end.

'Neither did I,' said Oliver mournfully.

'Oh Oliver,' said Van seriously. 'It's not so long now, and he'll be back.'

Everyone shrieked with laughter.

'What?' said Van crossly. 'It's not so funny.'

'Don't mind them darling,' said Oliver. 'They just don't understand about love.'

'Oh Oliver,' said Alabama, trying desperately to stop herself laughing. 'Don't go changing to please me.'

'I won't my sweet,' said Oliver tartly. 'Don't you worry.'

It was almost four o'clock by the time they had dispersed. All the other tables had been laid for dinner, and the waiter was reading a copy of *Sunday Sport* in one corner with a look of patent resignation on his face, only looking up when Sergei asked for another round of green chartreuse, which was what everyone seemed to want to drink, possibly because it is the strongest drink known to man apart from the kind of Polish vodka they make out of potatoes. It was Alabama who broke them up, since she had to go home and get ready for her tea. She still hadn't quite decided what she was going to wear for maximum effect, and she was going to need to feel at her most impeccable to face Max. Oliver took Xan, who still couldn't speak, off to see the latest art house film which was having a special preview that afternoon at the Gate, and which seemed to be starring every one of Oliver's friends from his German days, when he was studying at Heidelberg. Van invited Nicholas home to watch the afternoon matinée and have some tea. Nicholas, who had never spent a Sunday afternoon in front of the television in his life, and had never considered doing so, decided that it all sounded rather comfortable and just what he needed, and accepted. Besides, he rather liked Van. She wasn't Alabama, but she had a charm all her own. He could see exactly why Oliver had taken her up. Milo and Sergei decided to go off to the Tate to have a look at the late Picassos. They headed off purposefully down the street, arguing about Nietzsche with an intensity that made Oliver want to weep. Venice, thinking it was time to increase the pace, and feeling rather brave after three glasses of green chartreuse, large, with ice, asked Sebastian if he would care to walk in the park. Venice had never walked in the park in her life, but she had always thought it sounded rather romantic. It made her think of Holly Golightly and *Breakfast at Tiffany's* and Audrey Hepburn, and she thought that at this moment it was what she would like more than anything else. Sebastian, who walked in the park often, and had spent most of his time in Oxford in the botanical gardens looking at the orchids, accepted. As they left, Venice turned round, and favoured the assembled company with a vastly unsubtle wink.

'That girl,' said Oliver, 'I love her to death, really I do, but she's going to come to a Bad End.'

The park was perfect. The sun was growing lower in the sky, gilding the grass, emerging triumphant through the trees, shining off the water. Boys were playing haphazard games of football, and children were flying along the walks on shiny new bicycles, and couples were lying together on the grass. People were walking their dogs, and old men were taking their afternoon constitutional, and tourists were taking pictures of each other. Venice loved it.

'I love it here,' she said, taking her shoes off.

Sebastian looked at her, not quite sure what to do next. He would have rather liked to go and lie down in the sun, but he wasn't altogether sure that Venice was the kind of girl who lay down in parks. He didn't quite dare risk it. To tell the truth, he wasn't altogether sure what kind of girl Venice was. She had him confused. He decided to play it safe, so he didn't say anything, and they just walked.

They walked along the Serpentine, and they walked along Rotten Row, and then they went across to Kensington Gardens and walked round the round pond and through the sunken gardens and looked at the backs of the mansions on Millionaires Row, and then they walked back to the Albert Memorial, which Venice said was too vulgar for words. 'I read a book once,' she said inconsequentially, 'about a man called Albert Memorial Gates. Do you call that odd?' And still Sebastian didn't know what kind of girl she was.

'Well,' she said, looking up at him. 'Shall we go home?'

Sebastian was taken by surprise. Whatever he had been expecting, it wasn't this. He wasn't quite sure what to say.

'Mine or yours?' he said foolishly.

'Um,' said Venice, taking a chance. 'Mine?'

'Yours,' said Sebastian blankly. 'Of course.'

'That is,' said Venice, wondering if she had been too forward, 'if you wouldn't rather do something else?'

'No, no,' said Sebastian hastily. 'I wouldn't.'

'Well then,' said Venice, 'that's settled.'

'Yes.'

He took a deep breath, out of his depth. What was she expecting of him? Would she like him to kiss her now? Or did she just want to talk about Pinter? She was so full of everything. She was so self-assured, so at ease with all these glamorous people she surrounded herself with, who in their turn were so assured, so confident in their flippancy, in their wit, in their beauty. And then, she was so beautiful herself. Sebastian had never come across a creature like this before, and he wasn't sure how he should behave. His Oxford education had done nothing to prepare him for anything like this. How could she possibly have any interest in him, so young and callow and knowing nothing? Sebastian had become rather complacent at university, used to admiration, to being regarded as the shining star of his year, but now he suddenly realized what a beginner he was compared to these people. He felt that he was batting out of his league, that he would be out for a golden duck and have to retire to the pavilion in disgrace. He wondered if he should just make an excuse and go home.

Venice, who was rather breathless with her own audacity, decided that she had better get Sebastian into a taxi before he had a chance to change his mind. He hadn't sounded altogether enthusiastic about the idea, as if he were just being polite, so she had better get him home quickly before he had time to think up a plausible excuse. She raised her hand and a cab appeared from nowhere, as cabs had a habit of doing when Venice wanted one.

'Come along then,' she said to Sebastian.

Sebastian sat silently on the journey back to Belgravia, paralysed with indecision. Venice, in between surreptitiously checking her reflection in the glass partition, gave him quick glances out of the corner of her eye, and wondered what she could possibly have said to silence him so. Perhaps she had been too bold. Perhaps he really didn't want to come at all. Perhaps he wanted to go home and finish *The Last Tycoon*. And what would he say when he discovered that she was really a fraud, and not the brilliant intellectual she had been posturing as. He would be bound to find out sooner or later. She suddenly wished that she hadn't started this charade. Perhaps she should just have come clean at the start, and dazzled him with those fatal feminine charms that had always worked so well on everyone else. Except Sebastian wasn't everyone else, and he would have been sure to write her off as a bimbo and run off with a blue-stocking instead.

By the time they got into the house, they were both speechless with fear.

'Well,' said Venice, marvelling at herself. 'Well.' She had never been reduced to silence by a man before. It must be love.

'Well,' said Sebastian, equally at a loss.

Venice looked at the sofa, which suddenly seemed rather too big and awkwardly placed, and wondered how on earth she was going to steer them both onto it. That was going to be difficult. She decided to compromise, and start off in the kitchen. That was nice neutral ground, and might give them a chance to catch their breath and gather their wits.

'Come along,' she said encouragingly. 'I'll make some coffee.'

'Fine,' said Sebastian inadequately.

In the kitchen, Venice busied herself trying to find the coffee-making equipment, clattering about to disguise the lack of conversation. She had always been too much of a snob to have instant, but now she rather regretted it.

She couldn't look at Sebastian. She was going to have to tell him the truth, but how?

'Oh sod it,' she said uncharacteristically. 'I can't find the filter. Let's have a beer.'

'Fine,' said Sebastian again.

Venice got two cans out of the fridge and handed him one, still not quite looking at him. Now or never.

'Sebastian,' she said abruptly, forgetting to be winning in her consternation. 'I have to tell you something.'

'Yes?' Sebastian looked rather amazed. What could be coming? Perhaps she was married with two children and a mortgage.

Venice took a deep breath. 'I have to tell you that I am not all I seem.' She paused again, still not looking at Sebastian, unaware of all the hideous possibilities that were chasing each other round his head. 'I mean,' she continued, all in a rush, 'all that stuff about being interested in literature and reading the serious papers, and talking about Joyce and Proust, well, it's all an act.' She really didn't dare look at him now, but carried on in the cathartic rush of the confessional. 'Until I met you, I didn't read anything except *Vogue* and *Tatler*, and I thought that Joyce was a rather ghastly woman's name, and all I knew about South Africa was that it was where I got my peaches from. So you see, I'm the most shabby kind of a fraud, and if you want to leave now and never speak to me again, I'll quite understand.'

There was a terrible pause. Venice looked at her shoe. Then she looked at the other shoe. They were quite ravishingly pretty shoes, deep purple suede, with pretty old-fashioned curved heels. Venice loved them dearly. Finally she looked at Sebastian. He was smiling hugely.

'What?' she said furiously. How could he be so heartless as to laugh at her at a time like this? 'It's not funny.'

188

'But it is,' said Sebastian, smiling wider than ever. 'It's the funniest thing I've ever heard. You, the beautiful, the ravishing, the divine, the perfect Venice, wanting to impress ME.'

'It's not that funny,' said Venice sulkily. She wasn't sure that this was the response she had been expecting.

'But it is,' insisted Sebastian. 'Don't you see how terrifying it was for me? There you were, all assured and clever and witty, when I was expecting you to be a bimbo. I was absolutely terrified. I'd never met anyone like you before. I couldn't begin to deal with it. I was out of my poor tiny wits. Think.'

'You were frightened?' said Venice, who like most daunting women, thought of herself as an utter pussycat, not in the least bit alarming. 'Of ME? It's not possible.'

'I was paralysed with fear,' said Sebastian truthfully.

'Oh,' said Venice, smiling up at him, right into those dazzling green eyes. 'Oh. Well, fancy that.'

'And then what?' said Alabama sternly down the telephone.

'You guess.'

'He asked you to put on a nice rubber apron and thigh boots?'

'Much better.'

'He kissed you?'

'Of course.'

'Is he there now?'

'In a manner of speaking.'

'And I suppose you think that this is fooling him?'

'Possibly.'

'You do realize that he is bright enough to suspect that we're talking about him.'

'They say it's going to thunder tonight.'

'And don't you think that it's just a tad unsubtle to ring me up the minute you've seduced the poor boy?'

'Not at all. I know how you love storms. I wouldn't want you to miss it. They think just after midnight.'

'Venice,' said Alabama, more sternly than ever. 'You are the end. Are you in love?'

'Think of bright lights.'

'Incandescent?'

'That's it.'

'And what are you going to do about David? No, don't tell me. There's nothing like keeping it in the family.'

'I'm afraid not. They didn't say.'

'You are the utter limit. I'm going now, the doorbell is ringing.'

'Ah Max.'

'As you say. Go back to your ill-gotten gains.'

'Well,' said Sebastian, as Venice put the telephone back into its cradle. 'That was a most illuminating conversation.'

'Wasn't it,' said Venice happily.

'I suppose it was the weather you were discussing?'

'But of course,' said Venice blissfully.

'May I kiss you again now?'

'But of course,' said Venice ecstatically.

Sebastian kissed her.

'Tell me,' he said when he had finished, 'what was the bit about bright lights?'

Max stood on Alabama's doorstep looking moody. He was really getting awfully good at looking moody.

'Well,' said Alabama, throwing open the door, 'what a ray of sunshine, I do declare. Come in, why don't you.'

Max looked moodier than ever. He had been in two minds whether to come at all, and now he rather wished he hadn't. He had forgotten how difficult Alabama was.

All this new charm and old-fashioned carelessness was just as daunting as her previous arrogance. On the whole he rather preferred the old Alabama. He really didn't understand why she had to swan about as if she had just stepped out of an old film, these days. What had happened to the old jeans and the unpainted face? Why couldn't she wear something that covered her shoulder?

'So,' said Alabama, calm as you please, leading the way into the drawing room, 'what would you like to drink? There's beer in the fridge.'

'Fine,' said Max crossly. At least she wasn't going to make him drink one of those bogus foreign teas that no one could pronounce. He wouldn't have been at all surprised if she had gone the whole hog and had Crown Derby cups and cucumber sandwiches and a silver kettle on a spirit lamp like they used to before the war, but it seemed that some habits, at least, died hard. He took the beer she offered him, ignored the glass, ripped open the tab and drank it straight from the can. He stared at her balefully over the rim of the can. She ignored it.

'Well my sweet,' she said, in her best drawl, 'what has brought all this on? I haven't seen you since I can't remember when.'

Max was starting to regret his request in earnest now. He couldn't remember when he last felt at such a disadvantage. He had no familiar landmarks to orientate him. Even the house had changed: filled with roses and pot pourri, not a full ashtray or dead coffee cup or screwed up bit of paper cast aside to be seen. He felt as if he had just walked onto a stage and found that all his props had gone. This was all a terrible mistake. He didn't need her to tell him anything. He didn't need anyone. She could just go back to her ridiculous prince and her enslaved admirers and her flash dinners and her picture in the paper.

'It's the play,' he said unwillingly, almost before he could stop himself. What he had meant to say was that he was leaving and he wouldn't be coming back, but somehow it came out all wrong. 'It's my character. I think I've lost him.'

'Did you leave him in a taxi?' said Alabama. 'Or did you just forget him in Sabine's Bentley?'

Max stood up, really furious now.

'I knew there wasn't any point in coming here,' he said tightly, conveniently forgetting that it was he who had insisted. 'You're such a tough bitch, aren't you? For all your new airs and graces, you're still the same bitch at heart. You think you know it all, don't you? Don't you? Well, you can keep it.'

Alabama regarded him with amused eyes. He did so love making a scene.

'Sit down,' she said calmly. 'Don't leave. I'll apologize if you like. Why don't we just forget the bad blood and concentrate on getting this right? I'm more worried about my play than your affair with Sabine Borromini. Tell me what it is that bothers you in particular.'

Max looked at her for a long moment, as if he might see something behind those hooded eyes. How he longed to throw his beer in her face and stalk out. How he longed to put his hands round that lovely throat and strangle all that mean talk out of her. But he couldn't. For all his new-found success, for all his smart clothes and glamorous women and Bentley rides, he was still at a disadvantage. It was getting a longer fall all the time, and he had too much to lose. He sat down reluctantly, and drank some more of his beer, and lit a cigarette and stared at Alabama balefully through the smoke.

'It's just that . . .' he stopped, helpless. This was his job, and he couldn't do it. 'The first two acts,' he said slowly, starting again, trying to explain, 'are fine. I understand him perfectly. He's a real shit, he's easy.

But then, at the end, he goes wrong, and I lose him. Something isn't there.'

'Why?'

'I think he wants to keep the girl.'

It was Alabama's turn to stare. Max, wanting to get the girl. Next thing he knew, he'd be playing the lead in Oklahoma, the corn as high as an elephant's eye.

'Explain,' she said.

'I'll try.'

And he did explain. For more than half an hour, they argued back and forth. Bad blood all at once forgotten, Max told her of all his fears and frustrations, the ones that he couldn't tell anyone but her, because only she would understand, and only she could do anything to help him, if she chose. He had to make her choose. It was his neck on the line, more than hers, and he could feel the whisper of the guillotine, ready to strike, if he got it wrong. He had to make her see.

Alabama couldn't remember when she had last been so surprised. She listened to him, this petulant sulky boy, arguing with such intensity about his work and hers, and realized that he really minded. And that was odd.

'Well,' she said slowly, when he had finished. 'I'm going to need some time to think about this. Why don't you come round tomorrow night, and we'll talk about it.'

Max looked at her in surprise. He hadn't expected her to take him seriously.

'Talk,' he said. 'All right. But we open in three weeks.'

'That's not a problem,' said Alabama, smiling suddenly. 'I once wrote a whole play in three days, and this is only the third act.'

'Thanks,' he said, standing up to leave, suddenly awkward.

'Don't thank me,' said Alabama brusquely, feeling that she had given away quite enough for one afternoon. 'It's my play that's going to suffer if we don't get this right.'

After Max had gone, Alabama wandered about the house for a while, unable to sit still. She smoked a cigarette. It didn't help much. She could still see his dark furious face, trying its damnedest to convince her that he was right. She could hear the desperation in his voice. She wanted to take him in her arms and comfort him, but all he wanted from her was a script change. She supposed some people would call it irony. Out in the street, the church bells were chiming seven, hurrying the pious to evensong. Alabama knew that she should sit down and write, but she couldn't concentrate. She decided to go out, but with whom? Sergei was out with his racing cronies, and Oliver had flown to Paris for dinner. Alabama thought of ringing Venice, but she would be too wrapped up in her latest acquisition to think coherently. She rang Milo.

'Well,' he said. 'Hello. I thought I saw you at lunch.'
    'You always say that you can never see enough of me.'
    'It's a manner of speech. I'm in the process of being seduced by your high life friends, and I'm resenting it.'
    'They're not really MY high life friends, they're just window dressing, part of a greater plan.'
    'Yes,' said Milo, who had had a very illuminating little chat with Sergei in between the late Picassos. 'I know. Shall we dine? I presume you want to have dinner, or did you just ring me because the speaking clock was engaged?'
    'Don't be a bitch, Milo,' said Alabama in reproof. 'Let's go and get some spaghetti.' A girl could have

enough of nouvelle cuisine, after all.

'Oh all right, if you insist. Shall I bring a mac, or are you going to refrain from the story of your life?'

'Eight o'clock,' said Alabama firmly, and put down the receiver.

They met at the Italian restaurant they had been frequenting since they first met, in the days when they couldn't afford anything better. It was dark and stuffy, and the decoration was a bad hangover from the sixties, and the wine list was not everything it might be, but the spaghetti was the last word, and the waiters had been in love with Alabama long before she took up vamping.

'Well,' said Milo, who had been waiting some time, and already had three large whiskys under his belt. 'Is this the best St Laurent has to offer? I know that I'm not terribly up on couture, but shouldn't someone tell him that trousers should hide the knee, that most unlovely joint? Of course, he's getting on now, isn't he? Does this mean he's past it?'

'Don't,' said Alabama, looking down at her jeans with affection.

'I'm having a night off.'

'So I see. Not a hint of clever Bruce, or darling Jasper, whom we all love so dearly. Not even a dash of lipstick, I hardly recognized you. It really is rather galling to think that I'm the only person in London you don't dress up for. What does the dear young actor have that I don't, apart from appalling manners?'

'A girl cannot live by couture alone,' said Alabama, ignoring the last question. Milo really shouldn't drink so much whisky before dinner, if it was going to make him quite so disagreeable. He had never noticed her clothes before. 'Anyway, you've seen them before.'

'It's so long ago I can hardly remember,' said Milo,

staring gloomily into his glass. 'I think of you now as a latter day Lauren Bacall, or is it Ava Gardner. Who are you going to be next week? Betty Grable?'

'It's not that long,' said Alabama, annoyed to find herself on the defensive.

'A week is a long time in sexual politics. How long ago was it you met the ducky young thespian? Not to mention the slightly older, but remarkably well-preserved prince.'

'Oh really Milo,' said Alabama, irritably. 'I thought you'd taken rather a shine to the well-preserved prince.'

'That's what I resent,' said Milo, stabbing the air with a bread stick, like a lecturer who has got through the preamble and finally reached his key point, the utter crux of the matter, the argument on which his thesis would stand or fall. 'It's entirely your fault that I am now seen consorting with a man of whom I radically disapprove.'

'You disapprove of everyone,' said Alabama dismissively, quite unimpressed. 'Besides, you spend your life discussing Wittgenstein with him.'

'Exactly,' said Milo triumphantly, his theory vindicated. From across the room a waiter approached, ready to take their order, but seeing Milo's face, he thought better of it, and retired to the kitchen to have a soothing chat with the chef, who was the restaurant's resident oracle, and doled out endless universal verities in between making the bolognese. 'I should know better,' Milo continued. 'We live in a nation of *Sun* readers, philistines, barbarians who think that soap operas are a modern art form, and when I meet that rarity, a man with more than half a brain, a man who doesn't want to talk about property prices or Peregrine Moncrieff's salary, a man who doesn't know how to work a portable telephone and thinks that fax are something you look up in an encyclopedia, what do I find? He's a playboy.'

'What would you have him be?' asked Alabama, laughing at Milo's disgusted face. 'A don? A nuclear physicist? The editor of the *New Statesman*?'

'He could at least make a pretence. He could do something. Write for the *Spectator*, or something. Dilettante, but worthy. But a playboy? Come back the Aga Khan, all is forgiven.'

'Oh really,' said Alabama in exasperation, 'if you are going to turn into an intellectual snob just because you've had some good reviews, I shall have to cut you.'

'Oh will you?' said Milo, crumbling his bread stick to dust, his point lost, his thesis cast aside. 'How touching. That really is what friends are for. Of course, I suppose you don't really need me any more, now that you know how to let a man light your cigarette, and how to get out of cabs properly, and how to keep half of London at your perfectly shod feet. I am a positive dinosaur. I am obsolete.' He stopped, staring sadly at the pile of crumbs that had been his baton and the empty glass that had been his whisky.

'Well, you're not, that's all,' said Alabama, with something of an edge to her voice. She really did want a drink, but all the waiters seemed to have deserted them. She lit a cigarette instead, and blew a smoke ring. Milo always used to be impressed with her smoke rings. He had always said that she might have been a lousy playwright, but she could blow smoke rings to beat the band. She blew three in succession, one inside another, and watched them float away across the room, breaking up and losing their shape until there was nothing left but a faint blue haze. Milo didn't seem to notice.

'It's all right,' he said. 'You don't have to be charitable. Will I get a pension and a golden handshake, do you think? Perhaps a *bijou* little Cartier watch, nothing too flash of course, with "To Milo, for years of devoted service" engraved on the back in flowing copperplate.'

'Not if you go on like this,' said Alabama, who now needed a drink very badly indeed. 'I thought you were rather amused.'

'Was I?'

Alabama looked at him. He didn't look amused in the slightest. She couldn't remember him looking less amused, not since his first draft was rejected.

'Weren't you?' she said. 'What has brought all this on, all of a sudden?' An illuminating little chat and a little reflection in front of the work of a Spanish painter who probably had his first draft rejected too, if only she had known it, but she didn't.

'What indeed? Why am I talking like a character in a bad novel? You may well ask.'

'I am asking.'

'Ask away, do.' Milo held his arms wide, in the expansive gesture of a man who dares you to ask for the moon because he has it to give. 'Go on, ask me.'

'This is a ridiculous conversation, I never had such a conversation,' said Alabama, baffled and taking refuge in the society talk that Venice had taught her so well. She lifted her chin and looked down her nose, raising one eyebrow, in a way she had taught herself. 'If you are going to insist on having such an absurd conversation, can I at least have a drink?'

'Have a drink, do,' said Milo, more expansive than ever. 'Have several. Ask that waiter, he's longing for you to speak to him.'

The waiter had re-emerged from the kitchen, and was casting Alabama the most melting look he knew. People had told him he looked rather like Julio Inglesias. Alabama asked him for a bottle of house red. He looked a little disappointed that he hadn't been asked to cross deserts and mountains barefoot, but composed himself, manfully resigned to his fate. If the lady wanted a bottle of house red, she should have it. She should have anything she wanted, anything at all.

'So,' said Alabama, drinking her wine. 'What exactly is all this about?'

'Don't you think,' said Milo, looking at her very carefully, 'that there are limits?'

'Don't be obscure, Milo. Speed limits, city limits? What are you trying to say?' Alabama knew precisely what he was trying to say. She had known what he was trying to say since she had walked in. She didn't especially want to hear what he was trying to say, not just now, with things as they were, and she not feeling at her best, so she was busy fudging the issue. Having never been a great girl for fudging, she wasn't entirely sure how well she was doing. She longed for a nice stretch of sand to put her head into. After all, as someone terribly clever had once said, she couldn't quite remember who, who knew what the ostrich sees in the sand?

'I don't know if I shall bother,' said Milo. 'People never hear what they don't want to, have you noticed that?'

'Why don't you try me?' said Alabama, playing for time.

'All right.' Milo gave her another of those penetrating looks. She pretended not to see it. She rather wished that the kitchen might catch fire, or one of the other diners have a mild heart seizure, anything to distract his attention.

'Only because it's you,' he continued inexorably. 'If it were anyone else, I should just throw them in the river and be done with it. As it's you, I shall probably just throw myself in the river.'

'Well,' said Alabama, 'you'd better explain before you throw.'

'Ha,' said Milo obscurely, looking away from her to light his cigarette, which he did maddeningly slowly and with an inordinate amount of care.

'There's a thing. Do you remember those far-off days when I didn't have to explain things to you?'

'This is silly,' said Alabama, feeling herself approaching the petulant and despising herself for it. 'This is quite the silliest thing I've ever heard in my life.'

'Just hark who's talking. Don't you think it's time you stopped this amusing little game of yours?' Milo had at last come to the point, and Alabama wished he hadn't. She wanted to run away, to stop the match, to cry 'Take me out, coach,' to wake up and find herself in her own bed with Max beside her. 'Don't you think,' said Milo, into his stride now, 'that it's just faintly absurd to set Sergei up as some kind of performing dog in your vain attempts to turn that young actor into the charming prince he most certainly isn't? Don't you think that it is fractionally ridiculous for a girl of your intelligence to deck herself out in silks and satins and start calling everyone darling? Can you not see what a fool you are busy making of yourself?'

'No,' said Alabama, who saw perfectly. 'No. I can't. And what right do you have to censure my behaviour, anyway? Who are you to get on your high horse and start talking to me about the ridiculous?'

'Ah,' said Milo, in his blandest and most dangerous voice, 'so we're onto rights now, are we? I had rather hoped we wouldn't have to go through that.'

Alabama looked around for help, for a floating lifebelt, a plank of wood, anything. It was no good. She would have to get angry.

'Had you?' she said angrily. 'Had you really? I'm so sorry to interrupt the sermon for today, but I shall do exactly as I please. I thought that was the one perogative of a woman in love.'

'Love?' Milo snorted in derision. 'Is that what you call it? I shan't begin to tell you what I call it, or you might leave, and you haven't had your spaghetti yet.'

'I've stood you calling me absurd, so I should think I could manage to take the rest,' said Alabama, in her most withering tones. 'Or do you think I might swoon?'

'If you can take it so well, why are you quite so cross? You know I'm right, and everyone resents that, even you. People hate being told the truth, haven't you noticed? Although since you've given up being a writer I don't suppose you notice very much any more.'

'What makes you think I've given up writing?'

'Well, do forgive me, my sweet, but I haven't heard the tap tap tap of tiny typewriters of late. Or do you write in secret these days, in the still watches of the night, so that no one might guess what it is you really do and blow your cover?'

'I'll start again,' said Alabama, huffy now and on shifting ground. 'When I've got Max.'

'Got Max?' said Milo with a shout of disdainful laughter. 'Got Max. What a charming expression. What makes you so sure that you will get him? And providing you do, what makes you think that you can keep him? He strikes me as the sort who will run a four minute mile at the first glimpse of cellulite. What happens when you grow old and your looks go? Do you think he'll still need you when you're sixty-four? He might stay until he's more famous than you are, and then it will be stretch limos and yards of cocaine and bimbo city and where will you be?'

'Oh,' said Alabama in frustration, 'do you have to be so cynical about everything? Don't you believe in anything?'

Milo looked at her very closely. 'I used to believe in you,' he said gravely, 'but I don't think I do any more. I never thought I'd see you sell out.'

'I haven't sold out. Sold out, what does that mean anyway? I'm just adapting. I can't live in an ivory tower forever.'

'What does THAT mean? Oh really,' Milo flapped a weary hand at her, utterly dismissive, 'I'm tired of this conversation. I knew it would end up like this. You just go after your tatty little gigolo, and call it what you like, but don't expect me to send lilies to the wake of your grand passion.'

'I shan't,' said Alabama with dignity. 'I shan't expect anything of you. I think I'm leaving now.'

'Quite right,' said Milo approvingly. 'I'm glad to see some of those films you've been watching have come in useful. Make your grand exit, do, I long to watch. Mind you don't trip over your self-righteousness on your way out.'

Alabama threw a glass of red wine full in his face, pausing only for a moment to watch it run down his cheeks into little pools of claret on his white shirt, and then she left.

Alabama went home and cried. She knew that it was a cliché, but she seemed unable to think of anything more original to do. She cried quite hard, and she ruined her mascara, and then she cried some more. Looking round for distraction, she picked up a pretty piece of Venetian glass that Milo had given her years ago, and smashed it onto the floor. Then she cried even harder, because she had always loved it, and he had bought it for her on their first trip to Venice, in one of the long vacations from Oxford, in the days before everything had got so complicated. After she had quite finished, and she couldn't cry any more, she stood in front of the looking glass for a while, staring at her furious blotched face, and wondering what she could do next. There was no one to call.

She went and washed her face, and took her hair off her face, and put the answering machine on so she wouldn't be disturbed. Then she got her typewriter out, dusted it off, stood a bottle of bourbon beside it for company, and started to write.

CHAPTER

8

Sergei was the first to notice Alabama's absence. After spending two days calling her, only to be rebuffed by a very terse message on the answering machine, he went round to her house, only to find that the doorbell didn't answer either.

Oliver was the next to notice that all was not as it should be. He and Alabama had made a plan to go to the first night of a new production of *Hamlet*. Alabama wanted to see it because it was Shakespeare, who was the only playwright she would admit was better than she was, and besides, she had always loved *Hamlet*. All that repressed sexuality had always appealed to her worst instincts. Oliver had wanted to see it so that he could say he had seen it first, when it was sold out, and after all, he did so love plays about princes, especially tortured ones. After calling five times, with no success, he gave up and took Van instead, who turned out to be harbouring a deep passion for Kenneth Branagh, and insisted in sitting down on the pavement afterwards and writing him a note to say that he was the best thing since sliced bread and Olivier combined. Oliver was quite enchanted by such an ardent gesture, and took her off to the Caprice in high spirits, where he fed her champagne and quails' eggs and advised her not to waste herself on Nicholas. 'I do have the most sneaking soft spot for our columnist friend,' Oliver said, at his most conspiratorial, 'but I can't think he's quite the thing for an idealist like you, my angel.' Van listened to all this infinite sagacity with patent disbelief, and drank her champagne with a devil may care kind of smile, and told Oliver not to worry so. 'Well,' he said, 'no one can say I haven't warned you.'

Nicholas also started to think that something must be wrong after a week went by and Alabama still hadn't returned any of his seven calls asking her to go drinking with him. Alabama might not return his undying passion, but she always returned his calls. He had to admit that the attentions of Van, who had appeared in his life so unexpectedly and decided to stay, were going quite a long way to mitigating the pangs of despised love, but even so, it made him twitchy if he didn't see Alabama at least once a week. He wondered where she could be. His mind shied away from the possibility that she had had a reconciliation with the dreadful young actor and run off with him to some steamy little love-nest. (Nicholas, despite his affected disdain for the seamier of the tabloids, still couldn't help putting things in tabloid terms. If Alabama had run off, it could only be to a love-nest.) He sighed heavily and poured himself a large brandy. He would simply have to console himself by deciding which of the six parties he was invited to that evening would be graced with his presence.

Milo tried to ring Alabama to apologize for his behaviour. He wasn't quite sure what had come over him, and he wasn't altogether convinced that he wanted to know. He had never been jealous of Alabama before.

He must be getting old. On being rebuffed by the answering machine like so many before him, he gave up and assumed Alabama must be sulking.

Venice, needless to say, didn't notice anything. She was far too busy looking into Sebastian's enchanting green eyes to notice anything else. They were eyes that deserved a great deal of attention, after all. Venice had always understood how important it was for a girl to get her priorities right.

Max, on finding that Alabama wasn't answering her telephone, swore bitterly to himself, and wondered how he could have been so foolish as to think that anything had changed. Of course she didn't mean it about the play, she was just laughing at him. She was probably far too busy pandering to the whims of her absurd Russian. Max knew how demanding those old feudal types always were, damn their eyes.

As for Alabama, she was just writing, oblivious to all the speculation she was causing. She would re-emerge when she was good and ready, and it wasn't just yet.

After a week, Oliver called a meeting. Or rather, he gave a lunch party, which amounted to much the same thing. This was not merely a frivolous gathering, after all. Still, being Oliver, he got the caterers in, and ordered a crate of Crystal from his friendly wine merchant. However serious things might be, there was no excuse for giving people second-rate food. His one concession to the seriousness of the occasion was to arrange his own flowers. Besides, he sometimes thought that great bunches of orchids simply dumped in vases made a nice change from the elaborate arrangements he usually favoured. It was like a breath of fresh air. He considered wearing black as a mark of gravity, but thought that that might be jumping the gun just a little. They hadn't quite got to the stage of ringing the mortuaries yet. Besides, Oliver was an optimist. Alabama wouldn't go and do anything silly without letting him know.

The lunch was rather reminiscent of the police rounding up the usual suspects. Venice came with Sebastian on one arm. Nicholas came with Van on the other arm. Sergei and Milo arrived alone.

'Well,' said Oliver, handing out Margharitas like Smarties, 'where is she? Does anyone know?'

'Where is who?' asked Venice, who was, after all, in love.

'Your sister, my angel,' said Oliver, looking at her accusingly. 'She's disappeared.' He suddenly relented in the face of love, and smiled at Venice indulgently. How could she be expected to know? She had other things on her mind. Oliver had to admit that if he was Venice, he wouldn't have any time for anything else apart from Sebastian. Some things simply did demand all one's concentration, and this was one of them. Besides, Sebastian was looking particularly pretty today in an old naval coat. Oliver had always been susceptible to braid on a man. It reminded him of the heavenly soldiers he used to meet in his Italian days.

'Disappeared?' said Venice. 'How perfectly glamorous. Do you think she's eloped?'

'I hope not,' said Sergei. 'I have tickets to the opera next week.'

'And it would be a crime to waste those,' said Milo savagely. He was feeling guilty because he knew that it was all his fault. Besides, he hated the opera. He couldn't imagine anything less romantic than vastly fat women screeching at each other. They always reminded him rather painfully of his matron at prep school.

'Well,' said Sergei, calmly, 'it would rather. They are particularly difficult to get.'

'Perhaps she's just gone away for a while,' said Van reasonably. 'People do, you know.'

'She wouldn't go away without telling me,' said Venice, Oliver and Sergei in unison.

Van looked at Sebastian rather sorrowfully and rolled her eyes. Oxford certainly didn't prepare one for people like this. Van sometimes wondered what it did prepare one for, but she supposed that wasn't really the point.

'I don't understand a word of it,' she said.

'Don't worry darling,' said Oliver. 'Have another Margharita, and don't mind us.'

Lunch went on into supper, as they discussed the endless possibilities. Oliver was firmly of the opinion that the young actor was to blame.

'He was going there for tea, after all,' he said. 'I expect he's spirited her off somewhere.'

Sergei rather dashed this romantic vision by pointing out that the young actor was still in rehearsal. Oliver's face fell, but only for a moment. He had to admit that he was rather tired of the young actor, and that rehearsals were probably the best place for him. Nicholas was of the opinion that Alabama must have left the country. It was really the only reason he could think of that explained her not returning his calls. He had a horrible feeling that he might have said something that offended her in a careless moment, and that she was cutting him. Perhaps she was cross about Van. But that was so unlike Alabama. Neither Venice nor Sebastian had any helpful theories to put forward, so they contented themselves with doing the crossword. Venice couldn't do a word of the crossword, never had, but she did so love to watch Sebastian doing it. She thought it was terribly sophisticated. Oliver, half wanting to berate them for taking so little interest in the matter in hand, couldn't quite bring himself to do it. They looked so serious and pretty with their golden heads bent low over the paper, frowns of concentration on their smooth faces, that he didn't have the heart to disturb them.

Alabama finished another bottle and set it carefully beside the other two. She stared accusingly at what she had just written, made an expression of ultimate disgust, thought for a moment, and then ripped the page from her typewriter and threw it to the floor, where it joined the small sea of other discards. She had always been good at writing when she was unhappy, but this was not going as well as it should. Cooped up in her house, all by herself in the quiet, she found too many uncomfortable thoughts crowding in on her, too many distracting memories. She was surprised to find herself dwelling not on Max, not on the brooding dark eyes that had occupied so many of her waking moments for the last few weeks, but on Milo. Milo, angry and sneering, so unlike him, telling her that she was worthless, that she was a fool. No one had ever been less of a fool, everyone knew that. She was brilliant, respected, carelessly intellectual, without even trying. Alabama had been so used to being clever, for such a long time, that it hardly occurred to her that she might be capable of stupidity. To have it pointed out to her so brutally was not at all what she was accustomed to, and she wasn't at all sure she liked it. It had been so easy to slip into her new role, with Oliver and Venice and Nicholas and Sergei all so willing to play along with her every whim. It had been fun, she with her fellow conspirators, like playing at make-believe. And if sometimes she had a tiny inkling that the make-believe was just a fraction elaborate it was so terribly easy to dismiss that thought with another glass of champagne, and to concentrate on everyone telling her how wonderful she looked and what a transformation it all was, and how every other woman in London must be green with envy. It was so easy to expect to see one's face staring out of the paper every morning, with its complimentary caption. She had got rather used to being the brilliant AND beautiful Alabama Skye. And then Milo had to put in his tuppence worth, and everything was spoilt. She found herself sitting in the dark, not bothering to turn the lights on as the dusk gathered about the house, remembering the days when it had been her and Milo, *contra mundum*, in the days when they had both looked down from a great height and despised people who didn't know what was important. How clever and far above the crowd they had thought themselves, in the proper tradition of all undergraduates. They had been convinced that they knew the secret of existence, and perhaps, in a way, they had been right.

It was a week now, Alabama thought to herself. It was the first time in eight years that Milo hadn't called her every day, the first time he hadn't proposed to her every day. She missed it more than she could have imagined. It was so petty of him to have gone all self-righteous on her, so silly and pointless. She sighed impatiently, and lit another cigarette, her eyes drawn back to the blank sheet sitting balefully in the typewriter waiting to be filled. Her mind was quite wiped of inspiration. She felt twitchy and uncertain, as she did sometimes before a storm, except this time there was no thunder in the air. She wondered if she could have been taking him for granted. She had always believed that he would never desert her, whatever she did. She had tested him once before, and he had stuck by her then, without a murmur. But they had been so much younger then, and so much had rolled over them like water off a duck's back, barely ruffling their feathers. Perhaps it had all been easier then, when the future lay so golden in front of them, so much of it, waiting just for them, filled with endless promise. Perhaps. Alabama stood up and stretched her legs, and shook her head as if to clear it. If she wanted to have a perfectly respectable affair that was no business of anyone else's, and no one had any right to censure her behaviour. Even Milo. Especially Milo. Besides Max was a catch for any girl. Milo should be impressed that she had such good taste.

Alabama stared again at the fresh piece of paper waiting expectantly in her typewriter, and tried to drag her wandering mind back to the matter in hand. She had always been good at concentrating, at blocking the world and all its distractions out, at reducing the universe to the typeface in front of her. She couldn't think what had happened to her. It must be love, that was all. She frowned at the page in front of her. It stared unhelpfully back. It was so white and empty and fearsome. It dared her to mark its pristine state. It mocked her incompetence. Writers write, it said, in time-honoured fashion. Call yourself a playwright? It laughed at her in her hesitation. Alabama hated it. She hated it to hell and back. She tore it out with a grand gesture, and reached out for a new one.

The telephone rang, only to be cut off abruptly as the machine turned itself on.

'Hello Alabama,' said Max's surly voice, gruff and low and full of resentment. 'I suppose you're out whooping it up with your bogus Russian royalty. You can call me if you like.'

Typical, Alabama thought in disgust. Utterly typical that he should not mention his name, expecting her to know at once who it was. Of course, she did know who it was. There was no mistaking that furious voice. But it wasn't up to him to expect that. Did he think he was the only person who ever called her? Perhaps Milo was right after all. It was so unlike her to fall in love with someone so objectionable.

If Alabama had thought about it a little, she would have realized that otherwise perfectly sane women have been falling in love with terrible men for centuries. Cleopatra with Antony, Scarlett with Rhett, Josephine with Napoleon, the list was endless. However, Alabama had more pressing things to think of, so she carried on in her own incomprehension.

The next morning those who had attended Oliver's lunch woke up with varying degrees of hangover and reached for their telephones. Oliver had insisted that it was very important for everyone to call in each day, in case there had been any further developments. He had woken specially early, quite before eleven, and set up a situations room in his bedroom. This consisted of putting on a particularly fetching silk dressing gown, and arranging himself on his bed with a pot of coffee, three croissants, the paper, and a pad to take messages on. In this way, he wouldn't have to move from the telephone until it was time for him to get ready for lunch. He was beginning to think he would have been rather good in the war. He had always rather fancied the idea of himself in uniform, and really, who could have imagined this hitherto unperceived efficiency. If it wasn't for him, Alabama might have been lost for a month and no one would have taken the blindest bit of notice, let alone taken any action. He lit his first cigarette of the day, and sucked in the turkish tobacco appreciatively. He might even have

212

made a secret agent, except he wasn't entirely sure he would have cared for the Germans' nasty little habit of torturing their enemies. He knew all about their devilish methods of extracting information, pulling out fingernails and so on. Oliver regarded his own perfectly manicured nails and gave a little shudder. Perhaps not a secret agent after all. He knew he could never again grow such perfect specimens.

Nicholas was the first to call.

'Nothing, I'm afraid,' he said gloomily. 'Just that blasted machine. And, I might tell you, that dear Van has been giving me nothing but stick ever since yesterday, so I haven't had a very peaceful night.'

'Ah well,' said Oliver happily. He couldn't help but be vastly amused by such a stripling of a girl, barely out of university, lecturing such a worldly creature as Nicholas. He was so utterly clever to have discovered a free spirit, and in this day and age. 'Never mind,' he said to Nicholas, 'you know what they say. These things are sent to test us. Besides my dear, we all know how perfectly well-equipped you are to look after yourself.'

'I'm beginning to wonder,' said Nicholas, wondering if it were too early to have a drink. 'She makes me feel my age. All that fire and brimstone, it's almost more than a man can stand.'

'I know,' said Oliver gleefully. 'Isn't it utter heaven. I didn't think they made them like that any more. We'll have her on a soap-box next, think what a treat.'

'Don't,' said Nicholas. 'Imagine the embarrassment.'

'Oh really,' said Oliver. 'Don't be so middle class. It would be quite enchanting. You should be proud to have been taken up as her latest cause.'

Nicholas grunted non-committally. 'I had no idea that being a cause would be so tiring. She's convinced I'm really a thwarted novelist, and that writing the column is just a revenge on a world that doesn't appreciate the poetry in my soul.'

Oliver laughed helplessly. So many interesting developments in his life, it was enough to spoil him quite rotten. The idea of Nicholas having any poetry in his soul was almost too much to take in this early in the morning. His sides quite ached with laughter.

'Oh dear,' he said weakly. 'How utterly enchanting she is. Now get off the line darling, I'm expecting Sergei next.'

Sergei called in five minutes later. He too was taking his coffee in bed, and he too wore a silk dressing gown, one that would have made Oliver quite ill with jealousy had he had the good fortune to see it. It was the kind of dressing gown they don't make any more, and had belonged to Sergei's grandfather. It was the kind of garment that Oliver had aspired to all his life. Sergei, of course, simply wore it because it was a perfectly serviceable dressing gown, and very comfortable. He too, had nothing to report.

'Oh well, my dear,' said Oliver, 'it's heaven hearing your voice anyway.'

Venice, of course, didn't ring, but had to be called.

'What took you so long to answer the telephone?' Oliver asked pointedly.

'Doing the crossword of course,' said Venice with dignity. 'What can you want at this hour?'

'Darling heart, it's a full quarter to twelve, and your sister is still missing without leave. I want to know if you've heard anything.'

'Not really. Should I have done?'

'I can see there's nothing to be done with you,' said Oliver, not that he really expected anything else. 'Go back to your crossword, there's a good girl, and give that pretty boy of yours a kiss from me.'

'I shall do nothing of the kind,' said Venice. 'I don't want him getting ideas.'

Oliver lay back in his bed and drank his coffee, wondering what he should do next. The only sensible thing to do seemed to be to call everyone back and suggest they meet for lunch.

In Chelsea, Alabama was writing as if the devil were at her back. She had been at it for a good six hours. After a night spent alone with a bottle of Jack Daniels, she had indulged in another good fit of stormy crying, and was surprised to find herself awake at dawn the next morning, quite refreshed and with her head cleared. No wonder tragic heroines were always casting themselves on the floor and weeping as if the world had come to an end. Alabama was always surprised when tried and tested methods proved effective. Like playing hard to get, which Venice always swore worked like a dream.

She wrote all day. She wrote through lunch, unaware that she was hungry. She wrote without pause or hesitation, while across London Oliver rounded everyone up for lunch, and they went off to have Bloody Marys and several bottles of Chablis and talk about their hangovers and mourn Alabama's absence. She wrote and rewrote, and altered and improved, with Max's words ringing in her head, until the night had started to draw in, and she suddenly realized that she could no longer see the page in front of her. But it didn't matter any more, because she had finished, and it was perfect, and Max had been quite right after all, and now it was not just another Alabama Skye play, but a far far better thing than she had ever done before.

She sat for a moment, exhausted and exhilarated at the same time, giving herself a minute's silence for being so clever. Then she rang Max.

He arrived an hour later. Alabama had changed her shirt, and had a bath, and tidied her hair, but she still had her old jeans on and her face was unpainted. She was as Max remembered her, the first night he had seen her, standing outside his dressing room, lighting up the dank corridor of the little Croydon theatre. He remembered now why she had twisted his heart, and why he had taken her to bed, and he wondered how he could ever have left her for all the glamorous women and a taste of the high life.

The room too was as he remembered it, filled with ashtrays and empty cigarette packets, dead bottles and the boxes of A4, the floor littered with scrumpled paper, impatiently tossed aside.

'I see you're writing again,' he said, surprised.

'Yes,' said Alabama.

'That's good.'

'Yes.'

Alabama handed him a sheaf of paper.

'Here. It's the end of the play. I've rewritten it for you.'

'For me?'

'Who else?'

There was a pause. Then Max kissed Alabama, partly because he couldn't think of anything to say, and partly because he wanted to, and partly because it seemed like the most natural thing to do.

'Well,' said Alabama, when he had finished. 'That was nice. I'd almost forgotten what it felt like.'

Max smiled at her, with that heartbreaking twist of the mouth that she knew so well. She rather wished he wouldn't.

'So,' he said.

'So.'

It was late, and after all, there are only so many things that can be said when a man and a woman are alone together in the still of the night. They looked at each other for a long moment. Everything suddenly seemed very simple.

'I suppose you would like to go to bed,' said Alabama, who for all her new-found airs and graces, for all her designer clothes and Russian princes and smart restaurants and enslaved admirers, was still the same girl at heart.

'Yes,' said Max, who for all his new-found success, was still the same boy. Some things never change.

Alabama woke up late. It had been a long night. She reached over lazily to where Max should have been, only to find the bed empty and cold.

How utterly typical, she thought to herself, that having seduced her in such a pre-emptory fashion he should disappear as abruptly as he came. There was a note pinned to the pillow.

'Gone to rehearsal,' it said in that familiar black scrawl. 'Will ring later.' Not so much as a kiss, thought Alabama, trying to feel indignant. She got out of bed, smiling to herself, stretched in a pleased kind of way, admired her rumpled appearance in the glass, and decided that tomorrow really was another day. She turned the telephone on. It rang immediately.

'Hello,' said Venice, before Alabama could say a word. 'You're back in the land of the living at last. I knew you couldn't have gone far, except I did have a sneaking suspicion that you might have eloped, but Sebastian says that people don't go much to Gretna Green any more. Too many tourists he says, couldn't you die? He knows everything, he can even do the crossword. Where HAVE you been?'

'Writing,' said Alabama. 'I'm surprised you noticed.'

'I didn't,' Venice admitted. 'Oliver pointed it out. Really Alabama, half of London has been calling the missing persons office or whatever it is one calls in these circumstances. It's a very good thing that I am so in love, or I might have worried.'

'Well,' said Alabama, pleased to see that Venice was just the same as ever, only more so. 'Then it is a good thing.'

'Milo says it's all his fault,' said Venice, hardly pausing for breath. It wasn't often that she didn't see Alabama for so long, and she had so much to tell her she hardly knew where to start. 'Although I can't imagine why it should be, and he's being very close about the whole thing, to tell you the truth. Anyway, he says that he wouldn't be surprised if you never spoke to him again ever (you will, won't you?), and he's miserable now, because he says that you'll never marry him in a million years, and Sergei was livid, or at least the nearest he ever gets, because he had to take Van to the opera with him and Nicholas made a scene, and Van said that there was no point in all this fuss because she's utterly smitten by Chris Branagh or Charles Branagh, I can never remember his name, who is some actor she's never met, I ask you, and then Nicholas went off into quite a huff and said that's what comes with messing with juveniles, and I can't tell you what else. Not now, Sebastian, I'm talking to Alabama. And,' Venice paused briefly for breath, 'Oliver rings everyone twice a day to see if anyone has heard anything, and holds special council of war lunches, which you can imagine are his utter *raison d'être* at the moment, and he's rather miffed with Van at the moment too, although I don't expect it will last because really he thinks she's a slice of heaven, but she did refuse to come to the last lunch, saying that it's all too silly for words, and why couldn't you go off on your own if you wanted to, and then Nicholas stuck up for her, and there was almost another row, but Sebastian managed to calm everyone down by suggesting a round of poker, so we sat up until six in the morning, and Sebastian won £100, and I'm so in love with him I can hardly speak. So, what do you think of that?'

'I don't understand a word of it,' said Alabama, shaking with laughter. 'The moment I don't answer my telephone for a week, all hell breaks loose.'

'Odd, isn't it?' said Venice. 'All I can say is that I hope there would be the same fuss if I did it. I've half a mind to try it and see. Perhaps we should lunch?'

'I've a feeling,' said Alabama, thinking of Johnny's reaction when Max turned up with a new third act, 'that I might be a little tied up for lunch today.'

'Oh well,' said Venice. 'Let me know when you're free. I've got my perfectly scrumptious toy boy to keep me company.' Alabama heard a howl in the background, and Venice yelped down the telephone. 'Ouch,' she said, laughing. 'He hates it when I call him that.'

As soon as Alabama put the telephone down, it rang again.

'Alabama darling, thank the Lord that you're there,' said Johnny, in a harassed voice. 'I love you to death, you know I do, but what IS all this about rewriting the last act?'

'I felt it was wrong,' said Alabama calmly, lighting herself a cigarette and starting to smile.

'Well lovey, it's your play after all, and you know best, but we've only got ten days until we open, and to be brutally honest with you I've got Charlotta climbing the walls, and Sasha cursing the day you were born, and you know what a fan he is, usually, and Max is being no help at all, he just giggles, like dear Larry used to in the old days, and darling, really.'

'Johnny,' said Alabama, laughing. 'You can do it.'

'I can do it, my sweet, on my ducky little head, but can my cast do it? I mean, really love.'

'I'll come round, if you like,' said Alabama generously.

'Well, I hated to ask, but would you really? I mean, really, it would be such a help. You can take the heat and I'll get back to the directing, which is all I'm good at.'

Alabama smiled to herself as she dressed. It was nice, being back in the land of the living with such a bang. She had forgotten how much she enjoyed putting the cat among the pigeons, and she had to admit that she was rather looking forward to this particular rehearsal. She would have hell to deal with, but then, that rather came with the job. If she wanted a quiet life, she would have settled for accountancy.

She put on her old jeans and her boots, and tied a bandana round her head to keep her hair out of her eyes. It was like the old Alabama emerging from the ashes of unaccustomed finery. She couldn't even be bothered to paint her face, but she paused long enough to put some lipstick on, since it was Max. Then she gathered her wits and her resources and gave herself her best devil may care smile in the glass and went to rehearsals.

'Darling,' said Johnny, as she arrived. He looked as if he was the first to spot a lifeboat from the prow of a sinking ship. 'Thank God. Now people, here is the delicious Alabama, whom we all love, and she's going to explain everything.'

A chorus of disapproving voices broke out, the loudest of which was Charlotta's.

'Alabama darling,' she wailed, a pitch higher than the rest, 'I love your work, you know I do, as if it were my own, that's all, but what about my last speech, I mean it was the focal point of the whole act, and now it's cut, and just HOW am I supposed to make sense of my character now?'

Alabama tried not to look at Max, who was giggling in a corner, and being no help at all.

'All right everybody,' she said firmly, taking charge. She drew herself up very tall, and ran her eyes severely round the circle of mutinous faces in front of her. She was the darling of Broadway and the West End, she had been described as a prodigy by the most cynical critics in the civilized world, and she wasn't about to be given the run around by a bunch of neurotic actors and their egos. 'Let's just run through it. I think if you concentrate just a fraction you'll realize that it works much better than the original version. Don't forget that was written for an American audience.'

That touched the right nerve, as Alabama had known it would. She was only too aware of the disdain that American actors evoked, with their endless trumpetings about the Method and the importance of what they called their spirituality, whatever that meant.

'Well,' said Sasha loftily. 'No wonder. The Americans are heathens, no history, one must remember that.'

Everyone nodded in agreement, except for Charlotta, who was married to an American, if you could call it married, and Max, who just giggled more than ever.

'Now then,' said Alabama, pleased that this shot had gone home quite so successfully. She fixed them again with a gimlet eye, just to let them know who was the boss. 'Shall we start?'

'Places everyone,' said Johnny, clapping his hands. He gave Alabama a heartfelt look of admiration. She really did come up with the goods, in spades, he didn't care what anyone said.

It took two hours to bring them near compliance, and another two to draw the first cries of admiration, and by the time darkness had fallen outside, no one could imagine how they could have done the first version and ever held their heads up in public. It was, as they quickly recognized, something quite different. The changed third act had turned it from another clever caustic Alabama Skye piece of devilment into something exceptional. Alabama, watching it come to life, wondered quite where it had come from so suddenly. Inspiration like this was like lightning, it never struck twice in the same place. She was lucky that she had been at home when it happened.

By the time they had finished Alabama was exhausted, her shirt damp with sweat, and her back aching, but she had that old feeling of euphoria as she saw her work come to life. She had forgotten about that, with all the parties and the plotting and the lunches, she had forgotten about the excitement, the visceral thrill of seeing her words, written in black and white, leaping off the page, being translated into a look, a tone of voice, into something that could hold an audience spellbound. And this would hold any audience spellbound, or she would eat her hat, if only she had got around to buying one. It was going to be spectacular, and it was hers. It was almost better than sex.

'Well,' said Max, trying not to show how impressed he was.

'Well,' said Alabama. She could feel herself smiling in a way she hadn't for weeks.

'You were brilliant,' said Max, giving in. He had to take his hat off to her, this mercurial clever girl, if only he had ever got around to buying one.

'I was, wasn't I?' said Alabama, who had never believed in false modesty.

'I'd forgotten how arrogant you are.'

'You'd forgotten a lot about me,' said Alabama, not unkindly.

'Do you want to eat?' said Max, who didn't. He had only one thing on his mind, and no one was going to win any prizes for guessing what that was. He thought that at this stage he should still observe the formalities, for form's sake, and besides, he still wasn't quite sure whether Alabama had forgiven him completely. He didn't want to rush his fences just yet.

'Let's go,' she said.

The cast watched them leave together, question marks rising in each pair of observant eyes.

'Well,' said Johnny, who was as pleased as punch and very much needed a large whisky, no ice. 'That's it for today. You've all done superbly. Thank God Alabama is as good as she is.'

'I don't know,' said Charlotta, who was still smarting from the loss of her big speech, and had never believed in giving credit where it was due, whatever anyone said. 'Give me Pinter any day.'

'Oh shut up, Charlotta,' said Emmie.

'She was magnificent,' said Sasha. 'Lucky Max.'

Emmie gave him a very sharp look indeed, and Johnny turned away to hide a smile. Actors.

•

CHAPTER

9

It was, as Oliver was later to say with his usual knack
of summing things up, an eventful night.

Max took Alabama to a small French restaurant he
knew where they had a proper zinc-topped bar and
appropriately surly waiters, just like the ones in Paris.
Alabama found that she wasn't really very hungry after
all, so they ordered a great deal of wine instead of
food, and toasted to her continuing success. Max kept
staring at her as if he'd never really looked properly
before, and Alabama kept telling him not to. They
drank their red wine, without noticing much what it
tasted like, and then they had large brandies, and small
bitter cups of coffee, and some French cigarettes, and
Alabama blew a smoke ring or two, just to keep her
hand in. Then Max suddenly announced that he was
famished, and so they had to order scrambled eggs and
bacon to go with the brandy, and Alabama watched
him eat and smiled and blew another smoke ring,
just for the hell of it. They drew the evening out,
putting off going home, knowing where it would lead,
relishing the tension of expectation, pretending they
didn't really know quite what was going to happen.
They were so busy looking into each other's eyes

that they didn't notice Milo come in and leave just as abruptly.

Away in the ghostly white streets of Belgravia, Venice and Sebastian were having a night in. It was such a novelty for Venice that she was as excited as a child. She couldn't remember having had a night in since 1985. Overcome by her discovery of what she termed the Real Thing, she had even decided to cook. She had never learned to cook, but she was sure that all women could. It was an instinctive thing surely, like all men knowing about cars. Besides, she felt she owed it to Sebastian to try. A man who could do the crossword in under ten minutes was worth anything.

'Aren't you proud of me?' she asked as she went to take the chicken out of the oven. Everyone said that chicken was as easy as pie.

'I'm stunned,' said Sebastian truthfully.

'Shut your eyes then,' said Venice sternly, drawing on the oven gloves that she had gone all the way to David Mellor to buy. They were silver and three sizes too big. Venice rather enjoyed wearing them, like a knight in his gauntlets she rather thought. They made her feel like the real McCoy.

'Oh dear,' she said suddenly. 'Are you very hungry?'

Sebastian opened one eye. The chicken was very large, utterly succulent, corn-fed to a fault, and quite uncooked.

'I think,' said Venice slowly, standing up very straight and looking rather helpless in her vast silver gloves, 'that I must have forgotten to turn on the oven.'

'It couldn't matter less,' said Sebastian.

'Do you hate me?'

'Venice,' said Sebastian in his most sophisticated voice, 'I don't want to eat. Let's just go to bed.'

And that was where the trouble started, as Venice was later to relate at great length. If the chicken had been cooked, she and Sebastian would have been having a perfectly innocent dinner when David arrived, and nothing need have been said. After all, what could be more innocent than chicken?

As it was, when David did arrive, having spent several arduous weeks soothing the irate Moira's ruffled feathers, he found his son in bed with his mistress. Whatever he might have said to Sebastian about taking advantage of Venice's charms was forgotten in an instant. Seeing those two lithe young bodies locked about each other with such obvious and indecent enjoyment roused in David a jealousy he had no idea he possessed. His roar of fury roused half the neighbourhood, and brought two brave and bold policemen running to the door from their posts at the embassy next door, where they were after all having a very quiet night, and thinking that they could just about do with a little diversion.

It was fortunate for Sebastian that the embassy was so close. The police arrived just in time to witness David, armourclad in the best Savile Row had to offer, threatening to murder the naked Sebastian, who was fast discovering quite how vulnerable a man is without his clothes. Faced with the unexpected and charmingly diverting sight of Venice attempting to keep up a wayward sheet with one hand, while doggedly trying to hit David over the head with a Meissen vase clutched in the other, the two constables checked for a moment, as any red-blooded men would in similar circumstances, but they knew their duty. It took quite an unseemly scuffle to restrain David, but he was no match for a seasoned arm-lock, and at last they overpowered him. He was an unbecoming shade of puce and spitting with fury, but quite unrepentant.

'I shall kill him,' he insisted, with awful deliberation and a remarkable grip on his grammar, if nothing else.

'I shouldn't do that if I were you, sir,' said the police.

There was a pause, as everyone wondered what to do next. There was nothing about this in the police training manuals.

Venice hitched up her sheet. Sebastian had nothing to clutch about himself but his dignity. He stood up very tall and utterly contemptuous and looked down at his assailant.

'I think,' he said, 'that I shall go and dress now.'

'It was then that I really fell in love with him,' Venice told Oliver.

'I'm not at all surprised,' said Oliver, allowing himself the smallest twinge of lust at the thought of Sebastian unclad. Venice really was a very lucky girl.

It was late now, and Venice and Sebastian were drinking brandy in that late-night Mayfair bar that Venice liked. It had seemed the most sensible place to go, under the circumstances. They had found Oliver rather moodily ensconced at a table for one, since his bongo player was still out of town on his world tour.

Oliver needless to say, had been delighted to see them, and they had been equally pleased. Oliver had the ability to make the bubonic plague seem like a rather amusing trifle of gossip. They had been shaking rather when they arrived, but after half a bottle of brandy, calm was returning, and the hideous night was suddenly becoming rather funny.

'It was all that bloody chicken's fault,' said Venice. 'If only it had had the decency to be cooked . . .'

Oliver was enchanted. He so hated self-recrimination.

'Of course it was the chicken's fault,' he said. 'How could you know?'

'I wish you could have seen the policemen's faces when they arrived,' said Venice, starting to laugh at the memory. 'There was Sebastian, naked as the day he was born, with David's hands round his throat, and me with half a sheet on, screaming at them to stop, and trying to hit David over the head with his best Meissen vase.'

'They were terribly good and strong,' said Sebastian. 'They got Pa off in a second.'

There was a slight pause. It sounded so strange, Sebastian calling David 'Pa'.

'They thought we were quite mad,' said Venice, shrugging off a tiny shudder. 'There was David, swearing blue murder, and demanding that we got out of the house, and asking for his door key back, and Sebastian just looked down at him and strolled off to dress, and I had to explain that we really didn't want to press charges, but could they just go on sitting on David until we got out of the house. And then Sebastian came back, still as calm as you please, perfectly dressed and with his hair combed, and told David to remember his career, and to think what Moira would say if this ever got out.'

'Well,' said Oliver in admiration. 'Well.'

'That got him,' said Sebastian. 'He would lose the company and everything. So all at once he became quite reasonable, almost fawning, and said of course we were right, and that he'd had a hard day at the office, the dollar had lost a cent or something, and wouldn't it all be best forgotten.'

'All with the policemen still sitting on top of him,

growing more and more bemused by the minute, poor ducks,' said Venice.

'So then what happened?' said Oliver, who couldn't have been more interested.

'Then the sweet police got off, and David went into all sorts of contorted apologies, you never saw a man more embarrassed, and he started getting out his wallet, but one look from the police made him realize it wasn't such a good idea, and then I gave them some beer, which was all we had, and they stood around drinking it while I packed a bag, and then we got the hell out.'

'And came straight here?' said Oliver.

'Well,' said Sebastian reasonably, 'Venice needed a drink.'

Across London, unaware of all these momentous events, which would have kept his column in copy for quite a week, Nicholas stared at a bottle. It stared back. There could be something rather baleful about a bottle, especially when it was almost empty.

Nicholas and Van had had a fight, which was the reason he now sat alone. He was uncomfortably aware that it was all his fault, which didn't make anything any better. But really, how was he to know that she would take him so seriously? All he had meant to do was tease, just a little. If she would insist on going on about Kenneth Branagh and his list of unimpeachable perfections, what on earth did she expect? It was hardly flattering, after all. The generation gap had suddenly reared its ugly head and Van had gone off into a positive cloud of righteous fury, and started talking about the death of idealism and people selling out to Thatcherism. Nicholas wasn't quite sure how she had made the connection so quickly, but he had noticed that Van had a genius for lateral thinking that would leave de Bono gasping. He should have

229

known better than to argue with her, but he had been harbouring a secret crush on Mrs Thatcher for years, and he had become rather angry. Ideals were all very well, but people had to eat, and there was something infinitely seductive about paying less income tax. He had had the lack of judgement to say so, which had been the last straw.

'If that's what you think,' Van had said, sounding quite cold and utterly final, 'then I don't think that we have anything left to say to each other.'

She had left without another word. Nicholas sighed and contemplated the bottle more gloomily than ever. He really would never understand the younger generation. He blamed it on Oxford. Oxford never did a girl any good at all, in his opinion.

In Alabama's empty flat, the telephone rang. There was a pause as the machine turned itself on.

'Oh Alabama,' said Nicholas's voice, slightly distorted by the tape, but patently despairing. 'Why are you never at home when I need you?' He was very drunk by now. 'I wanted you to come out drinking with me, but I can see I shall have to drink alone. I die your utter slave.'

Van walked the streets, still buoyed up on her wave of anger. This always happened to her. She gave herself so utterly to people, and then they let her down. She wondered if she would ever learn. She was furious with herself as well as with Nicholas. Her absurdly optimistic nature led her to causes any other girl would know were lost. When would she stop trying to change people? Some people tried to change the world, but Van tried to change people. It was a terrible mistake.

She suddenly felt the fury die out of her. She was chilled and rather hungry and quite alone. She didn't want to go home where there was nothing waiting for her except last week's milk growing a beard in the fridge. She looked up, and realized that she was outside Sergei's house. There was a light on at the window, so she knocked on the door.

'Hello Van,' said Sergei, too well-bred to betray any surprise at being disturbed at such an unseasonable hour.

'Hello,' said Van rather wretchedly. 'Can I come in?'

'Of course.' Sergei held the door open for her, wondering quite what she wanted. She was a most unpredictable girl.

'I'm starving,' she said abruptly. 'Have you got anything to eat?'

Sergei led the way to the kitchen. It was not a room he frequented and he was surprised to notice how comfortable it was with its flagged floor and great scrubbed table. Copper pots and dried herbs hung on the walls, and Sergei was amused to notice a well-thumbed copy of the *Sporting Life* on the side.

'How lovely,' said Van, heading unerringly for the fridge. 'Can I help myself?'

'Please do,' said Sergei politely, rather glad that he wouldn't have to show his ignorance of his own kitchen by not knowing where things were. 'Would you like a drink?'

'Yes please. Brandy, if you have it.'

When Sergei came back with a bottle and two glasses, he found Van sitting at the head of the table, devouring a ham sandwich dripping with mayonnaise.

'Here you are,' he said, pouring her a drink.

'Thank you,' she said through a mouthful of ham, taking the glass and knocking it back in one. Sergei manfully repressed a shudder at the sight of lovingly aged Armagnac being gulped as if it were water. He gave her another shot. He supposed she couldn't be expected to know about such things. She was young yet, after all.

'Do you think I'm mad, staying with Nicholas?' she asked, plunging in as usual. It didn't occur to her to explain her presence at such a time of the night. She was used to Oxford hours, where people were there to be dropped in on, however late it was. Besides she liked Sergei. He took her to the opera. Any man who was not ashamed to be moved to tears by *La Bohème* couldn't be all bad. She wiped a blot of mayonnaise from the corner of her mouth with the back of her hand and stared hard at him, as if he could give her all the answers she wanted so badly.

'Mad?' said Sergei, taken a little off-balance. 'I'm not sure. Do you?'

'Tonight I do.' Van looked bleakly at him. Under her fringe, her blue eyes had turned almost black with consternation. 'I thought that under that tough journalist's exterior I should find a positive mine of thwarted hopes and dreams, but I think he's just in love with Mrs Thatcher. Another slave to materialism. There's not much I can do about that, is there?'

Sergei allowed himself a small smile. Personally he thought that the prime minister was a frightful jumped-up harridan who should be dispatched to the salt mines without delay, but it wasn't something he dwelt on often.

'Not a great deal,' he said. 'Does it matter so much to you?'

'But of course it matters,' said Van explosively. 'It matters. I wanted to make him mind about all the things that I mind about, but I couldn't have picked on a more hopeless case, could I? I thought that he must have had some terrible disappointment in life, like having a novel rejected, or a brilliant father he could never live up to. I thought that he needed someone like me to make him see that it was worth trying again, that one must never give up a dream, but he doesn't want to try. He just wants to go out all the time and watch the crowned heads of Europe having affairs with each other. His idea of heaven is going to a party full of people who have a page each in the *Almanac de Gotha*.' Van shook her head in utter frustration. 'I mean, REALLY.'

Sergei stopped smiling. This absurd child really did believe that she could change the way people worked. He wondered when he had stopped minding about things that much. He couldn't remember. Perhaps he had never minded. He looked at Van's furious blazing face, trying to come to terms with something that she could never make any better, and rather thought that he hadn't. Not like this, anyway.

'I think I must be awfully stupid,' said Van.

'But what about your first?' said Sergei gently.

'Oh that.' Van waved a dismissive hand. 'It's all very well. I used to think that it meant everything. And it did, at the time. I can understand about Napoleon and the French Revolution and every single one of the Angevin kings, but what good is that when it comes to real life? It's fine, Oxford, when you're there, but they fill your head full of wonderful ideas, and when you go into the real world, you find that none of them mean a damn. So then what do you do?'

Sergei shook his head a little hopelessly. It was ever since Alabama had come into his life. Up until then he had thought that he was settled in his ways, confirmed in his round of racing and skiing, taking lunch at his club with his cronies, stretching himself no more than a chapter of Voltaire required. He had never thought that he would be interested in any other kind of women than the polished pampered creatures that he courted so urbanely, the kind who didn't demand any more of a man than lunch at the Gavroche and a few pretty baubles from Cartier to keep them happy. But since Alabama had burst into his life without a word of warning, he had found himself drinking in seedy bars in Mayfair, aiding and abetting Venice and Alabama in their preposterous schemes of seduction, consorting with a gossip columnist, and now this. Now this strip of a girl, who arrived on his doorstep at some ungodly hour, needing to be fed, who sat in his kitchen, with her black suede jacket and her pointed boots and her great dark demanding eyes, drinking his Armagnac without a second thought, quivering with impotent rage, and asking him all the answers to life's questions.

'Why do you ask me?' he said.

'You?' Van looked at him in astonishment. 'Well, you know so much, don't you? I mean you're a man of the world, and you've travelled, and you know about philosophy, and you're a connoisseur of the arts, isn't that the expression, and you must know hundreds of people and see how they work, and Alabama thinks that you're wonderful, and she must be the cleverest woman I know. Who else should I ask?'

Sergei found himself touched by her faith, but a little baffled by it. He wasn't sure if he could live up to it.

'Well,' he said, not quite sure what to say, a state of affairs most unlike him.

'Oh I see.' Van stood up abruptly. Her nerves were raw tonight, and she misunderstood his hesitation. 'I'm boring you. I'm so sorry. I'll go.' She headed for the door, her shoulders hunched in dejection.

'Wait,' said Sergei, astonishing himself. 'Don't go.'

Back in their bar in Mayfair, Venice, Oliver and Sebastian were staring at each other with that ineffable fondness that the right amount of brandy can bring.

'So,' said Oliver, beaming at them both, and thinking that he had never in his life seen two such perfect creatures, 'what happens now?'

'Now?' said Venice, as if it were some obscure foreign word for deviant sexual practices.

'Well yes, darling. Now. I mean you can hardly go back to Belgravia after this little fracas, can you?'

'I suppose not,' said Venice reluctantly. She never thought about unpleasant things until they were forcibly borne in on her.

'So, where are you going to go?'

Sebastian suddenly drew himself up as tall as his bar stool would allow.

'We shall go,' he said grandly, 'to my place.'

'Your place,' said Venice with love, not even knowing where it was.

'Well,' said Oliver, impressed beyond words. 'Of course.'

They left the club, mostly because it was closing, and it was after all approaching the early hours of the morning and the poor tired waiters wanted to go to bed. Outside the streets were dark and shiny with warm summer rain. They walked round Berkeley Square a few times, because it looked so pretty with no traffic in it, and it was where the nightingale sang, so people said, and Sebastian hummed a little song that used to be the rage in the thirties, and Venice said that she simply couldn't love anyone more.

They were just about to go and get some bacon and eggs in a late café they knew up the road, when they found Milo at their feet having been thrown rather roughly out of a nightclub.

'My dear,' said Oliver, 'how perfectly enchanting to see you. I didn't think I knew anyone who got thrown out of nightclubs any more. It's nice to see that some people still know how to behave badly.'

Milo looked balefully up at them, and wiped some blood from the corner of his mouth. His eyes were crossing rather, and it took him two attempts to be able to speak.

'I feel dreadful,' he said at last.

'Well,' said Venice kindly, leaning down to give him her handkerchief, 'you don't look that ducky. Have you been rejected by the love of your life, or did you just decide that you had been sober for too long?'

Milo stared at her again, quite incomprehending.

'It's all right,' said Venice. 'You don't have to answer that question. Boys, I do think you should pick him up. He'll get frightful piles sitting on that wet pavement.'

Sebastian and Oliver dutifully picked Milo out of the gutter, while Venice did her usual trick with a taxi.

'Could you take us to Jo's please?' she asked. 'I know it's only round the corner, but one of us can't walk.'

Milo was bundled into the cab, where he collapsed with his head in Venice's lap. Sebastian tactfully looked the other way.

'Really, Milo,' said Oliver, dusting off his hands. 'Aren't you a little old for this?'

Milo muttered incoherently into Venice's left thigh.

'He says,' she interpreted, 'that a man is only as old as the woman he feels.'

After some effort and an unusual amount of profanities from Oliver, they managed to get Milo seated at a table in the late café.

A tired-looking waitress with drooping stockings shuffled over to take their order. She looked at Milo rather doubtfully, as he slumped in his chair, swaying slightly and muttering under his breath.

'It's all right,' said Venice. 'He's with us. What he needs is lots of very black coffee and some water.'

'And a sick bag,' Sebastian added reassuringly. 'Eggs for me please.'

Oliver started to laugh.

'Really,' he said. 'So much for a quiet night.'

'What ARE we going to do with you, Milo?' said Venice. 'No,' she added, seeing Sebastian's face, 'he is NOT coming back to your place.'

'She was married,' said Milo, with a sudden burst of clarity. 'That was it.'

'Oh dear,' said Oliver, shaking his head sorrowfully. 'It is always the most frightful mistake. I suppose you did your usual trick of asking if you could lay your tired head on her welcoming breast. I've always told you not to use that line in public.'

'Oliver used to be a nanny before this job,' Venice told Sebastian, who was happily tucking into his breakfast.

'Bloody good eggs,' he said. 'I wonder if they've got any tabasco.'

'Bring the boy some tabasco,' said Oliver joyfully. He was now of the firm opinion that Sebastian should have absolutely anything that his heart desired.

'But Milo,' said Venice, who was still determined to get to the bottom of this mystery, and was not to be deflected by something as fleeting as tabasco, 'what were you doing in a nightclub at three in the morning making passes at married women? It's not really you, is it? Nicholas yes, but not you.'

'Desperate,' said Milo, making a heroic attempt to focus on his coffee.

'Aren't we all, darling?' said Oliver tragically.

'Oh Oliver, do stop striking attitudes and sharpen your wits,' said Venice in her most businesslike tone, which was not particularly businesslike at all, but considering the lateness of the hour and the amount of brandy she had consumed, wasn't at all bad. 'Something is going on here that we are missing. This is not normal procedure. Oh good, here's my bacon.'

'Have some tabasco,' said Sebastian magnanimously. He had finished his eggs and had moved on to a Danish.

'Thank you,' said Venice, who never forgot her manners. 'Now Milo darling, what exactly are you desperate about?'

'Think I'm going to be sick,' said Milo, making a bolt for the door.

'Well,' said Venice sagely, 'it can't be that.'

Alabama and Max walked home. After the rain, the night had grown fine, even in Chelsea, and the moon was riding high. It was the kind of night the Italians write songs about. Alabama and Max loved it, it was so exactly right. Max held Alabama's hand and pretended he wasn't. Alabama let him.

Back at Alabama's house, where they had ended up by a silently mutual assent, the light flashed insistently on the answering machine.

'Just let me get that,' she said, as Max's hand slid its way down her back. Nicholas's melancholy voice came loudly into the room.

'Oh dear,' said Alabama in concern. 'Poor Nicholas. I must call him.' Among the other odd things that had been happening lately, one of the oddest was Alabama's growing fondness for Nicholas. She felt rather guilty that she had been neglecting him so much lately. He sounded perfectly desperate.

'What?' She turned to find Max staring at her in disbelief. She paused for a moment, her finger poised over the dial.

'Well, he's miserable, you can hear that.'

'Miserable?' Max stared at her even more. 'It's two in the morning.'

'So?'

'Hold on.' Max turned away and started pacing about the room. 'Hold on for just one minute. Are you telling me that you're going to call that shoddy little journalist at this hour of the morning just because he's had too much to drink?' Max hadn't forgotten the digs in the paper, nor the obviously smitten references to Alabama.

'I said,' said Alabama with rather alarming quiet, 'that he was miserable.'

'He's drunk,' said Max crossly. 'Any fool can hear that. He's probably passed out cold by now, with your name written across his heart in letters of fire.' Max was really getting into his stride now. 'And what's all that about being your undying slave? Just what has been going on?'

'Max,' said Alabama slowly. 'I'm not quite sure I understand you. Are you examining me?'

'Damn right I am,' said Max, who had seen the films, and knew how a man in a rage was supposed to speak. 'Since when did you get so buddy with Nicholas? Since when did you start calling him in the middle of the night? And what's all this guff about how miserable he is? What about me?'

'Well, what about you?' said Alabama, with even more menacing calm. 'You look perfectly fine to me. What difference does it make to you if I call him?'

'Plenty difference. You despise him.'

'Who says that?'

'You do.'

'I do? What do you suppose I say about shoddy little actors on the make?'

Max stopped in the middle of his pacing and stared at her, open-mouthed.

'What?'

'You heard.' Alabama started to laugh. He looked so ridiculous standing there, in the middle of the room, with his mouth hanging open. She wished Milo could have been there to appreciate how exquisitely funny it was.

'Shoddy little . . .' Max was lost for words. 'Stop laughing, for Christ's sake.'

Alabama laughed even more. From grand passion to utter absurdity, she couldn't help but think it funny.

'You look so silly,' she stuttered.

Max's sense of the ridiculous had never been very finely tuned, and it certainly wasn't working overtime this evening.

'Oh,' he said huffily, 'so now I look silly, do I? Thank you so very much. That really is quite charming of you.'

Alabama made a heroic effort to stop laughing, but she was finding it very difficult. She hadn't laughed for such a long time, and now she couldn't stop.

'Max,' she said, 'if I didn't know you better, I'd say you were jealous.'

'And what if I am? What then? Aren't I allowed to be jealous of strange men ringing up my woman at two in the morning?'

'I don't know,' said Alabama, rather taken off balance. Since when had she been his woman? She thought that he was taking rather a lot of things for granted all of a sudden.

'It's all very well for you,' said Max, who was by now

quite captivated with his own temper, and beyond noticing anything else, 'swanning about with half London at your feet, captivating princes and anyone who ever had a good review in the *TSL*.' (Alabama didn't like to point out to him that it was the *TLS*. She didn't think that he would appreciate the finer details of life at this moment.) 'And I don't know who else besides. It's all very well for you having half the national press dying of love for you . . .'

'It's only one gossip columnist, and he's hardly dying.'

'That's not the point. The point is, where do I fit in? Are you just taking me home on a whim, the way you did before? Is that all it is? You suddenly feel like a bit of low life, is that it?'

'No,' said Alabama, who was growing tired of this conversation, if you could call it a conversation, and wanted to go to bed.

'No?' Max was really working himself up to a pitch of fury now. This was a good scene, and like any actor, he wanted to wean the last drop of drama out of it. He was infuriated by Alabama's calm. He wanted to ruffle it, to make her scream at him, or throw something. If he had had production notes they would have read 'jealous fury, goaded anger' or something similar. 'No?' he repeated. 'Is that all you can say?'

'Well,' said Alabama reasonably, 'what would you like me to say?' With her legendary self-control, she forbore to point out that all this was rather a moot point, since it had been Max who had left in the first place, and that if anyone had a right to be jealous and angry, it was she.

'Don't you understand?' said Max, in something approaching anguish. He was working himself up to the really good bit now. 'Don't you understand that I love you?'

Alabama sat very still indeed. He shouldn't have said that.

'Don't you see?' Max continued, oblivious to his mistake, quite carried away on the tide of his own oratory. 'Can't you understand that you've been driving me crazy? Wherever I go, there you are, looking as if you've just stepped out of a fashion plate, with all your clothes practically falling off, being wined and dined by the most famous seducers in London. Do you think I haven't noticed the effect you have on people wherever you go? Do you think I'm blind? I can't offer you any of the things that they can. I can't offer you money or glamour or power. I can only offer you myself.'

He stopped, having played his last great speech. It would, Alabama reflected with a strange kind of detachment, have been rather touching had it not been said with the air of a spoilt child who is denied the toy he really wanted for Christmas.

All at once, she saw beyond the talent and the magnetism and the facile charm and the pretty brooding face. All at once, she saw the petulance, the selfishness, the insecurity, the narcissism. Scratch an actor, someone had once said, she couldn't remember who, and you'll find an actor underneath. Poor Max.

'You don't love me,' she said firmly.

Max looked at her, astounded. This wasn't the right line at all. This was her cue to fall into his arms and beg forgiveness for her feckless behaviour. He couldn't have played the scene any better, and now here she was spoiling it all.

'I don't?' he said helplessly.

'Of course you don't.' Alabama sounded as if she were chiding a small boy who has tried to eat yew berries in the mistaken belief that they would taste as good as they looked. 'You like the idea of being in love with me. And you're cross that you can't have everything that you want, when you want. Now you've played your little scene, and I think it would be best for both of us if you left.'

'You don't mean that,' said Max in his best cajoling manner. She couldn't mean it, surely? What on earth had he done wrong? He would never understand women. Especially not this woman. She was a law unto herself.

'I do, you know,' she said conversationally.

Max never knew when he was beaten.

'You can't,' he persisted. 'I mean, what about last night, and rewriting the play for me, and getting me the audition? What about all that?'

'That has nothing to do with it. You have a great talent. It shouldn't be wasted. But you don't want me, not really. You want a foil, someone to play out your scenes against, someone who will collude in your idea of yourself, who will always do what you want. I'm not that girl. I'm sorry Max. You nearly had me fooled. I almost fell for it. But it's not right.'

Max looked at her again, from his undefended position in the middle of the room. She sat there, quite calm and final and utterly certain. He could still hardly believe it. Where had he gone wrong? She had been ready to drop into his hands without protest, and now he had lost her. He looked at her unwavering eyes, and had to admit to himself that he had lost.

'Well,' he said baffled and beaten and not liking it. 'What do we do now? Am I to kiss you on your cheek, like a gentleman, and walk out of your life for ever?'

Alabama managed not to smile. His pride was in the dust, but he still insisted on talking like an old film, the kind they didn't make any more. Not for Max the ordinary walking out of the door and into the street of ordinary mortals. He was above such pedestrian ideas. When Max walked out of a door, he walked out of a life. Alabama was glad that she was right about him. He was going to be a world-beater.

'I think so, don't you?' she said. 'It doesn't have to be for ever, but if that will make you happy, you can think of it like that.'

'It doesn't make me happy,' said Max gruffly, trying his best to sound as if his heart was breaking.

'Well then, I expect we shall be able to see each other again without too much trouble.'

'It's easy for you,' said Max, with a rich vein of bitterness. 'It's always been easy for you.'

'Don't let's get uncivilized,' said Alabama coolly. 'Kiss me goodbye quickly and go, before you get angry again.'

Max kissed her.

'Goodbye then,' he said, as stiffly as he knew how.

'Goodbye.'

'I know my own way out.'

And he left, into the dark night, still shiny with the earlier rain, still with the moon riding high, and thought it was no longer for him, and decided to walk home, because a taxi was too pragmatic and would break the mood.

CHAPTER

10

Alabama woke the next morning feeling quite different.
It took her a moment to remember why. All she knew
was that she felt quite different. Rather light-headed and
perfectly irresponsible, and free. She stretched, liking
the warmth of the early sun on her limbs. She rolled
over in the bed, laughing to herself, liking the cool touch
of the empty linen sheets on her body. That was it. She
sat up in bed and laughed out loud. She had asked Max
to leave. Told him to leave, if she remembered correctly.
What a perfectly extraordinary thing to do, after all these
weeks of devoting herself to getting him back. What a
perfectly extraordinary girl she was. She had had him
exactly where she wanted him, and then she had told
him to go away. But really, how utterly typical of him
to make such a scene, and to declare passionate love
for her just when she didn't want it. And even had
she wanted it, how even more typical of him to do it
in such a way that made her instantly disbelieve him.

It was rather a waste, Alabama thought to herself. She
could have kept him for one more night, instead of
blowing him out quite so precipitately. It wasn't often
a girl came across such physical perfection. But still,
she did have some principles. She remembered what

Milo had said, and how right he was, and thought how pleased he would be with her now, and how he could start to call her every day again and everything would be all right. She decided she simply had to ring Venice.

Not very far away, Venice too was waking with the sun on her face, since Sebastian didn't seem to have any curtains. She wondered if that was out of choice or laziness. Perhaps it was absolutely the thing not to have any. She must ask him when he woke up. She looked fondly down at him as he slept, and thought how utterly irresistible he looked, with his face buried in the pillow. He didn't even snore, which was such a relief after David, who did rather.

She looked about the room with interest, still trying to get her bearings. She hadn't been in much condition to notice the finer points of the interior design the night before, what with one thing and another. There seemed to be a lot of bookcases, spilling over with books, and clothes scattered everywhere in a myriad of colours, and a large rather lovely looking-glass which needed cleaning, and a bust of Napoleon most uncharacteristically wearing a pair of Wayfarers, and a dressing table covered in studs and cuff-links and beer cans and cigarette packets and unopened bills and a copy of *The Last Tycoon*. Venice decided she loved it. Like Sebastian, it was perfect. She decided one could get a little tired of Meissen vases and Aubusson rugs.

The telephone rang, insistent into her admiration. It took her a little while to find it, but she finally discovered it in the dressing table drawer, hidden among Sebastian's handkerchiefs. What a perfectly clever place to keep the telephone, she thought.

'Hello,' she said, thinking how surprised the caller would be.

'Ven?'

'Al!' cried Venice in delight. Just who she wanted to talk to. 'What a perfect genius you are to know I was here. I wish you could see Sebastian's flat. It's the most to die-for thing I've ever seen in my life. Did you hear about the fight already?'

'What fight?' said Alabama, mystified. She had only used her common sense and realized that if Venice's number wasn't answering, she must be with Sebastian.

'Darling, you'll die, that's all. There's so much to tell, you wouldn't believe it. We must have lunch.'

Oliver, who had woken up with a blinding headache, but his priorities still intact, had rung all interested parties to let them in on last night's developments by the time he got around to Alabama.

'Darling,' he shrieked, back in his element with a vengeance. 'Have you heard? Could you die? Let's have lunch.'

So it was another of those lunches, the ones that now seemed inevitable whenever anything even vaguely momentous happened. As Oliver pointed out, it did save his telephone bill. As Sergei entered the restaurant, only to find Oliver pleading with the waiter, as usual, for more chairs, he wondered once again how on earth he had allowed himself to be dragged into All This, as he called it. All This was, of course, much more fun than lunch at the club and discreet dinners at the Gavroche with other people's wives, but he wasn't quite ready to admit that yet. He had some sort of reputation to protect, after all. Besides, he was feeling distinctly jaded after sitting up so late with Van, finishing off the Armagnac, and the Alka-Seltzers he had taken weren't working yet.

'Oh,' said Van, bumping into Nicholas in the doorway. 'What are you doing here?' She wasn't exactly feeling like a ray of sunshine herself, since, unlike Sergei, she wasn't used to Armagnac, and didn't know that it had to be drunk with respect. He could have told her, the rat.

He was probably laughing all over his face after her exhibition last night, but she had been so disappointed and angry, and he had been so sympathetic, when all the time he had probably been as bored as hell. And now here was Nicholas, looking as bad as she felt, and she didn't feel up to either of them.

'I expect I was asked,' said Nicholas equally coldly.

'Bully for you, buster,' said Van, lippy with her hangover. 'Are you going to put it all in your column, like a good little hack?'

'I might,' said Nicholas, standing on his dignity. 'What's it to you?'

'Not enough,' said Van crossly. 'Oh really, do let's make up and be friends. But I simply can't go to bed with you any more.'

Nicholas started to laugh, despite himself. She really was the most absurdly mercurial girl.

'Van really,' he said, 'only you could tell me something like that in the middle of the street.'

'Well,' Van smiled at him sheepishly, 'it's not the middle of the street. We're practically in the restaurant. And what does it matter anyway?'

'What about my poor broken heart?' said Nicholas soulfully.

'You haven't got a heart, everyone knows that.'

'So I haven't,' Nicholas looked reassured.

'And it did have to be said, even in the middle of the street.'

'I expect it did rather.'

'Well then,' said Van, vastly relieved that Nicholas

didn't want to make a scene or anything taxing like that. 'That's all all right then.' She reached up and kissed him on the cheek. 'Friends?'

'Friends.' Nicholas smiled down at her with great fondness. Later in life, he was to insist that Van had been the other great love of his life, apart from Alabama, but now he quite saw the impossibility of them staying together. She was too young and ardent and full of fire and brimstone for a battered old cynic like him. She needed a stronger man to keep her in order.

In perfect charity with each other, they went into lunch, only to find Oliver still pleading with the waiter for more chairs.

'Darlings,' he said, kissing them. 'Sit down quickly. This beast of a waiter doesn't believe that we need more chairs.'

Van stood on one leg and tried to avoid Sergei's eye, but to her amazement he pulled out the seat next to him and told her to come and sit on it.

'Good morning,' she said, trying not to blush. 'Did I bore you to death last night? I am sorry.'

'But not at all,' said Sergei truthfully. 'Although I do blame you very much for making me drink all that Armagnac. I feel distinctly jaded and quite my age.'

Nicholas and Oliver exchanged speaking looks. This was all getting almost too much, even for such seasoned campaigners as they.

'Why do we need more chairs?' said Alabama, who was only slightly piqued that her quiet lunch with Venice had turned into the feeding of the five thousand.

'Well,' said Oliver. 'There's Milo to come, although I don't know if we can rely on him after last night's performance. I did leave a message on his machine.'

'What performance?' asked Alabama, who still hadn't been filled in, and who felt like she had walked into a play in the second act. She certainly couldn't interpret the cryptic looks that everyone seemed to be exchanging.

'Well, darling,' said Oliver, sitting down and helping himself to bread. 'Only getting thrown out of nightclubs and trying to seduce other people's wives and getting legless drunk and sicking up on the pavement, that's all.'

'Milo?' said Alabama in surprise. 'The Milo that we know and love? Are you quite sure? He never did that, even at university.'

'Exactly,' said Venice in triumph. 'That's what I said.'

'We had bloody good eggs though,' said Sebastian vaguely. He wasn't quite feeling his best. He wondered when that nice waiter would bring him his Bloody Mary.

'Do shut up,' said Venice lovingly.

'Well,' said Alabama. 'Well, how perfectly extraordinary.'

Nicholas sat down next to Alabama, edging his chair a little closer than propriety allowed.

'Alabama,' he said with meaning. 'You look ravishing.'

Alabama, who hadn't made much of an effort that morning, what with one thing and another, was wearing all black and looked pale, if interesting. She smiled quizzically at him.

'No,' he protested, 'I mean it.'

'Sorry I was out when you called,' she said.

'Probably a good thing,' said Nicholas ruefully. 'I wasn't in much of a state for anything. It was just me and a bottle.'

'Secret drinking?' said Oliver, as usual picking up on the most interesting conversation. 'Nicholas, what is all this? Has Van broken your heart?'

'To smithereens,' said Nicholas, shaking his head sorrowfully. 'You see but a shadow of my former self.'

'It was an amicable divorce,' said Van. 'He gets the children and I get the castles in Spain.'

'How too interesting,' said Oliver, who couldn't quite believe that quite so many events of interest could have gone on last night without him knowing. 'Were you unendurably cruel, Van? Did you throw his poor pride in the dust?'

'Not at all,' said Van. 'You shouldn't be so quizzy. It doesn't become you.'

Oliver looked at her with love. She really was a find.

'So that's an end to it?' he said fondly.

'That's an end to it,' she said, relieved to have the subject closed. It wasn't so much that she didn't want to talk about it, but she was trying to concentrate on the infinitely more interesting development of Sergei's hand, which seemed to be covering hers, all of a sudden. Luckily for her, Milo arrived at that moment, diverting everyone's attention.

'Goodness,' said Oliver naughtily, 'you do look peaky, darling. Did you have a rough night?'

Milo looked about him with that bleary disoriented look that was always such a give-away. He still seemed to be wearing his dinner jacket, although he'd lost his black tie, and instead of his evening shirt he had on a white T-shirt with a picture of Lenin on the front. His eyes were mercifully covered with a very black pair of Ray Bans.

'Here,' said Alabama, taking pity on him. 'Come and sit down.'

Milo subsided into the chair next to her and groaned gently to himself.

'Get the boy a large Bloody,' said Oliver charitably. 'You really shouldn't do it to yourself, darling, it can't be right.'

'I know,' said Milo. 'I only wish I could remember what it was.'

'Oh,' said Oliver in delight, 'you mean to say you've forgotten already?'

'I have a hazy recollection of making improper advances on somebody's wife, not mine,' said Milo, 'but after that, it's rather blank.'

'Just as well,' said Oliver. 'We had to pick you up out of the gutter. It wasn't a pretty sight.'

'Oh God.' Milo passed a hand over his face. 'I feel awful.' He suddenly turned to Alabama, as if he'd just remembered something. 'Where's your nasty young actor?' he said accusingly. 'You were looking very cosy last night.'

Venice's face took on a knowing look. Some of the events of last night were suddenly becoming a great deal clearer. Who would have thought it, after all these years.

'I don't know where he is,' said Alabama, clearly.

'You don't know?' said Oliver, who was being a little slow. 'You mean to say . . .?'

'Well, I do rather,' said Alabama. 'We all make mistakes.'

Nicholas, Sergei and Milo all looked as if they'd just been told it was their birthday.

'Well,' said Oliver, who was rather pleased himself. He'd never thought that Max was up to much. 'When I think of all the trouble we went to.'

'And think how much you enjoyed it,' said Nicholas.

'There is that,' said Oliver, pretending to be mollified. 'But what made you change your mind, Alabama?'

'Oh you know,' she said airily, just as if she wasn't creating a stir at all. 'This and that.'

'Well,' said Oliver, 'you are the most extraordinary girl.'

Milo was grinning all over his face, like the Cheshire cat.

'And you can stop that,' said Alabama. 'After you were so appallingly rude.'

'Rude,' said Milo dreamily, 'but so right. May I lay my poor tired head on your delightful breast and go to sleep?'

'Yes,' said Alabama.

'Really,' said Oliver, 'I don't know how that boy gets away with it.'

'I'd love another Bloody,' said Sebastian, who hadn't been concentrating.

Since there was so much to tell, they didn't leave lunch until quite four o'clock.

Oliver took Nicholas off to a picture sale at Christies.

'I suppose it's just you and I now,' he said, 'until Carlos gets back from his world tour.'

'Don't worry,' said Nicholas blithely, 'we'll survive. How much do you suppose they'll get for that Monet? Divorce is SO expensive.'

Sergei took Van off to a private view, which had everybody shaking their heads in amusement.

'I'm not really dressed for it,' said Van, looking down at her jeans, which had seen better days.

'Don't worry,' said Sergei. 'There's plenty of time. We can go shopping on the way.'

Sebastian took Venice home.

'I suppose this will be the last taxi we ever take, now that we're poor,' said Venice, who had decided that what was David's should be returned to him, under the circumstances. 'Still,' she added stoically, 'I don't expect I shall mind being poor very much, as long as I can be it with you.'

Sebastian looked rather sheepish.

'Actually,' he said, 'we're not going to be poor.'

'We're not?' said Venice, who wasn't doing a very

good job of convincing herself that it was going to be too romantic for words, living on a shoestring.

'Well, no. I'm afraid I have a private income from my mother. Do you mind awfully?'

Venice looked at him with love.

'No,' she said, 'I don't mind a bit.'

Milo and Alabama stood together, watching everyone disperse. Milo was feeling a great deal better.

'So,' he said, looking at her.

'So?' she said, looking back and thinking how silly she had been.

'I suppose we had better go back to your place.'

'I suppose we had. But don't go getting any ideas.'

'I already have. And I think it will have to be St Margaret's Westminster, after all.'

Alabama smiled.

'I still prefer St James' Piccadilly,' she said.

THE END

CASTING
by Jane Barry

'Heartbreakingly funny . . . tremendously entertaining'
She

Dee Devlin is sick of rotating her underwear to the dictates of her diary, sick of watching men search for their socks at one in the morning – sick to the back molars of always being the mistress, never the wife.

Yet how does she locate Mr Single in a world full of married men? At forty, she's missed the boat on 18–30 holidays. A Lonely Hearts ad generates only one congenial companion from a stack of no-hope replies – a six-foot transsexual called Ann. And, despite her friend Gilda's advice, Dee fails to detect an Adonis amongst the would-be waiters and Father Christmases who daily audition for commercials at the Soho casting studio she runs. Is Gilda right – should Dee set up a casting session to find Mr Single? Or should she console herself with her five-carrier-bags-a-day shopping habit and the companionship of her designer cat, Mabel?

'Frothy, soapy and bags of fun. And, in between the laughs, she puts her perfectly manicured finger squarely on the agonies of being single in a world full of couples and married men'
Cosmopolitan

'Fast, furious, wise, full of hurt and funny – I loved it'
Fay Weldon

0 552 13648 4

A SELECTED LIST OF FINE NOVELS
AVAILABLE FROM CORGI BOOKS

THE PRICES SHOWN BELOW WERE CORRECT AT THE TIME OF
GOING TO PRESS. HOWEVER TRANSWORLD PUBLISHERS RESERVE
THE RIGHT TO SHOW NEW RETAIL PRICES ON COVERS WHICH
MAY DIFFER FROM THOSE PREVIOUSLY ADVERTISED IN THE TEXT
OR ELSEWHERE.

☐ 13648 4	**CASTING**	*Jane Barry*	£3.99
☐ 12869 4	**DREAMS ARE NOT ENOUGH**	*Jacqueline Briskin*	£4.99
☐ 13395 7	**THE NAKED HEART**	*Jacqueline Briskin*	£4.50
☐ 12850 3	**TOO MUCH TOO SOON**	*Jacqueline Briskin*	£4.99
☐ 13558 5	**AMBITION**	*Julie Burchill*	£3.99
☐ 10427 2	**BELLA**	*Jilly Cooper*	£2.99
☐ 10277 6	**EMILY**	*Jilly Cooper*	£2.99
☐ 10576 7	**HARRIET**	*Jilly Cooper*	£2.99
☐ 11149 X	**IMOGEN**	*Jilly Cooper*	£2.99
☐ 12041 3	**LISA & CO**	*Jilly Cooper*	£2.99
☐ 10717 4	**OCTAVIA**	*Jilly Cooper*	£2.99
☐ 13552 6	**POLO**	*Jilly Cooper*	£5.99
☐ 10878 2	**PRUDENCE**	*Jilly Cooper*	£2.99
☐ 12486 9	**RIDERS**	*Jilly Cooper*	£4.99
☐ 13264 0	**RIVALS**	*Jilly Cooper*	£4.99
☐ 13761 8	**CURRENT AFFAIRS**	*Barbara Raskin*	£3.99
☐ 13268 3	**HOT FLASHES**	*Barbara Raskin*	£3.99
☐ 13614 X	**AMBITION'S CHILDREN**	*Francesca Summers*	£3.99

All Corgi Books are available at your bookshop or newsagent, or can be ordered
from the following address:

Transworld Publishers Ltd, Cash Sales Department,
PO Box 11, Falmouth, Cornwall TR10 9EN

Please send a cheque or postal order (no currency) and allow £1.00 for postage and
packing for one book, an additional 50p for a second book, and an additional 30p
for each subsequent book ordered to a maximum charge of £3.00 if ordering seven
or more books.

Overseas customers, including Eire, please allow £2.00 for postage and packing
for the first book, an additional £1.00 for a second book, and an additional 50p for
each subsequent title ordered.

Name: ....

Address: ....